Cocky
Bastard

EXIT

Penelope Ward   Vi Keeland

ISBN-13: 9781682304280

COCKY BASTARD

Cover model: Nick Ayler Website: www.nickayler.com

Cover designer: Letitia Hasser, r.b.a. designs

Interior design & Graphics: Deena Rae @ E-BookBuilders

Table of Contents

To our husbands, the real cocky bastards.

Chapter One

I wondered if the vibration would feel good between my legs.

The sun caught the chrome of a Harley Davidson parked a few spots over, gleaming in the sweltering midday sun. I waited until Maroon Five finished playing on the radio, oddly fixated on the two-wheeled-man-toy as I fished in my purse for my cell phone. The motorcycle was simple—high gloss black and shiny silver, worn leather saddlebags with a skull embossed below the initials *C.B.*

How good would it feel to ride? Wind blowing through my long hair, arms wrapped around a man with a tough sounding nickname, engine purring beneath my jean clad thighs. Horse? Drifter? Guns? Wait. No. Pres. My imaginary biker was most definitely called Pres. And he'd look just like Charlie Hunnam.

I glanced down at my iPhone and found a half dozen new messages from Harrison. Inwardly, I smirked. Certainly, there is no one named Harrison that ever rode a Harley. Tossing my phone back in my bag, I cut the engine of my packed BMW and glanced behind me into the backseat. Boxes piled to the ceiling were beginning to make my full-size car feel claustrophobic.

A bus full of travelers pulled into the rest stop. *Great.* I'd better go in now and get my lunch, otherwise I'd never get out of here. Ten hours into a cross-country trip from Chicago to Temecula, California, I was somewhere in the middle of Nebraska with about another twenty some odd hours to go.

After a fifteen-minute wait inside for Pepsi and Popeyes fried chicken bites that I planned to eat back in the car, I stopped into the small souvenir shop. I was so tired and didn't really feel like driving the additional five hours I had to go before finding a place to sleep for the night. Yawning, I decided to stall and browse for a few minutes. Checking out some trinkets, I eventually picked up a Barack Obama bobblehead and shook it mindlessly, watching its maniacal smile as the head bounced up and down.

"Get it. You know you want it," a deep, raspy voice said from behind my shoulders. Startling me, it caused a knee-jerk reaction that resulted in the bobblehead slipping from my fingers and falling to the ground. The head broke off of the spring neck and rolled away.

The woman at the register shouted, "I'm sorry, ma'am. You'll have to pay for that. Twenty dollars."

"Damn it!" I spewed, following the path of the rolling head. As I bent down to pick it up, there was the voice again from behind me.

"And to think, some people say he's got a good head on his shoulders." He seemed to have an Australian accent.

"You think this is funny, asshole?" I asked before turning around and getting my first look at the man behind the voice.

I froze.

Oh. Shit.

2

"You don't need to be a fucking bitch about it." His mouth curved into a wicked grin as he handed me the bottom half of Obama. "And for the record, I did think that was really funny, yes."

I swallowed and seemed to lose my ability to speak as I took in the Adonis standing before me. I wanted to smack that cocky smile right off his face, though—his gorgeous, chiseled, scruffy face, framed by a thick head of copper-brown hair. *Fuck me.* This man was insanely hot, not someone I expected to come across out here. This was the middle of nowhere USA, not the Australian outback for Christ's sake.

I cleared my throat. "Well, I didn't think it was funny at all."

"Then, you need to take the stick out of your arse and lighten up." He reached out his hand. "Give it to me, Princess. I'll pay for the damn thing." Before I could respond, he grabbed the two broken pieces from me, and I cursed at the shiver that ran down my spine from the brief contact of his hand brushing against mine. Of course, he had to smell amazing on top of it all.

I followed him to the register as I fished through my messy purse for money, but he was too quick and had paid for it already.

He handed me a plastic bag containing the broken bobblehead. "There's some change in the bag. Buy yourself a sense of humor."

HUE-MA. That accent.

My jaw dropped as he walked away and out of the store.

What an ass.

It was. A fine one. A thick, juicy, round ass hugged tightly by his jeans. God, I really needed to get laid, because it didn't seem to matter that this guy had just insulted me to my face; my panties were practically wet.

After several minutes of staring into space at a shelf of Nebraska Cornhuskers t-shirts, I gave myself a mental kick in the butt. My reaction to the incident proved that fatigue had gotten the best of me; I wasn't usually that short-tempered. It was time to shake off the bizarre encounter and get moving. My stomach was growling, and I was looking forward to breaking into the fried chicken once I hit the road. I snuck a piece out of the box in my bag as I walked out of the building. My chewing ceased when I noticed *him* two spots down from my car—sitting on the very motorcycle I'd been fantasizing about earlier.

Approaching slowly, I hoped he didn't notice me. No such luck. Instead, when he spotted me, he flashed an exaggerated smile and waved.

Frantically searching for my keys, I rolled my eyes and muttered, "You again."

He snickered. "Did you end up buying a sense of humor?"

"I used the change to buy you some couth instead."

Chuckling, he shook his head at me. Running his hand through his hair, he put his shiny black helmet on and cranked the Harley. The rumble shook me to my core.

Getting in the car and slamming the door, I couldn't help taking one last look over at him, seeing as though I'd never see this guy again in my lifetime. He winked through the helmet, and my pathetic heart fluttered.

I watched through the rear view mirror as he backed out of the spot. I expected him to take off like a bat out of hell, but after moving away slowly, he abruptly stopped. He kept trying to rev the bike to get it to move, but nothing was happening. Eventually turning off the engine, he removed his helmet and ran his hand through his hair in frustration before getting off to inspect things. I should have just left, but couldn't take my eyes off him as he struggled to get it to run. *Man, that sucks.*

I dipped one of the chicken bites into the honey mustard sauce and popped it into my mouth, continuing to watch this like a spectator sport for several minutes. At one point, he took out his phone and made a phone call as he paced back and forth.

Putting his phone away, he looked in my direction and glared at me. Caught in the act of watching him, I let out a nervous laugh. I didn't mean to laugh at the situation, but it just came out. He raised his brow, and that made me cackle harder. He slowly walked toward me, clutching the helmet by his side. He knocked on my window, and I lowered it.

"You think this is funny, Princess?"

"Not really…maybe." I snorted.

"Well, I'm glad you finally managed to find your sense of humor."

HUE-MA.

God, his accent was sexy.

He arched his neck to look into the backseat and took notice of all the boxes. "You homeless or something? Living out of your car?"

"No. I'm in the middle of a cross-country move."

"Where you headed?"

"Temecula."

"California." He nodded. "Me, too."

I looked toward his Harley. "Well, it looks like *you're* not exactly headed *anywhere* anytime soon. I guess it's payback for calling me a bitch."

"Well, that would seem to be the case."

"That it's payback?"

"No, that you're a bitch."

"Very funny."

"You know what's even better than payback?" he asked leaning into the window, his cologne intoxicating me.

"What?"

He wiggled his brows. "Karma."

"What are you talking about?"

"Come around and have a look at the back of your Beemer."

BEE-MA.

I got out and walked around to the back of my car to find my right rear tire was completely flat.

What? This cannot be happening.

With my hand on my forehead, I looked over at his smug expression. "Are you kidding me? Did you know my tire was flat all this time?"

"I noticed it right around the time I caught you popping chicken and laughing at me, yes. It was real hard for me to keep a straight face at that point."

I didn't know how to change a tire to save my life. I couldn't believe what I was about to ask of him.

"Do you know how to change a tire?"

"Of course I do. What kind of a man would I be if I didn't know how to change a tire?"

"Will you help me? I know you have no reason to want to…after our little altercation, but I'm seriously desperate. I don't want to be stuck out here all alone at night."

"Let me ask you a question."

"Okay…"

He rubbed the scruff on his chin. "How badly do you want your tire changed?"

I backed away from him. "What exactly are you getting at?"

"Get your mind out of the gutter, sweetheart. I'm not fucking propositioning you if that's what you think. You're not my type."

"And what exactly *is* your type?"

"I typically go for women who don't have the personality of a door knob."

"Thanks."

"My pleasure."

"So, what are your conditions?"

"Well, as you clearly know from your laughing fit, my Harley is experiencing a technical malfunction at the moment. It needs a part that I don't have. I just called a tow company. But I'm on a deadline, and like you, I need to get to California."

"You're not suggesting…"

"Yes. Yes, I am. If I change your tire, you let me ride with you."

"Ride with me?"

"Ride me, yes."

"What did you just say?"

"You're hearing things."

I shook my head to rid the images now flashing through it. Did my tired mind only imagine that he just said that, or was he messing with me?

"I cannot drive hundreds of miles with a total stranger," I said.

"It's a fuck of a lot safer than driving alone."

"Not if you're a serial killer!"

"Look who's talking. You're the one who decapitated a U.S. president."

I couldn't help but laugh. This situation was seriously insane.

"Holy shit, Princess, is that a laugh at your own expense, I see?"

"I think you're making me delirious."

He stuck out his hand. "So, you in?"

I crossed my arms instead of taking it. "What choice do I have?"

"Well, you could always have *him* change your tire." He gestured to a large and scary-looking man who seemed to be watching us. This guy looked like Herman Munster in the flesh.

Letting out a deep breath, I conceded. "I'm in. I'm in! Just get me out of here."

"I thought you might say that. Please tell me you have a spare."

"Yeah. But I have to move some of my boxes so you can get to it."

He started to crack up when he got a load of the situation inside my trunk. "Damn, what the hell is all this crap?"

I looked into his eyes and answered honestly, "My entire life."

I temporarily piled the contents of the trunk onto the pavement. He got the spare out and immediately got to work.

As he was changing the tire, his white t-shirt rode up, exposing his tanned, rock-hard abs and a thin trail of hair that ran into his underwear line. Unwanted tension built between my legs. I needed a distraction, so I walked over to his bike and sat on it, gripping the handles and imagining what it would be like to ride in the wind. But all I could envision now was him in front of me, and that wasn't helping.

He slid his body from under my car. "Be careful, little girl. That's not a toy."

I hopped off and ran my finger along the letters emblazoned on the saddlebags. "What's C.B. stand for anyway?"

"Those are my initials."

"Let me guess... *Cocky Bastard*?"

"See...I would have told you my name, but since you're so clever, I think I'll just let you guess."

"Whatever, Cocky."

He lay back down on the ground. "I'm just tightening up these nuts, and we'll be ready to go."

"Nuts?"

"Lug nuts...on the wheel, dirty girl."

"Oh."

Hopping up, he lifted his shirt and used it to wipe his forehead. "All set."

Damn.

"That was quick. Are you sure it's on right?"

"I've got a few screws loose, darling, as you'll soon find out, but none of them are on your wheel." He winked and for the first time, I noticed his dimples. "We should probably stop tomorrow and get a new tire put on. This spare is really not meant for long term use."

Tomorrow. Wow. This was really happening.

"We should get going," I said. "I'll drive. I need to be in control of this situation."

"Whatever you want," he said.

I could feel the tension in my neck as I backed out of the spot. This was going to be very interesting to say the least. He wasted no time digging into my chicken bites.

I playfully slapped his hand. "Hey, lay off my food."

"Honey mustard? I prefer barbecue." He licked his thumb, and I swore at myself for getting turned on a little. This was going to be a long ride.

He smirked and lifted the plastic bag from the souvenir shop. "Did you even open it?"

"No. What's the point? It's just a broken bobblehead."

Handing it to me, he said, "Is it?"

With one hand on the steering wheel, I took out the bobblehead which was…in one piece.

"What the…how did you?"

"You seemed to like it, so I paid for the other and bought you a different one. You were too busy looking through your purse to notice."

I couldn't help but smile and shook my head.

"Well, whaddya know. A genuine smile." He held out his hand. "Here…gimme." When, I handed it to him, he took an adhesive strip off the bottom and stuck it to the dash. Obama's head was now bopping up and down with every movement of the car.

I broke out in laughter at the ridiculousness but also couldn't help the warm feeling that came over me with that sweet gesture. Maybe he wasn't really a bastard at all.

We were quiet for a while as he lay his head back and shut his eyes. Somewhere along I-76 after the sun set into a bright orange glow that illuminated the horizon in the distance, he turned to me.

His voice was groggy. "I'm Chance."

After several seconds of silence, I said, "Aubrey."

"Aubrey," he repeated in a breathy whisper, seeming to contemplate my name before closing his eyes again and turning his head away.

Chance.

Chapter Two

EXIT

66 **Y**ou just gonna keep letting that go to voicemail?" He narrowed his eyes on my cellphone buzzing on top of the center console. The damn thing was going off every half hour or so, but now the break between calls had shortened to ten minutes.

"Yep." It stopped dancing around, and I offered no further explanation. I'd thought maybe he'd let it go.

Of course he didn't. Five minutes later it buzzed again, and Chance grabbed it before I realized what he was doing.

"Harry's calling." He dangled my phone between his thumb and pointer, swinging it back and forth until I snatched it out of his hand.

"It's Harrison. And it's none of your business."

"It's a long ride, Princess. You know we're gonna talk about it eventually."

"Trust me, we won't."

"We'll see."

Only a few more minutes passed, and my phone was at it yet again. Before I could stop him, he had it in his hand once more. Only this time, he swiped and held it up to his mouth.

"Ello."

My eyes bulged from my head. I almost swerved off the road, yet I sat there like a mute.

"Harry. How's it going, Mate?"

The hint of Australian accent that lingered in the background was suddenly front and center. Harrison's voice rose through the cell, although I couldn't make out the words. I glanced over at Chance's cocky face. He shrugged at me, smiled, and leaned back into his seat, quite enjoying himself. At that moment, I decided our little road trip was over. As soon as we got to the next exit, his ass was getting kicked to the curb. That perfectly round mass of muscle could walk through bumfuck Nebraska for all I cared.

"Yeah, sure. She's here. But we're *kinda busy* right now."

I heard the next question loud and clear. Chance pulled the receiver away from his ear as Harrison roared, "Who the fuck is this?"

"Name's Chance. Chance Bateman. Some of my friends call me Cocky," he said with the perfect melody of intonation that I visualized causing the vein in Harrison's throat to throb a deep shade of purple.

"Put. Aubrey. On. The. Fucking. Phone." Each word was a short staccato burst of anger. Suddenly, I was no longer mad at Chance for answering the phone. I was livid that Harrison had the audacity to be angry at what *I* was doing.

"No can do, Harry. She's…indisposed at the moment."

Another growl of expletives came through the phone.

"Listen, Harry. I'm going to tell you this man to man, because you sound like a good chap. Aubrey has been avoiding your calls to be polite. The truth is, she just doesn't want to talk to you."

My anger was rapidly bouncing between the two men. Yet... *AH-BREE*. I wanted to strangle Chance, although at the same time, I really wanted him to say my name again. What in the hell was wrong with me? I missed Harrison's response, busy replaying the sound of my name spoken with an Australian accent. The way it rolled off that cocky bastard's tongue made my belly do a little flutter. I might have had a momentary lapse in time as I imagined it being whispered in my ear with a throaty strain. *AH-BREE*.

I blinked myself back to reality as Chance released an exaggerated sigh into the phone. "Okay then, Harry. But you're going to need to stop now. We're taking a nice long trip, and your constant buzzing is getting our girl's knickers in a twist. So be a good mate and knock off the interruptions for a while. Yeah?"

Our girl. That vein had to be ready to explode in Harrison's neck.

Chance didn't wait for a response before disconnecting the call.

For a full five minutes, neither of us said a word. He must have been expecting the tirade to come.

"You're not going to lay into me about my chat with Harry?"

My knuckles turned white on the steering wheel. "I'm processing."

"Processing?" His voice was almost amused.

"Yes. Processing."

"What the hell does that mean?"

"It means I don't say the first thing that comes to my mind. Unlike *some people*, I think about what I'm feeling and verbalize it appropriately."

"You filter shit."

"I do not."

"Yes, you do. If you're pissed off, say it. Scream it if you have to. But bitch once and get it over with, and stop *being* a bitch all the time."

The road was pretty barren, so it wasn't hard to slam on the brakes and pull over to the side of the road. I crossed three lanes and jerked to a stop. It was dark, the only light from my headlights and the occasional car passing. I got out and walked to the passenger side of the car and waited for him to join me.

Hands on my hips. "You have a lot of nerve. I save your ass at the rest stop and you proceed to get in my car, eat half my food, change my radio station and then, to top it off, you answer my phone."

He folded his arms over his chest. "You didn't save my ass, I ate *one* popcorn chicken, your taste in music sucks, and Harry with the stick up his ass was upsetting you."

I glared at him.

He glared right back.

Oh My God. The light from a passing car lit his face, and there it was. Number thirteen. His angry eyes were *exactly* the color of number thirteen. I used to have to peel the paper off *Cadet Blue* in the Crayola sixty-four pack before the other crayons had even lost their points. I liked it so much, it wasn't just the color I'd shaded the sky. There was a whole year of my life when all the faces in my coloring books were that beautiful blue with a mysterious touch of gray. I'd never seen the color in real life on anything, especially not eyes.

I was half gone. And then he took the other half.

"Aubrey." He stepped forward

AH-BREE.

Damn him. I didn't say a word. I was busy…processing.

"I was trying to help. Harry needed that. I don't know who he is to you, but whoever he is, he's obviously done you wrong. And you don't want to hear his apologies anymore. They're bullshit, and you know it. Let him stew on the thought of you taking a trip with another man for a while. Woman like you, he should know men would be circling. Shouldn't need reminding."

Woman like me?

I tried to keep up the façade of being pissed off, but I just wasn't feeling it anymore. "Well, don't touch my phone again."

"Yes, Ma'am."

I nodded, needing to feel some sense of victory. I couldn't just let go of my anger because he had a sexy voice and number thirteen eyes. Could I?

"How about I drive for a while?"

My night vision wasn't great to begin with, and I was starting to get a little blurry eyed. "Okay."

He opened the passenger side door and waited for me to get in, then closed it and jogged around to the other side. Before slipping into the driver's seat, he bent down and picked something up from the street, dropping it into his bag in the back before adjusting the seat where he wanted it.

"What did you pick up?"

"Nothing." He blew off my question. "Driver picks the music." We pulled away from the curb.

"You changed the station every five minutes while I was driving."

He shrugged and smiled. "It's a new rule."

Being in the passenger seat gave me an opportunity to study him. God those dimples were deep. And the bit of stubble starting to shadow his chiseled jaw worked for me. *Really worked.* There was a good chance he'd be driving an awful lot.

Three hours later, it was almost midnight when we decided to stop for the day. We'd made it as far as I'd planned, even with having to waste a few hours getting a new tire.

The woman at the reception desk of the hotel was busy playing a game on her phone and barely looked up at us when we approached.

"We'd like a room for tonight, please?" Chance said.

"Ummm…two rooms, please," I clarified.

"What? I was going to get one with two beds."

"I am *not* sharing a room with you."

He shrugged. "Suit yourself." And turned his attention back to the front desk clerk. "She's afraid if we room together, she won't be able to keep her hands off of me." He winked at her. She had dark skin, but I could see her blush anyway.

I rolled my eyes, too tired to fight with him again and spoke to the clerk, "Can you make my room facing west, not on the ground floor, and an even number, if possible?"

"I'd like mine with a bed, toilet and television, if that's possible." He grinned, bating me.

"I can give you rooms 217 and 218. They're right next to each other."

"Perfect. She likes to be close to me."

I wasn't sure if his egomaniacal sense of humor was growing on me or if I was just slap happy from so many hours in the car, but I actually laughed a little.

He looked pleased.

The clerk handed us our keys along with a warm chocolate chip cookie each. On our way to the elevator, I offered him mine. "Want my cookie? I'm not going to eat it."

"Sure. I'll eat you."

"What did you just say?"

"I said I'd eat yours."

I *really* needed to get some sleep. And perhaps a nice cold shower.

He toted both our overnight bags to our rooms, and it wasn't lost on me that he let me in and out of the elevator before him. Cocky Bastard had manners to go with his arrogance.

"Night, Princess."

"Night, Cocky."

I was glad he didn't say my name; I was bothered enough just sleeping next door to him.

Fifteen minutes later, I'd completed my bedtime ritual and slipped into bed. I took a deep breath in and out and let myself sink into the softness of the mattress.

A knock at the door made me jump.

With a huff, I got out of bed and stood on my tiptoes to look out the peephole. Why were those things always so high on the door anyway? I was surprised to find no one standing on the other side. Maybe I'd imagined it.

Another knock.

I flicked on the lights. The sound wasn't coming from the entrance door. It was coming from an interior door I hadn't even noticed before.

Chance's door.

I unfastened the top lock and cracked it open just enough so I could see what he wanted. And there he stood.

Shirtless.

Wearing only dark gray boxer briefs that hugged him like a second skin.

It took a minute to understand what he was doing there, even though he was holding up a toothbrush in question.

"I thought we had established I wasn't a serial killer already."

I opened the door wider.

He smiled.

Oh lord. Stop that. Right now.

"I must have left my toothpaste in my saddlebag in the car."

I swallowed hard. "Uh huh."

He cocked his head to the side, and his brows dipped in. "Can I borrow yours?"

"Oh. Yeah, sure."

He walked past me and let himself into my bathroom. I waited at the door.

"You got an awful lot of girly crap in here for one night," he said with a jumbled mouth full of toothpaste from the bathroom. "Private Collection Tuberose Gardenia."

He was reading my Estee Lauder perfume bottle.

I heard him rinse and spit. Then there was a gargling sound. He used my mouthwash, too. *Sure, help yourself.*

He walked out and flicked off the bathroom light. "Is tuberose a rose?"

I shook my head, still confused by the whole situation going on.

"That's why," he murmured.

"Why what?"

"I couldn't figure out what you smelled like all day. Not sure I ever smelled a Tuberose before." He shrugged and walked back into his room but not before turning back. "Even those little black lacy underwear smell like tuberose."

My eyes bulged. I'd taken off my bra and panties and left them on the bathroom counter.

"You…you—"

"Relax. I'm teasing. Do I look like an underwear sniffer to you?"

Yes.

No.

Maybe?

"Night, Aubrey." He graced me with a dimple and disappeared.

AH-BREE. Damn him.

I locked the door and checked it twice, unclear if it was for my safety or his. His voice saying my name was on audio replay inside my head, getting softer and softer like a soothing lullaby with each breath as I drifted off to dreamland.

Until the knock came again.

I think I might have actually fallen asleep for all of three seconds before getting up to open the door. Again.

"Wanna watch a movie?"

My room was pitch dark; he had every light in his room on. It took my eyes a minute to adjust. And when they did, they focused right on his underwear. Instead of saying no and shutting the door, I argued with him. Again.

"I'm not watching a movie with you in your underwear."

He looked down and back up at me. "What? It's not like I have an erection."

My eyes widened at the inappropriateness of his comment, but then I started picturing him in his ridiculously tight underwear *with* an erection. Suddenly, I had no place to look. If I looked down, I was staring at his package. If I looked up at him, he'd surely see what I was thinking.

He chuckled. "I'll put shorts on."

I had no idea why I was even negotiating, when I really had no desire to watch a movie. He disappeared and came back a minute later with a pair of loose hanging shorts. I could still see the rim of his Calvin Klein underwear band sticking out. And now that there were no tight undies to focus on, I realized the shorts actually made it worse. They hung from the valley on his narrow hips where a deep V was carved. Covering up his tight buns only left me to pay more attention to the details of his chest. And his ridiculous abs.

"Your turn," he said.

My eyes asked for clarification.

"If I can't be in my underwear, you have to change out of that night shirt."

"What's wrong with my shirt?" My voice was defensive.

His eyes dropped to my chest and the corners of his lips curled to a delicious wicked grin. "Nothing at all. By all means, keep it on."

I looked down, having forgotten that I was wearing a thin white shirt with no bra. My nipples were standing at full attention, trying to pierce through the sheer fabric.

We argued over what to rent for twenty minutes before deciding on a horror movie I didn't really want to watch. Five minutes later, wearing a sweatshirt over my nightshirt, I fell asleep with Chance sitting on the twin bed next to me.

The next morning, he was back in his own room when I woke up, the interconnecting doors left open on both sides. I overheard him on his phone telling someone his plans for the day. Clearly, the entire day of activities was a lie, since I was pretty sure he wouldn't be staying within Los Angeles County all day.

Chapter Three

W e decided to stop at a diner down the road from the hotel for some breakfast.

I placed my drink order first. "I'll have a nonfat three-pump vanilla latte, low foam and extra hot."

Chance squinted his eyes at me and turned to the waitress. "Did you get all that? She'll have a hot two-pump chump with extra cream."

Bertha—as her nametag indicated—didn't look a bit amused. "We just have coffee, decaf or regular," she said monotonously, holding a carafe.

"I'll take a black coffee then."

"Make it two," he said.

She poured it into our cups. "I'll be back to take your order."

Chance was laughing at me as he shook a sugar packet.

I crossed my arms. "What's so funny?"

"You."

"What about me?"

"Did you really think you could order your frou-frou drink in a place like this?"

"Who doesn't have lattes? Even McDonald's has them!"

"We'll get you a latte and a Happy Meal for dinner then—with a little toy inside. Will that make you happy?"

Shaking my head, I perused the menu. There was nothing here that I could eat. "Everything is so greasy."

"Mmm. Bacon. A little fat once in a while won't kill you."

"I've already had my monthly allowance of fat...the chicken bites from yesterday."

"Monthly allowance?"

"Yes. One cheat meal a month." I sighed. "There is not one healthy thing on here. I seriously don't know what to get."

"No worries. I'll order for you."

"What? No."

Chance lifted his finger. "Bertha, babe? We're ready over here."

God, he even had the ability to make that mean waitress blush.

"What'll it be?"

He pointed to the menu. "I'll have this dish you call *heart attack on a platter*. She's just gonna have an order of plain rye toast, hold the butter."

"Comin' right up."

"All I'm going to be having is dry toast?"

"No. You'll be eating off my plate in no time. You just haven't realized it yet. The toast is merely my way of showing you that you don't really want the things you say you do. And many of the things you deem bad are really those that—deep down—you want the most."

"Oh, really..."

"I see through you. The harder you try to be good, the more you're starving to be bad. Not only are you going to eat some of my greasy food, but you're going to eat it with my cock sauce all over it and love it."

"Excuse me? Your what?"

Chance bent his head back in laughter before unzipping the pocket to his jacket. He slammed a small plastic bottle down on the table. It had a rooster on the front.

"Cock sauce. Also known as Sriracha—a Thai chili sauce. I never travel anywhere without it."

Bertha brought over an oval plate piled high with scrambled eggs, home fries, sausage links, bacon, Canadian ham and corned beef hash. She placed it in front of Chance before handing me the small plate of toast.

He wasted no time squirting lines of the red sauce across the top of his food. He dug in, watching me as I looked at him.

Staring him down, I crunched my toast in an exaggerated bite, determined to keep myself from wanting any of it. Admittedly, I was famished.

To prevent myself from looking at the plate, I pried my eyes upward, focusing on his baseball cap. He'd bought it at the hotel gift shop and was wearing it backwards. It was a good look, really worked for him with his hair sticking out of the sides. A ray of sun streamed through the window of our booth, accentuating number thirteen blue again.

Damn.

His voice snapped me out of my thoughts. "You know you want it, Aubrey."

Huh? Did he catch me checking him out, or was he talking about the food?

He cut a sausage link in half and attempted to feed me with his fork as he flashed a sexy smirk. "Come on. Just one piece."

It smelled spicy…and delicious. Unable to resist, I opened my mouth and let him feed it to me. "Mmm," I said as I chewed the juicy link slowly, closing my eyes and savoring every bite. When I opened my lids, Chance's gaze was fixated on my lips.

"You want more?" he whispered huskily.

Saliva gathered in my mouth. "Yes."

This time, he lifted a piece of bacon and fed it to me from his hand. I hated to admit it, but he was right about that sauce. It was so good on everything.

"More?"

I licked my lips. "Yeah."

Chance fed me three more bites. When I let out a moan, he dropped his fork, and it made a loud clanking sound. "Jesus Christ. The food is good. But it's not *that* good."

My mouth was disgustingly full. "What do you mean?"

"When was the last time you were really good and rooted?"

"Rooted? What?"

"Fucked, Princess. When was the last time you were properly fucked?"

"What does that have to do with anything?"

"There is no way you could possibly have that kind of reaction to food unless you were completely hard up." He wiggled his brows. "Prince Harry didn't quite do it for you, did he?"

"That's none of your business."

"Your face is turning redder than this sauce." Chance leaned in and whispered, "Aubrey…when was the last time you had an orgasm during sex?"

"It doesn't matter."

His tone became more insistent. "How…long… has it been?"

"College," I practically coughed out. *What the hell did I just admit?* "I can't believe I just told you that. Now, I'm embarrassed."

He let out a deep breath. "Don't be. But I'm not gonna lie. I'm truly shocked. A woman like you should be with a man that knows what he's doing."

"Why do you care? You keep saying that, a 'woman like me.' I didn't even think you liked me very much."

Chance leaned back into the booth and glanced out the window before looking me in the eyes. "As much as you're a pain in my ass…I do like you, Aubrey. You're funny. Not funny ha ha…but funny. You're conscientious. You're quick-witted. You're smart. You're damn cute…" He looked down almost to stop himself from going any further. "What happened anyway?"

"With what?"

"Why are you running from that tool Harrison?" When I hesitated, he flagged down Bertha. "Can we have more coffee, please, gorgeous?"

I didn't know what came over me. Maybe it was the hot sauce. A part of me just wanted to let it all out. After Bertha poured two fresh mugs, I started to open up to him.

"Harrison was a partner at the law firm I worked at back in Chicago. I was an associate. Patent and trademark law. He and I were a couple for a little over a year. We'd moved in together. About two months ago, I found out he was cheating on me with one of his interns. So, yeah…"

"So, you moved out?"

"Yeah. I also left my job. Harrison has spent every day of the past several weeks trying to convince me that I'm making a mistake, that I'm throwing away my career because he would have made me partner sooner than I could do it on my own. I left everything behind, took the first position I got, which happened to be at a small startup firm in Temecula. I'm scared. I don't know anyone out West, and I don't know if I'm making the right decision. I'm not even sure if being a lawyer is what I even want anymore. I feel very lost." Admitting that last part made me start to tear up a little.

Chance's eyes held a serious intensity that I hadn't previously seen from him. "What are you passionate about, Princess?"

Thinking for a bit, there was only one thing that really came to mind. I let out a nervous laugh. "Not much except…animals. I love anything to do with them. I'd wanted to be a vet, but my father was a lawyer, and he pressured me to follow in his footsteps."

"You probably feel like you relate to them better than humans, huh?"

"Sometimes I feel that way, yes."

He scratched his chin and smiled. "You'll find your way. You will. The shit that happened back in Chicago is still too fresh for you to think straight. When you get out to California, the change of environment will do you good. You can take your time, look inside yourself and decide what it is you really want, then make a plan to get there. You are in control of your destiny—except in the next twenty-four hours. I'm in control of it for now." He winked and flashed a devious smile. "You're stuck with me whether you like it or not."

"I guess I am." I smiled. This guy was starting to grow on me, and that was making me really uneasy. I didn't even know anything about him. "Your turn. Who are you, Chance Bateman? How long have you been in the U.S.?"

"I was born here, actually. I'm a citizen. I moved to Australia when I was five. My father was recruited into professional soccer in Australia to play and eventually coach. I grew up in that world."

"That's really cool."

"It was for a while...until it wasn't anymore." He swallowed, his expression turning sullen.

"What do you mean?"

"It's a bit of a long story."

My phone rang, interrupting the conversation. It was Harrison. *Shit. Shit. Shit.*

I flipped it around to show Chance the caller I.D.

He took it from my grasp and answered, "Harry! You wanker!"

Harrison's voice was muffled. "Put Aubrey on the phone."

"Aubrey and I were just talking about you! We're out to brekky, and she picks up one of these tiny sausage links and says, 'See this here? This is just about Harry's size.'"

He sounded irate through the phone. "You fucking asshole. Tell Aubrey if she's taking up with trash like you—"

Chance hung up the phone. "Ready to go?"

"That was awesome." I high-fived him after he lifted his hand. "Yeah, I'm ready."

"Bye, Bertha!" Chance winked at our waitress.

"Bye, hot stuff."

Rolling my eyes, I shook my head in laughter as I followed his hot ass out the door.

It was a beautiful, clear afternoon. I told Chance I wanted to drive this round. In all honesty, I needed a break from staring at his eyes and stubble for a while. My unwanted attraction to him was really starting to make me uncomfortable. Having control of the radio was also a plus to being in the driver's seat.

"Michael Bolton? Really, Princess? You're gonna make me sit through this?"

"What? He's good! His voice is...hearty...robust!"

Chance started singing loudly over the lyrics to *When a Man Loves a Woman*. He sounded horrible. The impromptu duet between Chance and Michael was enough to make me switch to another song.

Soon after, we stopped for gas, and Chance went inside the mini-mart to get us some snacks after he finished pumping my fuel.

When he reentered the car with a large paper bag, I looked over at him and froze just as I was about to turn the ignition.

He had powder under his nose.

Shit! Was he a coke head? Had he gone to the bathroom to snort it?

"Are you gonna start the car sometime today?" he chided.

My breathing became labored as I geared myself up for a major disappointment. "Tell me the truth."

"Alright..."

"Were you doing drugs in the bathroom?"

His eyes darkened. "What the fuck?" He was angry. "Why would you ask me that?"

"You have powder under your nose!"

He closed his eyes and suddenly erupted in laughter that lasted for at least a minute. He'd never laughed so hard in the time I'd known him. Chance kept trying to speak but would keep losing it, having to clutch his chest. He looked at himself in the sun visor mirror and swiped the powder from above his lip.

Practically shoving his finger into my mouth, he said, "Taste."

I pushed it away. "No!"

"Taste!"

I hesitantly ran the tip of my tongue along his finger. It tasted like grape Kool-Aid or something. "It's sweet."

He opened the paper bag and took out one of those Pixy Stix with powdered sugar inside and threw it at me. "Your cocaine, madam."

Relief washed over me. I also felt stupid. "Pixy Stix? You like these?"

"I love them, actually."

"That's pure sugar. I haven't eaten one of these since I was a kid."

"They were all out of Fun Dip, so these had to do." He looked down. "I can't believe you thought I was snorting coke. I'm not perfect by any means, but I've never done drugs in my life." Chance looked seriously hurt by my assumption.

I still hadn't started the car. "I'm sorry for jumping to conclusions. It's just...I don't really know you."

"So, get to know me," he said softly.

We were silent for a while before I spoke, "Why are you headed to California?"

"I live there."

I knew what I really wanted to ask but wasn't sure why it mattered so much. My heart started to pound. "Who were you talking to on the phone this morning?"

He looked startled by my question. "What?"

"I overheard your conversation from my room. You were telling someone your plans for the day. You lied and said you were in Los Angeles."

It took him a while to answer. "It's complicated, Aubrey." Then, he seemed to shut down and turned toward the window.

"Well, this was a good conversation. I'm glad I asked," I said bitterly as I started the car and took off toward the highway.

We sat in silence for a long while. Chance looked tense and kept sucking down the Pixy Stix one by one. After about a half-hour, I decided to break the ice. "How do you keep a body like that eating the way you do?"

"Is that your way of saying you like my body? You like what you see?"

"I didn't say that exactly."

"Not exactly, but you implied it."

"Jackass."

"Lots and lots of sex, Aubrey. That's how I do it."

"Really? That's it?"

"No. I just wanted to see your face turn that pretty shade of pink it does when you're embarrassed." He snickered. "In answer to your question, I work out a lot, and I don't eat like this every day. But on road trips, all dietary rules go out the window. You need to be able to eat what you want to keep sane."

"Well, from what I see, you're pretty insane, so it's not working."

He smiled at me, and I returned it. The aftermath of our tense conversation from earlier finally seemed to have faded away. "Give me one of the packages of pretzels, please."

He took one out of the paper bag and handed it to me then looked behind his shoulder to my packed backseat. "What do you have in all these bags back here, anyway?"

"Don't touch my stuff."

"I bet there are some treasures in this junk that would tell me everything I ever needed to know about you."

He started to blindly grab things out of my bags. "Oh, a book! *Happy Bitch: The girlfriend's straight-up guide to losing the baggage and finding the fun, fabulous you inside.*"

"Put that back and don't touch that bag again!"

"Alright. But what exactly are you hiding in this one that's so bad?"

Shit.

Chance kept digging. "What's this now?"

Oh no!

He pulled out my lifelike flesh-toned vibrator. "Princess…is this a silicone cock in a bejeweled case? No wonder why you didn't mind that Harry couldn't do it for you. You were taking it into your own hands and into your own—"

"Give me that!"

He took it out of the case. "Oh…this thing is pathetic. We could do a lot better than that."

"Chance…seriously, I'm not joking. Hand it over…now!"

"It's nothing to be ashamed of. We all pleasure ourselves."

The events that followed seemed to happen in quick succession. He kept waving the dildo around as I tried to grab it. A truck driver that noticed it honked at us. The car was swerving. Then, I saw it. It was standing in the middle of the road with frightened eyes, frozen like a deer in headlights. I suddenly cut the wheel hard to the right, driving straight into an embankment, not knowing if I had killed him.

66 Is he breathing?" I held my own breath hovering over Chance until I saw the rise and fall of its little stomach. It had shaggy long hair and was spotted like a cow, but its eyes bulged from its head more like a frog. The poor goat was only a baby. One I'd just raced into with my car while fighting over a damn vibrator.

At first, I didn't actually think I'd hit him. But then I watched in horror as he fell straight over, all four legs standing straight up stiff, like something out of a bad movie. Now we were both standing over him, waiting for something to happen, neither of us quite sure what to do.

Without warning, the goat flipped himself and was suddenly standing on all four feet. Startled, we both jumped back. Chance's arms spanned wide as if to protect me from a killer beast.

The baby goat took a few cautious steps, and then proceeded to walk directly into my BMW, as if the two-ton mass of steel wasn't even there. "Oh my God. I must have hurt his head. Look how confused the poor thing is." I reached out to touch the wounded animal, and Chance grabbed my arm, stopping me.

"What are you doing?"

"I'm going to pick him up. Look at him. He's hurt. I ran him over." I skirted around Chance and leaned down on one knee, extending my hand in peace to the sweet little goat. "And it's all your fault."

"My fault?"

"Yes, your fault. If you hadn't been distracting me, I would have been paying more attention to the road, and this would have never happened." The goat nuzzled into my hand. "Oh my God. Look how cute he is." I petted the top of his head, and he snuggled even closer.

"It's not my fault. If you weren't so uptight about your sexuality, you would have been calm when I found your magic wand."

I stopped petting the goat's head. "I am *not* uptight about my sexuality."

Chance folded his arms across his chest. "Admit that you pleasure yourself then. I want to hear you say it."

"I will do no such thing."

"Uptight."

"Pervert."

"A pervert is someone who has sexual behavior that is wrong or unacceptable. That's your problem. You think pleasuring yourself is wrong. I find it perfectly acceptable. In fact, I rather like the thought of you using your little magic wand."

I was pretty sure my eyes resembled the poor goat's—bulging from my head. Just then, a truck whizzed by us. One of those double trailers that always made me nervous to drive near. A whoosh of wind in its wake reminded me how close to the road we actually were.

"Come on. It's dangerous out here," Chance said.

"What are we going to do with Esmerelda?"

"Who?"

"Him." I scratched my nails behind the goat's ear, and he made a low humming noise that sounded like he was saying, "mommmm."

"Let him go." Chance waved his arm in the direction of the wooded area behind him. "Back where he came from. He's fine."

"He's not fine."

"Looks fine to me."

"I think he has a head injury."

Chance shook his head. "He's fine. Watch." He clapped his hands and made kissing sounds as if he were calling a dog. "Come on buddy. This way."

Esmerelda made no effort to move, quite content with her head pressed against my chest and her body between my legs.

"You need to let go of him."

"I'm not holding him here."

"Not physically. But he's got his head buried between your cleavage and his body between your thighs. No male is going to walk away from that willfully."

"See. Told you. Pervert."

Another truck flew past. This time he sat on his horn as he breezed by, and I went from squatting down to tumbling back onto my ass. The goat...well, he took one step and fell over again—all four legs stood straight up in the air. I couldn't believe I'd damaged such an adorable baby goat.

"See. He's hurt. We can't leave him here."

"What do you expect us to do for him? Belt him into the backseat of the car and take him to a veterinarian for a full work up?"

Two hours later, we were finally pulling off the highway in Sterling, Colorado to take our passenger to the Sterling Animal Hospital. It had taken Chance nearly a half-hour to unpack and repack the back of my car to make room. He wasn't happy about it.

"Snowflake?"

"No."

"It's from the children's book…"

"Heidi. Yes. I know."

"You do?"

"What? You just assume I'm uneducated because I don't walk around with a stick up my ass like your Harrison?"

"That's not what I meant."

"Oh yeah? So what made you assume I wouldn't know a classic literature story?"

"I don't know. You just don't seem like the type."

"Well maybe you should stop typecasting people. Not everyone fits into neat little compartments you know."

We were both silent for a while, with only the woman's voice from my GPS interrupting occasionally to direct us to turn.

"Mutton."

"Excuse me?"

"For the goat. A name."

"We are not naming him mutton! That's sadistic." We'd been arguing over names for the last hour or so. I favored names from Greek mythology or classic literature, whereas Chance wanted to name him one of the many dinners the poor baby could be turned into.

We arrived at the animal hospital, pulling up to an open spot right in front of the door. I made Chance carry the little guy, even though the door was only about ten feet away. Holding Esmerelda Snowflake, he looked…hot.

Was I that demented? Because I actually thought he was even sexier carrying a goat.

Inside, the women at the front desk confirmed it wasn't just me. Their eyes feasted on the bulge of his biceps as he carried our injured passenger to the front desk. He was quite the sight. I started to smile. Until he spoke.

"My friend slammed her BMW into this little guy while she was trying to get a grip on her vibrator." He smirked at me and winked at the receptionist. She blushed. I wanted to punch him.

"I'd like to get him checked out. I didn't think I hit him, but he just seems…off."

Chance snickered and mumbled under his breath, "He's not the only one."

Fifteen minutes later, we finally saw a doctor. He checked out the goat as if it were an everyday occurrence. One hand held him down on the examining table, the other pressed on his belly, checked his eyes, and wiggled all four legs. It seemed like a thorough physical to me.

"Everything seems to check out just fine. He has the usual congenital myotonic symptoms, and he probably suffered from a thiamin deficiency at some point. But those conditions don't come from a car accident. In fact, I don't see any signs that this little guy was even hit. It was probably just the fainting."

"The fainting?"

The doctor chuckled. "This here is what is commonly known as a fainting goat. It's a genetic disorder. Popular around these parts. Some farmers even show them. They faint when they get nervous. All the muscles in their bodies freeze up, and they basically just tip over. Only lasts about ten seconds. Doesn't cause any pain, but it's unusual to see for the first time."

"But…he's confused, too. When he got up, he walked straight into my car. And kept banging into things during the drive here."

"Well, that's likely because he's blind, too."

"Blind?"

"Thiamin deficiency, I'd guess. Unfortunately, it's becoming a more common problem. Improper feeding, particularly too much grain and too little roughage. Greedy farmer trying to fatten up the animal quickly. One of the side effects of the deficiency is blindness."

"Let me get this straight," Chance said with a skeptical tone. "We didn't hit the goat, but he faints when he's scared and he's blind."

"That's right."

Chance erupted in laughter. It was the second time I'd seen him lose it in the last twenty-four hours. His chest heaved, and a deep throaty sound echoed through the room. I couldn't help it. It got to me. Next thing I knew, I was hysterically laughing. too. We laughed so hard, tears streamed down our faces.

"What are we supposed to do with him?" Chance chuckled as he spoke to the doctor.

"Whatever you want, I suppose."

"Where do we bring him?"

"Bring him?"

"Is there, like, a shelter for animals we can bring him to?"

"For goats? Not that I'm aware of. Although there are quite a few farmers around. You can probably get one of them to take him in as part of their herd."

"The same type of farmer that tried to fatten him up to make a quick buck and blinded the poor thing?" I asked.

"Well, there are good farmers out there and bad. Just like anything else."

"And how do we tell the good from the bad?"

The doctor shrugged. "You don't."

We'd been in the car almost ten hours already. Chance was driving, and our new passenger was sound asleep in the back seat, actually snoring. I didn't even know goats snored. "We should stop soon. It might take us a while to find a hotel that allows pets."

Chance's eyebrows shot up. "Pets? You think we're going to find a hotel in the middle of nowhere that accepts goats?"

"What choice do we have?"

"He's staying in the car tonight, Aubrey."

"He most certainly is not." I folded my arms over my chest. "He cannot stay locked in a car overnight."

"Why not?"

"Because…" I was angry he was ready to leave the goat in the car without so much as a blink of an eye. "Because what if he gets scared?"

"Then he'll faint." Chance chuckled.

"That's not funny."

"Sure it is. Come on, Aubrey. Lighten up. Your being uptight is what got us into this mess in the first place."

I had no idea where it came from; the confession just blurted itself from my lips, "I pleasure myself. Okay? Does that make you happy to hear?"

Chance grinned. "As a matter of fact, it does." He shrugged. "I pleasure myself too, Aubrey. In fact, the next time I rub one out, I'm going to picture you."

He did not just say that? I was appalled. But also sort of turned on. I opened my mouth to say something back to him, then closed it. Then opened it.

Chance glanced over at me and then back to the road. "Well, well, well. Aubrey, babe. Whatta ya know. You fancy me pleasuring myself to your pretty face."

"I do not."

"You do, too."

"I do not." *I totally do.*

Surprisingly, Chance let it drop. He pulled off to the side of the road into a parking lot of what looked like a nicer version of Wal-Mart. It was an oversized warehouse of a store, only the front had a stone façade. *Cabela's The World's Foremost Outfitters.*

"What are we stopping for?"

"Supplies." He parked the car. "I'll be out in ten minutes. You can stay with Billy the Kid so no one steals him."

I was outside the car stretching when Chance returned, both of his arms filled with bags. I bent at the waist, finishing a rotation of stretches and leaned to my right to greet him.

"What is all that?"

He didn't respond for a minute. I bobbed up and down slightly, leaning into my bend and then looked up at his face to find what had made him quiet. He was looking right down my shirt. It wasn't his fault; I was basically putting it on display right before his eyes. My shirt gaped in the front giving him an eyeful of my cleavage. I stopped bouncing. Eventually, his eyes lifted and found mine

42

watching him. Our eyes locked. I knew that look. I'd seen it before. *In the mirror after I'd gotten a look at his ass.*

He shook his head and blinked a few times. "Gear."

"What kind of gear?"

"Tent, lantern, kindling wood, sleeping bags." He shrugged. "Basic camping supplies."

"For what?"

"Camping."

"You're going camping?"

He shook his head and shoved the bags wherever he could find any free space. The trunk and backseat were packed to the brim when I started this trip. And now I had an extra passenger, a goat...and apparently camping gear. "*We're* going camping."

"Ummm...I don't camp."

"Then Curry over here." He pointed to the backseat. "Is sleeping in the car." Chance closed the trunk, and his hands went to his hips. "What's it going to be, Aubrey? Camping or he sleeps in the car alone."

Apparently I was going camping. There's a first time for everything.

66 **I** take it you've done this before?" We'd only been at the campsite for a half hour, and Chance had already started a fire and was almost done pitching the first tent.

"Every summer with my family. My dad took my sister and I camping every year in the Outback. Best memories of my life. It wasn't fake camping like this, either."

"Fake?"

"No numbered campsites, bathrooms and security. We did real camping. What about you? What soured you to camping?"

"Nothing. I've just never done it before." Chance finished putting up the first tent and stepped back, admiring his handywork. "That tent's huge."

"Not the first time I've heard that," he snickered.

I shook my head. "Why did you buy such big tents?"

"Damn it!" Chance yelled as he swatted a mosquito from his face. The boisterous sudden rant scared poor Esmerelda Snowflake, and she froze in place and proceeded to tip over and faint. We got a good laugh over that one.

Chance threw some more wood on the fire and sat down. "What about the other tent?" I asked, looking over the fire at him. I really hoped he wasn't expecting me to attempt to figure that one out myself.

"What other tent?"

"You only bought one tent?"

He pulled a Pixy stick out from his back pocket and tilted his head back, shaking some of the sugary powder into his mouth. "Tent has two rooms. There's a divider. You and your son can sleep on one side. I'll sleep on the other."

I didn't really have a right to complain, seeing as he was doing all the work and paid for all of the supplies. So I didn't, for a change.

We munched on what would normally be a month's supply of carbs for me and sat around the campfire. Chance peeled a stick with a pocketknife and popped a marshmallow on the end before offering it to me. He really was good at this stuff.

"So, I'll be sharing a tent with you tonight, we adopted a pet together, and I don't even know what you do for a living?"

"I guess you can say I'm retired."

"Retired?" At what? Twenty-six, twenty-seven?"

"Twenty-eight," he corrected.

"Oh. Well that makes it better." It was dark, even with the light of the fire. I lifted my roasted marshmallow to check it. The color was browned nicely on one side, the other side was still white. "So what did you retire from?"

"Soccer."

"You played professionally?"

"In Australia. Yes. Well, not for long."

"What happened?"

"Torn ACL."

"It couldn't be repaired?"

"I had a few surgeries. But it tore again."

"I'm sorry. How long did you get to play for?"

"One game."

"One game? You mean you tore it in your first professional game?"

"I did. First and last professional game, both on the same day."

"How long ago was that?"

"I stayed on the roster for my three-year contract. Had a few surgeries…never really could make it back to the level I needed to be at. Retired at twenty-four."

"Wow. That sucks."

He smiled.

"But what do you do now?"

"I still get royalties, so I don't have to work a nine to five or anything. But I spend my days making junk art."

"Junk art?"

"Some people call it recycled art."

"I went to an exhibit like that at the Guggenheim. I loved it. I'd love to see your work sometime."

He nodded. Very noncommittal.

"Can I be nosey?"

"You mean more nosey?"

"You're the one who told me to get to know you. Before you made me crash into poor Esmerelda Snowflake, that is."

"You didn't even crash into that thing. And his name is *not* Esmerelda Snowflake."

My marshmallow was on fire. I blew on it, then slipped it off the stick and took a bite. It was almost liquefied. "Mmmmm."

I noticed Chance was watching me intently. "You want a bite?"

He shook his head slowly.

"Why not? You're the sugar addict."

"I get more enjoyment out of watching you eat it than I would eating it myself." He swallowed. The sight of his throat working made me warm, and it had nothing to do with the fire.

"Anyway. How can you be living off royalties if your contract was only three years?"

He looked away. "Posters and stuff."

"Posters? You mean of you?"

"Haven't we talked about me enough? Harry's been quiet today, hasn't he?"

"Not a chance, Cocky. You blew me off once, and I let you off the hook."

Turned out, I wasn't the only one that thought Chance Bateman was ridiculously hot. Even years after retiring from professional sports, legions of women in Australia were still keeping his poster and jersey sales alive enough for him to live off of. There was something very endearing about him being a little embarrassed of the whole thing.

After a few more hours of sitting around the campfire, we decided to call it a night. Chance set up my sleeping bag for me and then zipped the divider of our two-room tent down. He left me with the lantern, so I could change first.

My clothes smelled like campfire, so I stripped everything off. There was something exciting about standing naked with only a flimsy piece of nylon between us. I might have lingered an extra minute before I put my bra and panties back on. When I was all done, I unzipped the corner of the tent and handed the lantern to Chance.

He gave me a sly grin and zipped the divider back into place. My side of the tent went dark, but as I climbed into my sleeping bag, I realized I could now see everything on his side. It was a shadow, but a *very detailed* shadow.

He was facing me, standing very still. I wasn't certain, but it felt like he was looking right at me. It was impossible to actually see me through the vinyl divider, but I sensed his eyes on me nonetheless. He reached down to the hem of his shirt and slowly lifted it over his head. The shadow of his body was broad at the shoulders but tapered to a narrow waist. Even though I couldn't see the detail, I imagined what I knew was there. The ridges of his muscular abs, the hard plains of that carved V. My mouth was suddenly dry.

He stood there again for a long moment and then began to strip out of his pants. The sound from the slow unzip of his jeans made the hair on the back of my neck stand up. His thighs were thick and muscular; his boxer briefs hugged his legs like a second skin. I held my breath when his thumbs hooked into the top of his boxers, and he began to peel them off of his body. He bent to slip them off and then stood.

Holy mother of all cocky bastards. *He was hung.* The thing was dangling more than halfway to his knees. I took a sharp breath in, realized it was audible, and quickly slapped my hand over my mouth. I kept it there until he was completely dressed, afraid a moan might slip out.

When he was finally done, I watched him climb into his sleeping bag. He rolled onto his side and faced my direction. It made me wonder if he was looking at me. Then he flicked off the light.

"Night, Aubrey."

AH-BREE

Perhaps I could have been imagining it, but his voice sounded as thick and needy as I felt.

"Night, Chance."

I took a deep breath and shut my eyes, attempting to regain my wits. Then it dawned on me for the first time...had he just watched me give him the same show and returned the favor?

Where am I? That was the first thought that came to mind as I woke up. After a few seconds, everything registered. Sunlight attempted to permeate the tent. I lightly patted my bedside before my hand tapping on the ground turned frantic.

Where was the goat?

I jumped up out of my sleeping bag. "Chance!"

"Hmm," he moaned groggily from behind the divider.

"The goat! He's gone." A rush of panic tore through me. "He's gone!"

I zipped the divider down without a second thought.

"Relax. He's here with me."

"Baa." The goat let out that single sound as if to confirm that I had overreacted. My pulse immediately slowed down as I held my hand over my pounding heart. "Oh, thank God."

Chance sat up and ran his hands through his messy hair. Blinking when he looked up, he seemed to freeze. "Jesus Christ. Are you trying to kill me?"

I looked down at myself and crossed my arms over my chest. I'd run over so fast that I hadn't thought about the fact that I'd only slept in my bra and panties. "Shit. Sorry. I was so panicked. I wasn't thinking straight and didn't put anything on."

Utterly embarrassed, I returned to my side and spoke through the closed divider as I started to get dressed. "So, how did he end up over there with you?"

"You were out like a light. He started rustling around, trying to break through to my side. The bugger wouldn't calm down until I let him over here. Slept next to me the rest of the night. Worst fucking breath I've ever smelled in my life."

I couldn't help but crack up at that.

"You think that's funny, eh, Princess?"

"I really do." After throwing my last item of clothing on, I unzipped the barrier again.

Chance was standing before me half-naked only wearing his tight boxer briefs. He glared at me. "Privacy much? What if I'd just walked in on you like that a few seconds ago?"

He'd never looked so sexy, with his bed head and that almost angry look. My eyes unapologetically trailed down the length of his torso, down the thin line of hair leading into his underwear and stopped on his…massive erection.

Oh, God. Now, it made sense why he was suddenly modest.

Clearing my throat, I said, "You…you're…"

"Hard."

"Yes."

"It's called morning wood. I can't be responsible for how I wake up…especially under these conditions."

"Sleeping next to a goat. Did it turn you on?" I laughed.

"I was referring to your impromptu striptease a few seconds ago. And now, you barged over here again before I had a chance to calm the fuck down from it."

"Oh."

51

"I can only take so much." Chance slipped his pants on.

His stare was burning into mine. He looked even sexier with his arousal straining through his jeans. As much as I'd felt awkward for putting him in this situation, I loved the idea of being the one responsible for his hard on. In fact, my ability to handle my attraction to him was dwindling pretty fast. With each second that passed, the muscles between my legs were tightening from just the way he was looking at me. These were times I was grateful to be a woman because at least my excitement could be hidden. Still, this wasn't a good predicament. I needed to break the ice.

Clearing my throat, "What are the plans for today?"

He slipped a shirt on. "We need to eat."

"So, we'll get breakfast out?" I stupidly asked.

"Yes, breakfast. What else would I be eating out?"

Uh.

Choking over my words, I said, "No. Breakfast is good. I'm hungry. You?"

"Starving." The look in his eyes implied that he wasn't necessarily referring to food.

I was starving, too.

"Okay, then," I said as I retreated to my side of the tent to cool off.

It took us about an hour to break down our campsite and pack everything back into my car.

We opted to stop for takeout breakfast at a fast food place that was just before the on ramp to the highway. Chance had gone inside to order our huevos rancheros breakfast burritos and coffee. I used the opportunity to take my phone out and typed into Google: *Chance Bateman Australia.*

There he was. A plethora of pictures popped up. There was one in particular where he was shirtless, wearing nothing but a white t-shirt draped around his neck, and you could see just a tease of the top of his juicy ass. The picture showcased his signature sexy smirk that made me squirm in my seat. *That cocky smile.* Goddammit, he was handsome. That same image seemed to be the one that came up the most. It was also the one that was being sold as a poster for a cool $19.99 plus shipping and handling. There was even a picture of some girl standing next to the poster on her wall pretending to bite his ass. I suspected there were other people out there playing their own twisted versions of pin the tail on the Chance.

Knowing he'd be back any minute, I was reading through old articles and message boards so fast that my eyes hurt. It was definitely evident that Chance was more well-known for his debut game injury and his looks than anything else. I couldn't help but feel a sense of pride for how he'd turned lemons into lemonade, though. Scrolling down, I came across some pictures of him at various events with the same attractive blonde model. *Piper Ramsey.* A twinge—well, maybe a boatload—of jealousy developed in the pit of my stomach.

A knock on the window startled me. I tossed the phone aside, and it fell into the driver's seat. Well, more like I *threw* it over there.

"Open up for your coffee," I heard him say through the window. I took my cup from him as he walked around and got into the driver's seat. "What were you looking at?"

"Um, nothing. I was just…"

Shit.

Before I had a chance to explain myself, he lifted the phone, scrolling through the pictures with his thumb. He then threw it down onto the center console. "Well, now you've seen it all, haven't you?"

"Yes…and it's…pretty amazing."

He let out a single angry laugh. "Amazing, eh?"

"Yes!"

"And tell me, Aubrey, what exactly is so amazing about working practically your entire life for one single moment and seeing it all go up in flames on the very first try? What is so amazing about being more famous for your failure than your success? You know what *was* so nice about this trip with you up until now? You didn't see me as *that* guy that everyone*thinks* they know, and now you do."

Shit. I'd really upset him.

"I'm sorry, but I wasn't thinking those things at all."

"What *were* you thinking then?"

"I was thinking about how wonderful it was that you could stand up proudly in the face of adversity and still make a name for yourself on your image alone. I was also thinking about how striking you are, if you really want to know. And I was wondering who that girl Piper was. I was curious about everything, yes, but not in a bad way. Not once did I think anything negative."

Chance let out a long, deep breath and muttered, "Let's just go."

I felt so horrible for upsetting him and even though the internet was public, it somehow felt like I had invaded his privacy. More than anything, I felt like I had hurt him, and that hurt me, because whether or not I wanted to admit it, there was an unwanted ache in my chest. I could feel myself falling for him, and that scared me.

An uncomfortable silence clouded the air for the better part of an hour. The only time he'd move his hands from the wheel was to feed Esmerelda Snowflake pieces of hash brown patty dipped in cock sauce. Even the goat liked cock sauce.

At one point, he finally looked over at me. "I'm sorry I snapped at you."

"It's okay. I'm sorry that I made you uncomfortable."

"I probably would have done the same thing if I were you. It's just…all the stuff online, it's all bullshit. That's not the way to get to know me. If you want to know something, just ask me. Those people that post shit don't really know me."

"I do feel like I know the real you."

"You probably know more than most people. I've been nothing but myself with you from the moment we met. Even though I give you shit, I feel comfortable around you, and that's rare for me."

There was that feeling in my chest again.

"I feel the same about you, and I don't really understand it. I just know I'm really glad that we crossed paths."

He tapped the bobblehead. "Just think…if you'd never picked up Mr. Obama here, who knows where we'd both be right now?" He pointed to the backseat. "Where would this beast be right now?"

"Probably passed out on the side of the road."

Chance glanced back at the goat. "Instead, he's eating our food and sleeping with both of us. No thanks to me. It was all you." He flashed a sexy side glance and startled me when he put his hand on my knee, triggering a sudden rush of desire. "You're sweet. You have a good heart. That prick, Harrison, is gonna be sorry someday." When he took his hand away, I longed for its return. What he'd said also sent shivers throughout my body. An indescribable feeling overwhelmed me. I didn't know how to respond, so I turned on the radio. *Good Vibrations* by the Beach Boys happened to be on.

Chance turned up the volume. "Look at that! They're singing about you and your magic wand, Princess."

I covered my mouth in laughter, and we both cracked up. We'd finally broken through the earlier tension, and that gave me a sense of relief.

After we stopped for lunch and had driven for several more hours, Chance turned to me. "Are you in a rush to get to Temecula by a certain time?"

"I don't start my new position for another week, and the house I'm renting is fully furnished, so not really. Why?"

"Care to take a little detour before darkness falls?"

"Sure. I'd be up for that. What do you have in mind?"

"Somewhere rock hard and deep." He winked.

Well, that piqued my curiosity.

Chapter
Six

EXIT

We parked the car near the perfect spot overlooking the steep rocky walls of the Grand Canyon. Its beauty was overwhelming.

"Oh my God, Chance. I can't believe I hadn't thought of stopping here myself. I've always wanted to see it in person. It hadn't dawned on me that it was right on our way. It's so breathtaking."

I looked over at him and saw that he'd been staring at me instead of out toward the majestic peaks.

"Yeah. It's very beautiful," he said in a low voice.

"Let's take a picture."

With the Canyon as the backdrop, Chance snapped a selfie of us with his phone. He then texted it to me so I'd have it. The snapshot came out so good. The sun was shining into the blue of his eyes, and we both looked so happy and at peace. It made me wish this moment could go on forever, that we never had to leave this place.

As we sat looking out into a blaze of red colors while the sun set over the panoramic scenery, Chance suddenly said, "Tell me about your family."

"My mother lives back in Chicago. She wasn't happy about me moving at all. I'm her only child. But ever since she remarried, I've felt like she hasn't needed me as much. My father died a year after I graduated from law school, so at least he got to see me live out his dream, which was that I become a lawyer like him."

"It was his dream, but not yours…" he said in understanding.

"No. It's really not what I wanted."

"What is your dream?"

"I just want to be happy and fulfilled, but I have no clue what that even means anymore or how to get there. So much is up in the air right now for me. I feel like I'm at a crossroads in my life."

"That's not the worst thing in the world. Sounds like a good time to find yourself, especially since no one is tying you down."

"Yeah, I suppose."

"Speaking of which, I think we definitely scared off Harry Balls for good."

Our laughter at his comment caused an echo.

I stretched my arms and stared up at the sky. "You know what? I'm definitely happy right now. This—our little adventure—has been good for my soul."

He flashed a sincere smile. "You have a good soul. I could see that about you straight away despite your little bitch façade. You know why you're happy?"

"Why?"

"Because you're finally loosening up."

"I guess you took the stick out of my ass while I was sleeping in the tent last night then?"

"Yup. Burned it in the campfire." He nudged me with his shoulder.

I smiled and changed the subject off of me. "What about your family? Where are they?"

Chance paused and scratched his chin. "Like you, I also lost my father. He died of pancreatic cancer a few years after my injury."

"I'm so sorry."

"I just have one sister, Adele. She's two years younger. With Dad gone, my mother and she decided to move back to the states, but I stayed back in Melbourne. I never planned to move back here with them, but Adele got into some really bad shit. She needed me. I had no choice but to leave everything there behind to come handle things here."

"What happened?"

"It's a long story, but basically, she took up with a drug dealer and started using as well. It was a fucking nightmare."

"God, that's awful."

"I felt a lot of guilt because with my Dad gone, I was supposed to be the man of the family, looking out for her. I had my head stuck so far up my ass in Melbourne that I didn't know how bad things were with Adele."

"Where is she now?"

"Hermosa Beach…lives near me."

"Is she okay?"

"She's straightened up a lot, although she's still a work in progress. She's not with that motherfucker anymore. That's the main thing."

"And your Mom?"

"I was coming back from visiting her when I ran into you, actually. She's living in Iowa temporarily now to be closer to her mother. My Gram is dying. But my mother was also living in California near us before Gram got sick."

"I'm sorry to hear about your grandmother."

"Thanks."

"I think that was very selfless of you to drop everything and move back here for your sister."

"Well, my life had been nothing but selfish up until then. Nothing should ever come before family. I learned that the hard way. Adele and my mother mean everything to me."

"They're lucky to have you. I wish I had a bigger family."

"You'll have one of your own someday."

"I'd like to, but I'm not sure it's in the cards for me. I haven't had the best luck with men."

"Don't tell me there were bigger douchebags than Harrison?"

I chuckled. "Along the same lines."

"Let me guess. After you broke up, I bet they all came running back. Am I right?"

Pausing, I said, "Now that I think about it…yeah. I've only had a few serious boyfriends, but they all did come back at one point or another asking for a second chance. How did you figure that?"

"Wild guess."

"I don't understand."

"Girls like you are hard to find."

"Girls like me? Explain."

"Okay. It's not hard to find a beautiful woman, right? Definitely not hard to find a smart woman. And there are definitely some women with good hearts. But in my experience, it's extremely rare to find the whole package."

"Don't even try to say you have trouble finding women, Chance Bateman. You could have anyone you wanted."

He squinted his eyes at me. "Is that what you think?"

"Am I wrong? You're not a chick magnet?"

"Crazy psycho bitch magnet, maybe."

"You've never found the whole package?"

"The one time I thought I had, it turned out I was dead wrong. I thought it was love, but in retrospect, it was merely infatuation."

"Was that Piper?"

His expression turned sullen as he looked down. "Yeah."

"What happened?"

"Piper was my fiancé."

"Wow. You were going to marry her?"

"Yeah. Proposed to her three months into the relationship. Not too smart."

"She's gorgeous."

"You're prettier," he said without hesitation.

"And you're a fucking liar."

"I have no reason to lie. I've seen her without makeup. I've seen you without makeup. I'm telling you that you're prettier."

From the pictures I'd seen, Piper was blonde, thin and conventionally beautiful. With my unruly auburn waves and curvy frame, I looked nothing like her.

"How can you say that? She's a friggin supermodel. How can I possibly compete with that?"

"Your beauty is more natural. You don't need a drop of makeup. Your hair is out of place and wild. Sexy. The freckles scattered across your nose give you character. I mentally play connect the dots with them. When you move, your tits move with you because they're not fake. And don't get me started on your ass. Shall I go on?"

Feeling suddenly shy, I grinned nervously and briefly looked away before asking, "What happened with her?"

"Well, as you know from your stalking me, Piper's a small celebrity in her own right. I'd met her at a nightclub right around the time I was first signed to the team. She stuck by me for a while after the injury. She really enjoyed the limelight that came along with my sudden and odd fame. But as the months went on, her excitement started to wear off. I wasn't enough for her anymore. When I'd gone through a bit of a depression, I stopped wanting to go out. She kept on with it and eventually took up with one of my teammates behind my back. She's married to him now with two kids."

"Wow. What a cunt."

Chance bent his head back in laughter. "Princess, did you just use the C word?"

"Yup. First time in my life, but it was worth it."

"I didn't know you had such a dirty mouth."

"Neither did I, but damn, it felt good to say it."

"I liked hearing you say it. I think you should shout it out into the vast wide open canyon in fact."

"You think so?"

"Yeah. Do it. Do it! Shout it out."

"Cunt!"

"Say it again louder!"

"Cunt!" my voice echoed.

"Again."

"CUNT!" I screamed at the top of my lungs.

We heard a thump against the window coming from the car parked just behind us. Chance hopped up to check on things. "Ah, crap. You scared the shit out of Mutton. He just dropped down."

"Oh no."

"That's not all."

"What is it?" I got up and ran toward him.

"When I say scared the shit out of him…I now mean literally. Bugger took a dump all over your backseat."

"What?"

After Chance did his best to clean the mess with some Wet Ones wipes, the mood of our Grand Canyon excursion had officially been ruined. It was getting too dark to enjoy it anyway.

"Do you mind if we don't camp tonight?" I asked. "I'd like to shower and sleep in a bed."

"What do you say we go find a hotel near here, have a nice dinner, hot showers and call it a night. I'd like to sleep in your bed, too."

"What did you say?"

"I said I'd like to sleep in a bed, too."

"Oh."

"What if we can't find a hotel that will let us take him in?"

"We definitely won't. So, we're gonna have to sneak him in."

Chance stopped at a drugstore on the way to the hotel while I waited in the car. When he returned, he handed me a plastic bag containing bottles of water, snacks, duct tape and…diapers.

"You bought diapers?"

"Yes. Huggies Pull Ups. We're figuring out how to put one on him, especially if he's got the runs, and we're taking him into a nice hotel."

"I can't believe I hadn't thought about this problem before. Had he not gone to the bathroom all this time?"

Chance pointed back behind us. "Did you see how much he shit just now? He was backed up for days!"

We both broke out into hysterical laughter, wiping tears from our eyes. When we finally calmed down, Chance started the car and drove toward the highway.

Somewhere in the middle of Arizona, Chance pulled into the parking lot of a pretty high end hotel about ten minutes off the interstate. After I got our room keys, we came up with a plan where I would distract the front desk clerk while Chance snuck the goat in. He'd wrapped him in one of my comforters and sped past the desk and into the elevator.

Chance had the door adjoining our separate rooms open when I got upstairs.

He'd already managed to put two Pull Ups on Esmerelda Snowflake, wrapping some tape around the top to secure them. Chance hadn't noticed me, and I watched as the goat jumped into his arms and licked his face.

"Alright, buddy. Calm down. You're a good mate, you know that? A good mate."

"You're being so sweet with him."

Chance turned his head toward me suddenly, surprised to see me standing there. "Bugger's growing on me."

"I know the feeling."

Because you're growing on me.

"I was thinking I'd go out and get us something nice to eat. Do you like wine?"

"I do. I've actually been dying for a glass."

"What kind do you like?"

"Any kind of white."

"I like red. I'll get both."

"That sounds great." I smiled. "Do you know where you're going?"

"This map here says there's a strip of restaurants and a liquor store about two miles down the road."

"Alright. I think I'll take a shower while you're gone."

"Okay. Any special requests for dinner?"

"Surprise me."

He left, and I retreated to the luxurious bathroom. As the hot water poured down on me, all of the emotions I'd been struggling with the past few days seemed to pummel me all at once. It hit me that we were on the final leg of this trip now. I still had no clue if Chance and I would simply go our separate ways once we got to his stop or if he was interested in more. Based on that phone call I'd overheard, clearly, there was something he was keeping from me. I never flat out asked him if there was currently someone else when he admitted to a "complicated" situation. Even knowing that was a possibility, I couldn't help my feelings for him. Chance was the only thing that felt right about my life right now—the only thing that felt like home for as long as I could remember.

I threw a t-shirt on along with some cotton shorts and tried to watch a little HBO while I waited for Chance. Esmerelda Snowflake hopped on the bed next to me. An hour went by, but Chance hadn't returned. With each passing minute, an uneasy feeling grew in my gut.

What if he never came back?

It was a foolish thought. He'd given me no reason to believe that. Still, my reaction was one of slight panic suddenly. Maybe I was just exhausted from the trip, a little delusional. When another half-hour passed, I called his phone. There was no answer.

With each minute, the panic grew, and my eyes started to swell. I couldn't help it. I knew it was probably an overreaction, but I'd already lost control of my emotions in the shower, and his not returning was adding fuel to the fire.

The door suddenly opened, and I rushed to wipe my tears.

"My God, that was a cluster fuck," he groaned.

Chance was holding two bags and dropped them down on the desk in my room when he noticed me frantically wiping my eyes.

"Aubrey, are you crying? Did something happen?"

"No. No, I'm fine. It's nothing."

He walked toward me. "It doesn't look like nothing. What the hell is going on?"

"You were gone so long. I called your phone, and there was no answer. I started to think maybe…"

Shit.

He blinked repeatedly. "You thought I wasn't coming back?"

"It was just a fleeting thought. Deep down, I knew it was ridiculous but couldn't seem to help it. It's been a long trip, and I think I'm just tired."

Chance gently wiped the tears from my eyes with his thumb. "I'm sorry you got scared." He took my chin in his hands and turned my face to meet his eyes. "I wouldn't do that to you."

My heart raced as he pulled me into him. My body seemed to melt into his solid, warm frame. His heart thundered against mine as he hugged me tightly. I never wanted him to let me go. *Don't let me go.*

When he pulled back, cold air replaced the warmth of his body. "Can we please erase this from memory? I asked. "It was a lapse in sanity." I wiped the last of my tears and sniffled. "What took you so long, though?"

He didn't answer. He was still just looking at me with a serious expression as he examined my face. He seemed to be contemplating something. I couldn't recall him ever looking that serious before. Finally, he said, "I had to go to two different restaurants. The first one told me it would be an hour wait, and the second was no better." He lifted his phone out of his pocket and connected it to a charger. "My phone died. That's why you couldn't reach me."

I shook my head, muttering to myself, feeling so stupid for overreacting.

He handed me a cup. "Let's forget this and have a nice dinner, eh?"

Trying my best attempt at a genuine smile, I said, "That sounds good."

We sat across from each other at the small table in my room as we ate in silence. Chance had ordered three entrees from an Italian restaurant: eggplant lasagna, chicken parmesan and pasta primavera.

He poured wine into the two paper cups. "I know it's a lot of food, but I figured he'd want to eat as well," he said, placing a plate of food on the ground for Esmerelda Snowflake.

The tension in the air never let up all throughout dinner. I just kept pouring more Chardonnay to numb my feelings.

Chance went straight back to his room after we cleaned up. That left me feeling empty and confused, like maybe I'd freaked him out with my crying episode. Having had too much wine, I lay on my bed and stared up at the ceiling, which seemed to be slightly spinning. With my buzz granting me false courage, I got up and opened the adjoining door.

The shower was running while the goat waited outside the closed bathroom door. Lying down on Chance's bed, I curled into the thick down-feathered pillow. When he emerged from the bathroom, he stopped short of the bed.

He was wrapped in nothing but a white towel. His thick hair was wet and slicked back. Droplets of water slowly ran down his chest. So overcome with pent up desire, I licked my lips. My heart was beating out of my chest.

"What are you doing in here, Aubrey?"

I sat up suddenly. "Do you not want me here?"

He closed his eyes briefly then said, "It's late. I think it's better if you go back to your room."

That was not like him.

My stomach dropped. Humiliated couldn't even begin to describe how I felt as I said, "Oh. Yeah. You're right. I didn't realize how late it was."

He just stood there, towering over me with his large hands gripping his sides as I walked past him.

I returned to my room alone, tossing and turning as I ruminated over why all of a sudden he'd turned cold. Chance had sent me so many signals today that he wanted me. We'd opened up to each other. We'd laughed. He'd told me I was pretty. Maybe I misread everything. Maybe he was just being nice. Maybe he was attracted to me but didn't really *want* me for himself. Maybe the crying freaked him out. I was more confused than ever. The only thing that seemed certain: by the end of this trip, I was going to end up hurt.

Chapter Seven

EXIT

The next morning was awkward, but not the type of exciting awkward we'd encountered yesterday in the tent. I'd slept like crap, and last night's rejection that left me feeling sad had morphed into anger. We sat at a Waffle House filled with truckers and retirees. I stirred my coffee and let the spoon clank loudly on the table.

"Everything okay, Princess?"

"Fine." I avoided eye contact and stared out the window as I sipped my coffee. It was bitter…and so was I.

Chance leaned back against the booth and splayed his arms along the top of the seat. "I may not be an expert in women, but I know enough about them to know that *fine* means *definitely not fucking fine.*"

"Well, apparently you don't know me. Because fine means fine."

He ignored me and continued with his analysis of one simple word. "And the speed at which the *fine* is delivered is directly proportional to the level of pissed off." He drank his coffee and tipped the mug in my direction. "And your *fine* came pretty damn quick."

The waitress interrupted as we glared at each other. "Everything okay here?"

"Fine," I snapped. My response came so fast and sharp, the waitress was taken aback.

"Sorry. It's her time of the month, and she gets like this." He shrugged, and the waitress looked at him apologetically. I think she actually felt sorry for him.

I waited until she walked away. "Could you not do that?"

"Do what?"

"Make up stories about me."

"I'm not sure it actually was a made up story. You're quite the fucking bitch this morning. Maybe that's your problem. Is it your time of the month, Aubrey? Is that what's bothering you?"

"I'm not a bitch and no…that's not what's bothering me."

"So you admit something is bothering you then?"

"What is this, a deposition? Are you a lawyer now? I thought you were an ass model."

Chance glared at me; I glared right back. At least I'd sufficiently pissed him off enough to shut him up for the rest of our meal. We ate in unhappy silence and then Chance took the goat for a walk before we started back on the road.

He took the first shift driving. Five minutes into the trip, my phone was buzzing. Harrison's name flashed on the screen. "Aren't you going to talk to loverboy?" He asked facetiously, but I answered with honesty.

"No. I make it a point to only be an idiot once. He showed me who he truly was with his actions. It doesn't matter what he says with words now."

His eyes flashed to mine and then back to the road. We were quiet for another hour after that.

"What do you think about another detour? Sin City for a night or two?"

It made me sad to answer, but spending two more nights with him wasn't a smart idea. I was already feeling something he wasn't; putting some distance between the two of us was the right thing to do. "I should probably just get to California."

He actually looked sad about my answer, which confused me even more. "Okay. If that's what you want."

Hours later, knowing it would be our last full day together, a feeling of melancholy settled in. We stopped to fill up and, as usual, Chance was sucking on a Pixy stick when he returned to the car.

"Want one to suck on?" He whipped a fistful of long purple sticks from his back pocket.

"No thanks."

"You sure? You look like you could use a good suck." He winked at me.

"Why do you do that?"

"Eat sugar?" We loaded back in the car. Chance was driving again.

"No. Make remarks with sexual innuendo to them all the time."

"Guess my head is always in the gutter when I'm around you." He pulled away from the pump and navigated out of the parking lot.

"Except last night." I mumbled under my breath, apparently louder than I intended.

"What's that supposed to mean?"

"Can we not rehash last night? I felt like an idiot enough. You don't have to pretend to be attracted to me to make me feel better today. I'm a big girl."

"What?" His brows drew together. "Is that what you think? That I'm not attracted to you?"

I shrugged and rolled my eyes.

Chance muttered a string of curses and pulled off to the shoulder of the road. We hadn't even made it a mile since the gas station stop. At this rate, I'd never get away from him. He threw the car into park and got out, slamming the door hard behind him. The whole car shook with the strength of his anger. I watched from inside as he paced. He tugged at his hair as he walked back and forth on the dirt, grumbling something to himself. I couldn't make out what he was saying, but I didn't need to in order to be sure it was a whole lot of four letter words.

What the hell was he angry for? Because I called him on his crap? Because I'd made him feel bad for rejecting me? I was glad he was pissed…because so was I. After a few minutes, I got out of the car, too.

"You know what, get over yourself. Someone finally called you on the little game you play. Being rejected sucks," I scoffed. "Although, I'm sure you don't know the feeling at all."

Chance stopped pacing and stared at me. The muscle in his jaw ticked and he looked like he was near blowing. I wanted him to blow.

"You know what else? Plenty of men find me attractive. I don't even care that you don't. You're no different than Harrison. Saying one thing and doing another."

Well that did it. The explosion came. Although, it definitely wasn't the one I saw coming. Chance stalked to me. He looked so angry. I backed up until I was against the car with nowhere else to go. Then he invaded my personal space. One arm reached out on either side of me, caging me in between him and the car. He lowered his face to mine and spoke with our noses only inches apart.

"You're right about one thing, Princess. I'm not attracted to you."

I refused to give him the satisfaction of seeing tears, although inside my heart was slowly breaking. Then he continued.

"Attracted was what I was when I saw you that first day in the store. Playing with that little bobblehead. I thought you were beautiful. Gorgeous even. But now, I'm not attracted to you anymore. Now that I've gotten to know you, it's not attraction."

I wanted to tell him to go screw himself. But even as he was saying terrible things to me, I was mesmerized by him. The way his eyes turned from blue with a hint of gray to gray with a hint of blue when he was angry. The way his chest heaved up and down and damn if he didn't smell good, too. I stood there and waited for the rest of his rant. Because, let's face it, I wasn't capable of doing anything else.

"Now that I see what's really behind that bitchy façade—a woman who was hurt badly yet still willing to put herself out there because deep down she's a romantic— attraction doesn't come close to what I feel when I look at you. You really want to know what I feel when I look at you now?"

Somehow, I managed to nod my head.

"Attraction is way too tame for what happens when I look at you. I want to fucking conquer you. Watch your beautiful face as I sink deep inside of you so hard it borders on pain. I want to bury myself so far that you won't be able to walk for days. The only thing that could possibly be more beautiful than your face when you smile at me, is your face with me inside of you."

He closed his eyes and leaned his forehead against mine. "So yeah, you're right. I'm not attracted to you. It's more like I'm captivated by you."

I was pretty sure he had to feel my heart thundering in my chest, even though our chests weren't touching. "I don't understand then."

Chance lifted one hand to my face and cupped my cheek. He caressed my face tenderly before his hand slid down to my throat. A long moment silently ticked by. My heartbeat was under his thumb when he finally spoke. "I wish things were different."

The next few hours of the drive, my emotions were in turmoil. We were both quiet, although there was no longer an angry tension in the air. I was confused, to say the least. When we started to see the signs for Las Vegas, the only thing that was clear in my jumbled head was that I wasn't ready for this trip to be over.

"If the offer is still open, I'd like to take the detour." My voice was quiet, almost hesitant.

Chance glanced over at me, a solemn look on his face at first, then a slow grin spread wide. "You want to sin with me, Princess?"

Did I ever.

I couldn't believe we'd found an animal boarding facility to take a goat. The woman at the front desk didn't even bat an eyelash when we'd asked if she could keep our passenger for a night or two. Something told me they'd seen a heck of a lot stranger stuff in Vegas.

We parked at the end of the strip and decided to walk along Las Vegas Boulevard until we found a hotel that jumped out at us. The sun was scorching hot as we walked along the pathway that traveled from one end of the infamous strip to the other. I pulled off my white t-shirt, leaving only a very tight nude colored tank top. I didn't usually walk around that exposed, but the sweat was already beading down my back. Laughing, I draped the t-shirt around my neck and walked ahead of Chance, glancing at him backward over my shoulder.

"Remind you of anything?" I teased, posing exactly how he was positioned in the poster I'd found for sale all over the internet.

"Cute." He shook his head and chuckled. My mood was growing better as we walked. A street mime surprised me as we passed and took my hand. He pulled a flower out from up his sleeve and presented it to me, holding my hand up to his mouth for a kiss. Chance grabbed my hand and tugged me away before his lips could reach my skin.

"Hey. What did you do that for?"

"We're in Vegas, not Kansas. You don't let strange guys put their lips on you." My initial reaction was to be annoyed. Then I realized Chance hadn't let go of my hand after grabbing it. We were walking hand in hand, so I figured why argue if you like the end result.

At the Mirage, we visited the white tigers, at the Bellagio, we watched the water show set to music. We walked for what felt like miles in the hot sun before we stumbled upon the Monte Carlo. A huge sign for the The Pub at Monte Carlo hung from the side of the towering hotel.

Arrogant Bastard.

It was a beer, and we were hot and thirsty. What other sign did we really need to know we'd found where we should stay?

The cold air conditioning inside The Pub hit my sweaty skin causing a chill that shook its way through my body, leaving a small tremor behind. Goosebumps broke out on my arms and legs, and I didn't have to look down to know they weren't the only thing protruding from my skin.

Chance's eyes lingered on my pebbled nipples for a moment but then rose to meet mine. I arched an eyebrow but said nothing.

"Can you put those things away?" He shook his head and forced his eyes down to the bar menu.

"I can't help it. They have a mind of their own. They stand at attention whenever they want."

"I know the feeling," he grumbled while shifting in his seat.

"What can I get you two?" the scantily clad waitress asked. Chance didn't look up but responded quickly.

"Two arrogant bastards, please."

I liked that he didn't even notice the waitress. "So. What do you want to do tonight?"

"The usual. Blackjack, boobs and booze."

"Pardon?"

"When you come to Vegas, you come for three things: playing cards, half-naked women and partying like a rockstar."

A busboy brought us utensils and smiled at me. Chance noticed.

"We already got the half-naked woman covered," he grumbled.

"So, let me get this straight. You like half-naked women. Just not when one of them is me?"

The waitress brought our beer, and Chance chugged half of the oversized mug in one long gulp. God, what is it with me and that Adam's Apple? Watching it, I felt it bobbing in the pit of my stomach.

"I like you half-naked. Just…in the car or a closed tent. Not prancing around town for everyone else to see."

"Were you dating Piper when that poster of you hit the stores?"

He squinted. "That's different."

"Oh yeah? How?"

"My being naked from the waist up, doesn't have the same effect as you walking around with that little flesh-colored tank top with your massive tits bouncing up and down."

I sipped my beer. "Wanna bet?"

Chance's eyebrows shot up. "Princess. Are you being brazen again?"

"Do you like brazen?" I asked with a sinister smile.

He chuckled and shook his head. "You're trying to kill me. I knew it."

We both ate ridiculously large hamburgers and washed them down with our even larger mugs of beer. I was going to need a month long cleanse after this trip.

"So what do you want to do tonight?" Chance asked as we headed to the lobby to book rooms.

"Whatever you want."

He stopped short. "That's a dangerous offer, Princess. You might want to amend your answer before I take you up on it."

Between his admission earlier today and the beer leaving me feeling a little tipsy, I was feeling bold. I walked into Chance's personal space and smirked. "Whatever you want. I'm yours to do with what you please tonight."

He groaned, and I pretended I didn't notice him adjusting his shorts a few times as we checked in to the hotel.

I took less time to get ready for the senior prom than I did getting ready to go out that night. Normally, I tried to tame my naturally wavy hair, but instead I encouraged it to be wild. Smokey eyes and glossed lips matched the sexiness of my open toe high-heeled shoes, and the simple black dress showed off my figure in all the right places. Finally, toting around everything I owned had a perk.

My look wasn't really me, and it definitely wasn't how I'd normally go out at night. But when Chance knocked and I opened the door, any apprehension I'd felt went out the window.

"Fuck." He raked his fingers through his hair.

Inwardly, my peacock feathers fanned. "I just need to grab my bag. Come in."

"No, thanks. I'll wait out here."

If I couldn't have him, I was damn straight going to make sure to rub in his face what he was missing.

A group that looked like they might have been a bachelor party stumbled to the elevator bank as we waited. I sort of loved it when Chance put his hand on the small of my back in an understated possessive gesture. I really loved it when he didn't take it away, even when we walked out on the strip.

"Where are we going?"

Chance hailed a cab and opened the door for me. He answered by means of directing the driver, "Spearmint Rhino, please."

Five minutes later, we were pulling into a parking lot. The neon sign read Spearmint Rhino. But beneath it explained more: *A Gentleman's Club*. "We're going to a strip club?"

"We are. You said it was my choice all evening." He winked.

Oddly, although I'd never been inside of one, I was more intrigued than put off. The interior was nothing like I'd imagined. I suppose I expected darkness and sticky floors. But instead, I was surprised to find two floors, a grand stage and opulent décor. At first, it seemed more like a swanky nightclub than a place where women took off their clothes. The main stage had seating all around it, and there was a section with long couches for larger parties. Other areas could be curtained off for privacy. Some of the curtains were closed; others were open and inviting. I watched as two attractive women led a man by his hand into a private area behind a door.

My eyes took in everything around me, but when I looked at Chance, he was only watching me.

"Have you been here before?"

He nodded. "A mate's bachelor party last year."

"You mean you don't frequent this place with your dates?"

Chance chuckled and took my hand. "Just you, babe. You still think I'm a womanizer, don't you?"

I let him lead me to a booth in a corner. It was quiet, private almost, but it didn't stay that way for long. A dancer wearing only a g-string, with a body I could only dream about, smiled as she approached. "Would your date like a dance?"

He looked at me, caught my widened eyes and declined graciously. "Not just yet. I think we're going to have a drink first."

He turned his attention to me. "Still okay with me picking what we do all night?"

I rose to the challenge. "Of course."

We shared a bottle of wine that was grossly overpriced, and I actually forgot where we were for a while.

I looked around and sighed. "Where do they get all these perfect women from?"

Chance emptied his glass. "I only see one."

"That's sweet. But I can't lift my leg over my shoulder like that one." I pointed to a woman who had to have been double jointed. "So I think she definitely has me beat."

"Thank God."

"Thank God, she has me beat?"

"No. Thank God you can't lift your leg over your shoulder. There's only so much a man can take before he breaks." There was an intensity in his eyes that made me feel like if I pushed a little harder, I could break him. Only, I didn't want to break him. I wanted him whole.

"So. Have I passed your test yet? Or do we have to pay a hundred dollars for another nine-dollar bottle of wine?"

"Just one more thing. Then we can go."

I was almost afraid to ask. "What's that?"

"I'm going to buy you a lap dance."

"And that will prove I'm not uptight to you once and for all?"

"No. But it will sure as hell make my night."

The lap dance was nothing like I expected. It sort of…turned me on, and I didn't know how to process that. I liked men. I never had any interest in women, so it left me feeling a bit confused on the way back to the hotel.

"What's going on in that head of yours, Aubrey?"

The strip was jam packed like it was nine in the morning in midtown Manhattan, even though it was almost one in the morning in Las Vegas. I'd had a little too much truth serum…I mean wine. I leaned my head on Chance's shoulder in the back of the cab and took an audible breath. "Say my name again, Cocky?"

"Princess."

"No, my real name."

"Oh. Uptight Princess."

I jabbed him in the chest with my elbow and laughed. "No really. I like the way it sounds when you say Aubrey."

"Oh yeah?"

"Yeah."

"Alright, Aubrey." He wrapped his arm around my shoulder and pulled me close.

AH-BREE.

Snuggled tightly to Chance's side, I dozed for a few minutes in the car. His raspy voice saying my name with that incredible accent, made me warm all over. It felt so right, it almost hurt to think we wouldn't be with each other all the time soon enough.

Chapter Eight
EXIT

The knock at my door came at eight in the morning. I was awake but definitely not awake enough to go into a gym. What was I thinking when I'd agreed to go? I was way too amenable last night. The alcohol had smoothed out my edges temporarily, but this morning I was feeling wrinkly again.

"It's too early," I groaned after finding Chance already dressed in his workout gear. He looked sexy as all hell in his low hanging running shorts and sneakers, but even that wasn't enough to help my dragging ass. He caught the door as I turned back to my bed and slipped back under the cover.

Chance ripped the toasty blanket off of me.

"What the hell?"

"Rise and shine, Princess."

"I don't feel like getting up."

"You'll feel better after we do it."

I cocked an eyebrow and he smirked. "Ah. I think I've corrupted you. Who's the pervert now?"

"A pervert is someone who has sexual behavior that is wrong or unacceptable." Word for word, I recited the definition he'd given me when we were arguing over my not admitting to masturbating.

He chuckled. But also scooped me up from the bed and carried me to the bathroom. "Did you see the size of that burger you ate yesterday? I need to go the gym, and you're coming with."

I pouted. "Are you telling me I'm fat?"

"Not at all. I'm telling you I like looking at that shapely ass of yours and I'm selfish. I want to keep it that way."

I rolled my eyes but went into the bathroom and washed up. When I came out, Chance was lying in my bed, both his hands behind his head as he leisurely watched a European soccer game.

"Do you miss playing?" I asked. It was a stupid question. I regretted it the minute it came out of my mouth.

"I do."

"Can you get back into it somehow? I don't mean playing. Maybe coaching or managing a team or something?"

"I've thought about that."

"And—"

"I never actually finished my education. I went pro in my second year of college. Most universities and even high schools want their coaches to be educated. Sets an example for the students."

"So go back to school."

"I suppose I could. Might keep me busy for the next two or so years."

I walked to the suitcase and got out my little workout top and matching spandex leggings. "I'll just be a minute. I need to change."

Inside the bathroom, I pulled my hair back and dressed in my workout gear. I yelled to Chance through the bathroom door as I brushed my teeth. "What are we doing? I like yoga."

"Yoga isn't a real workout. I usually weight train and run on the treadmill for forty-five minutes for my cardio."

"Okay. Maybe the gym will have both, and we can do our own thing." I opened the bathroom door and walked out, ready to go.

"That's what you're wearing to the gym?"

I looked down. My tummy was bare, but I didn't think it looked too suggestive or odd. "What's wrong with this?"

"Nothing." He turned off the TV and grabbed my hand on the way to the door. "Guess I'm doing yoga today, too."

We actually compromised in the gym. He took a yoga class with me, and then we ran on side-by-side treadmills for a half an hour. After, we were both starving. Last night, we'd talked about staying another night, so I broached the subject on the way to breakfast. "Were you serious about wanting to stay again tonight?"

"I'd stay forever if we could." Those little things he said gave me hope, even though he'd all but written the words *never gonna happen* on my forehead.

"Well, then tonight is my night. You got to pick what we did last night. Now, it's my turn."

Chance squinted and held my gaze for a heartbeat too long. "I'm game."

"Great." I smiled. "I want to go visit Esmerelda Snowflake this morning. She's probably scared."

"We're paying a pampered pet place eighty dollars a day to babysit that thing. They give him three squares, and it sleeps in air conditioning, when it normally lives outside and walks in front of speeding BMWs. And you're worried it's scared this morning?"

"It's my day. Did I complain when you got to pick whatever we did?"

"I only got a night. Why is it that you're getting a whole day and night?"

"Because."

He chuckled. "Good answer, Counselor. Do you argue that well in court?"

"Shut up." I grasped for something. "I get a whole day and night because you made me go to a strip club and get a lap dance."

"Table for two," Chance said as we arrived at the hostess station of the buffet. Then he turned his attention back to me. "You liked it. I think you even got a little turned on."

"I did not." My face reddened.

Chance spoke to the hostess as she seated us. The woman was probably in her late sixties, not that he cared. "She got a lap dance from a stripper last night and won't admit to liking it."

The woman smiled and shook her head. Her Jamaican accent was thick when she spoke. "No shame here, sweetheart. What happens in Vegas, stays in Vegas. You enjoy a little shakity-shake if you want to. Can go back to being your conservative self on Monday. I'll grab you some coffee, and you can help yourselves to the buffet whenever you're ready." She walked away.

"Come on. Admit it. You liked it. That woman's ass grinding down on you." Chance shrugged. "I know I liked it."

"Why do you enjoy making me admit things that are embarrassing?" I'd already confessed one embarrassing thing; I had no intention of offering anything else.

"You mean like when you admitted you pleasured yourself?"

I felt the temperature on my face heat. I stood to head to the buffet line, even though I'd just sat down. But Chance grabbed my wrist and stopped me. "Don't ever be embarrassed by pleasuring yourself or enjoying a lap dance. It's beautiful, and so are you."

Taking an early afternoon stroll, we'd just returned back from visiting the goat. Sweet boy got really excited and jumped all over Chance, licking his face when we arrived. Poor thing probably thought we were never coming back.

"Esmerelda Snowflake was so cute when he saw you."

"My face is still sticky from that attack."

"You know you missed him." I chuckled.

"What are we gonna do with that thing anyway?"

"That *thing*? Don't refer to him like that. He's like our adopted child."

Chance came to a halt and looked up at the sky, cracking up. "Our child?"

"Yes! He has no one but us in this entire world."

"Seriously, though, Aubrey. After we part ways, what *are* you going to do with him? You can't keep him."

My heart suddenly dropped.

After we part ways.

My mind was trying to grapple with the fact that he'd implied that this trip was definitely it for us. In typical Chance fashion, just when he'd given me a little bit of hope that something was developing between us, he'd go and ruin it.

I was silent for a while before I forced myself to speak. "I'm gonna try to find a farm that I trust. I'll keep him with me somehow until I'm certain it's the right fit."

"Fair enough. He's lucky to have you." He was searching my face, trying to read my sullen expression. "Have you thought about what you want to do for the rest of the afternoon?"

"You know what? I really don't care. You decide."

Chance stopped walking again and turned to me. "Wait. You want to forfeit your ability to choose whatever we do today? Why on Earth would you do that?"

Because you just basically admitted that I mean nothing to you, and I don't really want to be around you at all right now.

"I'm just not in a decisive mood."

"There's a dark cloud in the air, Princess. I don't know what I did or said this time, but I feel like I know you well enough now to know that something suddenly pissed you off."

"Drop it, Chance, okay? We don't have much time left here. Don't waste it trying to read me. Sometimes people get into bad moods. End of story. Just pick something."

His face turned serious. "Are you alright?"

"Yes. I promise."

"I know I was joking about it earlier…but *is it* your time of the month?"

"No!"

He scratched his chin as we stood facing each other in the crowded promenade. "I think I have just the idea of what you need, something that's going to relieve all of the tension that has been building up inside of you over the past few days."

"Oh really?"

He wiggled his brows. "Oh yeah. Wait here." He walked away to make a phone call out of earshot.

As I stood there in the middle of the dry heat, I vowed to try to keep my mood in check moving forward. I had to accept this situation for what it really was—a road trip, nothing more, nothing less. I needed to enjoy these last hours with him and stop overreacting.

Upon his return, his mouth spread into a wide smile. *Those dimples.* A reminder that my new stance wasn't going to be easy.

Grabbing my hand, he said, "Come on."

I had no idea where he was taking me. I couldn't have told you if it was out to ice cream or up to his bedroom. After a five minute walk, we ended up back at the hotel. Following him into the elevator, I noticed that he pushed the button for a different floor than where our rooms were located.

"What's on the third floor?"

He winked. "You'll see."

When the doors slid open, I saw the sign: *Tranquil Waters Spa.*

"We're going to the spa?"

"Well, we're getting you a rub down."

Before I could ask him to elaborate, he walked up to the receptionist. "Couples massage appointment under Bateman."

I couldn't help but laugh and shake my head. "Couples massage?"

"Yes. We're getting one together. I could use some tension relief myself."

An attractive woman approached and batted her eyelashes at Chance. "Right this way."

Bitch.

We followed her down a long hallway and into a room with dimmed lighting. "Take off everything but your underwear and wrap yourself in these towels," she said. "Your masseuses will be in shortly."

It was completely quiet except for the sound of soothing instrumental music. The room smelled like mint, and there were flickering electric candles sparsely arranged around the space. It would normally be a relaxing experience were it not for—

"You heard her. Take off your clothes," Chance said gruffly.

A chill ran through me upon hearing the dominant tone of his voice.

"Do you really think I'm going to just disrobe in front of you right now?"

Instead of answering my question, he grabbed at the material of his shirt. I watched every movement of his rippling ab muscles as he slowly lifted it off. If that vision were a gif on tumblr, I would have replayed it over and over.

He unzipped his jeans and slid them down before tossing them on a chair. He stood before me in nothing but navy boxer briefs as he blatantly stared at my chest. "Your turn."

"Turn around then," I said softly.

"Do I have to?" he joked and flashed a wry smile before he moved to face the wall.

Removing my tank top, I stared at the defined muscles of his back and then down to his ass. He was standing right under one of the bulbs of the recessed lighting. It shined onto his delicious derriere like a spotlight. The crack in the middle of it was perfectly outlined through the fabric. He had the most phenomenal ass. *I wanted to bite it.*

When I unsnapped my bra and threw it on top of where his jeans were strewn, his breath hitched.

I wrapped myself in the plush white towel and lay down stomach first onto my table. This was supposed to be a relaxing experience, but I definitely felt a little nervous.

"You can turn around."

"You're no fun," he said as he lay down on the table next to me.

"What did you expect me to be standing in front of you stark naked?"

"One can only dream."

We were both on our stomachs with our heads turned toward each other. His eyes would occasionally travel down the length of my body.

He whispered, "You okay, Princess?"

Something about the tone of his question tugged at my heartstrings. I mentally cut them with an imaginary scissors. I was going to stick to my vow to keep my feelings in check if it killed me. "Yeah. I'm okay." When he raised his eyebrow skeptically, I smiled. "Really. I am. This was a good idea. Thank you."

"I'm glad you're pleased."

After ten minutes of waiting, I was starting to wonder if they'd forgotten about us when the door slowly creaked open. A small Asian woman named Anna walked around to the other side of Chance. To my left was a large, muscular man who resembled the actor Joe Manganiello.

Chance's eyes darkened, and he turned to the woman. "*He's* gonna do her?"

"At least someone's gonna do me," I muttered under my breath.

"Yes. We find that it works best this way. Men tend to be more comfortable with a female masseuse, and our female clients really enjoy James. Is there a problem?"

Chance was just looking at me, his mouth agape.

"No. No problem at all," I answered, looking straight into Chance's eyes. "I prefer a man."

James' voice was low and deep. "Please unwrap your towel and slide it off. You can stay on your stomach."

This was too good to be true. Cocky's plan totally backfired.

Chance's eyes were glued to every movement as I removed the towel from under me. Then, his gaze landed on the sides of my bare breasts pressed against the table.

Anna dripped hot oil down the length of Chance's back. He should have been closing his eyes and relaxing. Instead, he was looking straight at James pouring the same oil on me. I could see his back rising and falling as his breathing quickened.

James started to rub the oil into my skin. At one point, his hands were massaging the very bottom of my back and were practically kneading the top of my ass. Chance's gaze then turned into more of a death stare. He was seriously pissed, but I couldn't help feeling happy about it.

Watching the woman touching Chance in the same way was also getting me very riled up, but I was too preoccupied with his observing me to figure out whether I was jealous or turned on. Probably both.

After several minutes of watching Chance follow every movement of James' hands, I couldn't help but ask him, "Are you okay?"

His voice was hoarse. "No."

He was seriously burning with jealousy. I couldn't figure him out. If he only knew that the entire time, I kept imagining it was *him* touching me. I wanted that more than anything.

"How much longer?" Chance asked the woman.

"Try to relax, sir. You're extremely tight."

Forty-minutes later, our massages ended. Chance hadn't taken his eyes off James' hands the entire time. I suppose the only reason I knew that was because I hadn't taken my eyes off of *him* watching me.

Things were extremely quiet when Anna and James left us alone to get dressed.

Chance's back was toward me when I asked him, "How do you feel?"

"Tighter than when I walked in."

"Why is that?"

"Because I just paid 350-dollars to watch a man touching you for an hour."

"It's okay for a woman to touch you but not okay for a man to touch me?"

He suddenly turned around before I was dressed, prompting me to cover my breasts with my shirt.

"It's not okay for a man to touch you when I fucking can't," he snapped before turning back around, allowing me to finish getting dressed. After several seconds of silence, he finally said, "I'm sorry, Princess. I acted like a fucking asshole."

I really loved his jealousy.

"You're lucky I'm drawn to assholes. Cocky bastards, too." Pulling my arms through my shirt, I said, "Turn around, asshole."

"Since I'm batting zero, I'd like to give you back your pass to choose what we do for the rest of the day."

"I'll take it. I think we both need to cool off. Plus, we're all sticky from that oil. Why don't we just hang out at the pool?"

"I'm down for that."

"Wait…we don't have swimsuits."

"We'll buy them at the shop downstairs. My treat if I can pick yours." He winked.

"Deal."

"Really?" He looked surprised. "You trust me?"

"Yeah." I smiled. "I do."

This was the new Aubrey. Carefree. I wasn't going to get attached. I was going to loosen up and have fun with him.

"Alright."

Chance surprised me with his choice of bikini. There were some really skimpy string ones, but he chose one with a modest sports bra top and a bottom that covered most of my ass. It was white with little black polka dots and had a small ruffle over the back of the bottom. He also bought a pair of sleek black swim trunks for himself that hugged his ass beautifully.

We found two white lounge chairs next to each other and had brought snacks and magazines. It was late in the afternoon, so the pool area wasn't as crowded. We'd both taken a dip together before returning to our spot to chill. So far, this might have been my favorite part of the trip.

"What do you want to drink?" he asked.

"Something frozen and fruity."

Chance got up to head to the bar. A few girls were ogling him as he sauntered toward the other side of the pool. He didn't seem to notice how often people checked him out. Maybe he noticed but just wasn't affected by it.

After he returned with two daiquiris, we drank in silence.

Playing with the paper umbrella in my drink, I looked over at him. "This is nice."

He smiled. "I'm pretty sure if there was anything I could choose to be doing in the world right now, it would be this."

"This pool is beautiful."

"It's not just the place. It's the company."

As he looked over at me in that moment, his eyes were telling me a story. They were telling me that he'd truly meant what he said. I believed that Chance wanted me, that he wanted to be with me, but that he truly couldn't. Whatever it was that was holding him back was something out of his control. Those pesky feelings I'd been trying to suppress began to creep up again, so I buried my face in an InTouch Weekly magazine. Chance was sucking on a red Pixy stick when I got a sudden craving for sugar and asked, "You have any more of those?"

"I just might," he said, winking as he dug into the plastic bag we'd brought and handed me one.

I started to suck on it and barely anything was coming out. Then, I looked down and noticed that there was a hole at the bottom end of the stick. The orange powder had spilled out onto my stomach.

Chance laughed. "Messy girl."

"Do you have a napkin?"

"No need," he said. "Let me."

Faster than I could blink, Chance leaned over me and lowered his head to my stomach. He slowly ran his tongue along my navel, licking upward in one straight line to just inches from my breasts. I writhed under him, feeling a total loss of control as he lapped up all of the powder.

"Mmm," he moaned as he sucked the last bit of sugar off of my skin and licked his lips.

My breathing was ragged when he returned to his spot on the lounge chair. He'd left me sitting there, completely aroused but in shock. We didn't talk about what he'd done. He said he had to use the bathroom at one point and disappeared for a bit.

Just like that, all of the resolve I'd built up today was obliterated.

Since the upper hand in choosing our activities was still mine, I decided I wanted to try a really nice restaurant for dinner.

We ended up at the Foundation Room, which had a killer view that was sixty-three stories up, overlooking the strip. It was themed like an old country house with a cozy vibe.

After we devoured the crab cake appetizer, Chance opted for the steak while I ordered the grouper.

Trying hard not to think about how it felt when he licked the sugar off me earlier, it was to no avail. Every time I looked up at his lips, I could still feel them on me.

We'd ordered two bottles of wine, which seemed to flow endlessly along with the conversation. We talked straight for at least two hours. Chance spoke to me about growing up in Australia and talked more about his years in training for a soccer career that never happened. We'd shared stories about our fathers' battles with cancer. I'd divulged a lot of the details of my breakup with Harrison.

I was feeling even closer to Chance. By the end of the night, it was as if I knew everything there was to know about him, except where his life stood now. That seemed to be the big black hole.

Further adding to my angst, he'd gotten a phone call in the middle of dinner which caused him to get up from the table. I was pretty sure whoever it was had something to do with why he was holding back with me.

When he returned to his seat, my heart was racing as I asked, "Who was that?"

He looked me dead in the eyes, his tone serious. "No one important, Aubrey."

Instead of grilling him, I poured myself more wine. With each sip, a false sense of happiness overrode my insecurities. I became happier and happier.

By the time we left the restaurant, Chance had to put his arm around me just to keep me balanced. I wouldn't say I was piss-ass drunk, but I was definitely intoxicated. So was Chance.

We were laughing about nothing. At one point, we stumbled upon a chapel. There was a sign that read, *Fake Weddings Here.*

Chance stopped me in the middle of the sidewalk. The vapors of alcohol on his breath infiltrated my nostrils as he spoke close to my face. "Marry me, Princess."

"What?"

"We have an illegitimate goat—a fake child together." He laughed. "It's only proper that we partake in a fake wedding ceremony to make you an honest woman."

"You're insane!"

"Shit, we can text a picture to Harry. How fucking awesome would that be?" His mischievous smile sent tremors of desire through me. "Come on, it'll be fun." He led me by the hand into the small white chapel.

A large man dressed up as Elvis stood alone in the entryway. "It's a good night for a wedding," he greeted monotonously.

"Do you need a reservation?" Chance asked.

"We're slow tonight. We can take you right now if you want."

Chance looked at me, his semi-drunken eyes glassy. "What do you say?"

I shrugged. "There's no license. It's not real. So, no harm, right?"

We each filled out a form with some of our basic information. For a cool $199, we ordered the full wedding experience that included a ceremony, five digital images, souvenir rings, a silk bouquet and my choice of borrowed dress. Before I knew it, I was being whisked away by a woman named Zelda with a mop of frizzy red hair. She brought me to a back room where there was a rack of assorted white dresses in different shapes and sizes. She had me try on a few different ones, and I ended up picking out a strapless, lace mermaid style gown that was a little too long. My boobs were also spilling out of the top. It was the one dress that I liked, though.

Zelda helped me do my hair into an updo with tendrils framing my face. I had no idea what to expect when I walked back out there.

Music began playing. "Are they starting?" I asked.

"Your boyfriend must have picked a song, so yes."

"We're supposed to pick the song?"

"We have a library of music, and we usually let the groom choose while the bride is getting dressed. That's the best use of time."

I recognized it as *Marry Me* by Train. Even though the whole thing was staged, I couldn't help the butterflies that

99

were swarming inside of me as the music played. As much as I knew this was fake, my nerves seemed every bit the same as they would have been were this a real wedding.

This is ridiculous! Why am I so nervous?

Zelda handed me my small bouquet of silk calla lilies. "Ready?"

A deep breath escaped me. "Sure." Suddenly, I could feel myself starting to sober up. This was not the time to lose my alcohol high.

When I appeared at the threshold that led to the small aisle, Chance was waiting with one hand crossed over the other. He was still wearing the same fitted black button-down shirt he had on at dinner, except a small boutonniere was now pinned to the front. He looked so handsome and…*nervous*, too. This was the weirdest experience.

As the music played, I took very slow steps toward him. My heart was beating through the tight lace fabric hugging my breasts. Halfway down the aisle, I tripped over my dress and nearly wiped out. Chance snorted and started to crack up, and I couldn't help laughing, too. That definitely lightened the mood for the rest of my trip down the aisle.

Zelda gestured for my bouquet as she positioned herself diagonally behind me. Apparently, she was my maid of honor, too. Elvis started to speak.

"Dearly beloved, we are gathered here today to witness the union of Chance Engelbert Bateman and Aubrey Elizabeth Bloom in holy matrimony…"

"Engelbert?"

He winked and whispered, "Not really."

Elvis continued, "Which is an honorable estate that is not to be entered into unadvisedly or lightly, but reverently and soberly."

"Not exactly soberly," Chance cracked.

"If anyone can show just cause why they may not be lawfully joined together, let them speak now or forever hold their peace."

We both looked behind us to the empty seats. You could have heard a pin drop.

"Who gives this woman to be married to this man?"

Zelda spoke from behind me, "I do."

"Will you be using standard vows, or do you have your own?"

We answered at the same exact time.

"Standard," I said while Chance blurted out, "I have my own."

"You have your own?" I whispered.

"Yeah." He grinned.

"We'll start with the bride then." Elvis recited the standard vow, and I repeated them word for word after him.

Then, it came time for Chance to speak.

He paused, closed his eyes briefly then looked into my eyes as he took my hands in his. "Aubrey, from the moment you opened your smart mouth and called me an asshole in the first few seconds we met, I knew you were a pistol. At first, I thought it was the stick up your ass. I later realized it was just a protective mechanism. You'd been hurt, and you didn't want to let anyone in. Sometimes, those who put up the biggest shields are those who are protecting the biggest hearts. My Gram used to always say, if you want to know the size of a person's heart, look at how they treat animals or those that can offer them nothing in return. For some reason, you decided to trust a random bloke long enough for me to figure out that you have the biggest heart there is. You are just as beautiful on the inside as you are on the outside. You turned what started out as a miserable trip into the adventure of a lifetime. You can't begin to understand how much this time with you has meant to me. If you take nothing else from this, please remember that you deserve to be happy."

Tears were stinging my eyes.

Oh. My. God.

He'd caught me so off guard with that speech that it stunned me into silence. It was beautiful, but also sounded awfully like a cryptic goodbye.

There wasn't a trace of humor in his expression. He'd meant every word.

I heard nothing else that Elvis said up until, "By the power vested in me by the state of Nevada, you may now kiss the bride."

I wasn't looking at Chance anymore. I just shook my head repeatedly to let Elvis know he should skip that part, that Chance and I wouldn't be doing that. "We're not gonna kiss."

The next thing I knew Chance's big, warm hands had cupped my face as he leaned in and growled over my mouth, "The fuck we aren't."

In an instant, his lips devoured mine. My legs went almost totally limp. My heart was beating out of control as he pressed his body into me. He nudged my mouth open unabashedly with his tongue as it went in search of mine. Unable to get enough of the sweet taste of his breath, I opened wider, letting him in. He moaned into my mouth as I moved my hands upward to tug on his silky hair. He stopped kissing me long enough to lightly bite my bottom lip before releasing it. The kiss then became hungrier. I had no idea how long it lasted because a sense of time didn't exist for me anymore.

Elvis coughed. "Alright. That's nice. We have another couple now waiting to get hitched."

Chance pulled away.

Completely dazed, I looked up at him. His hair was all messed up from my fingers running through it. His stare was penetrating, and he looked just as bewildered as me.

What the fuck just happened?

The mood changed as we exited the chapel and found two couples waiting in the lobby. The first couple looked like they might skip the wedding and go straight for the honeymoon—right there in the lobby. The groom was dressed in an American flag suit consisting of red pants, a blue jacket spotted with stars, white shirt and a red and white striped tie. When he released his vacuum suck of his future fake bride's face, he lifted her into his arms, and I saw that she had on a matching outfit, only hers was an American flag bikini.

"Do you speak Russian?" he asked Elvis, who had followed us into the lobby with Zelda in tow.

Elvis shook his head. "Bilingual services are extra. You need an appointment."

"How much extra?"

"One hundred and fifty dollars. We have to pay the translator."

The patriotic groom reached into his pocket and pulled out a small wad of bills. He frowned, and his fake bride started shouting something in what I could only presume was Russian. She stamped her foot and flailed her arms as she ranted.

Chance snickered and leaned into me. "And I thought you were a bitch."

"Hey." I smacked at his abs.

He smiled, and I was torn between being sad that the sexual tension had ebbed and being relieved we seemed to be back to our version of normal. Chance held his hand out to me. "Mrs. Bateman?"

Shit. I liked the sound of that. A lot.

I put my hand in his, and Zelda ran over. "Would you like to do your wedding photos inside or outside? We have a lovely gazebo and pond out back. There's even a swan in the pond. She has an injured wing, but she looks beautiful in the background of photographs."

"We'll do them inside," Chance responded quickly.

"But the swan sounds nice."

"We don't have room for another pet. I'm not letting you near that thing."

I rolled my eyes. "We can just skip the pictures."

"Not a chance, Princess. Harry needs one of those babies." A dirty grin tempted at the corner of his lips as his eyes dropped to my chest. I had some serious cleavage trying to spill out in that form fitting dress. "Plus. You…in that dress…that's top of the toilet tank material right there."

"Pervert."

We posed for four pictures; it was reminiscent of dreadful prom photos. The last photo, Zelda made a suggestion. "How about something romantic now?"

I cocked my head and challenged Chance, laughing. "Yeah, sweet talker, how about something romantic?"

Zelda changed the background we were standing in front of. No longer were we standing in front of the famous old, neon Las Vegas sign. We were now transported to a honeymoon suite of some sort. The background had a photo of a large bed filled with rose petals and candles were lit all around the room. It was so ridiculously cheesy, I couldn't help but laugh. "Come on. It's our fake honeymoon night. There's our bed. Don't you have something romantic to say?"

Chance glanced back, got a load of the scene and turned back to me. "I'm not exactly the romantic type."

"What a surprise."

Chance's eyebrows lifted and then he stared at me for a second before he leaned in to whisper in my ear. "How's this for wedding night romance. If that were our bed, and I was lucky enough for you to be my wife." He paused and took a breath in, exhaling warmth on my neck. "If I was lucky enough to get to have you, I'd own every inch of that body. For the first time in your life, you'd give up that control you cling to so tightly. I'd demand it, and you'd willingly give it to me." He practically growled the rest. "That bed. I'd fuck you full of romance." He pulled his head back to look at me. Our noses were touching, but neither of us leaned in to formalize the connection. It wasn't necessary.

Zelda interrupted, "Beautiful. I think I captured the moment. I guess you're a romantic after all, Mr. Bateman."

Chance smirked. I stood in place, unable to move. "Lucky for me, it seems my bride likes my brand of romance after all."

Chapter Ten

EXIT

We were both sober by the time we arrived back at our hotel, although a big part of me still felt off kilter. I was drunk, just not from alcohol any longer. We were both still wearing the cheap metal bands that were keepsakes from our fake wedding, and when we arrived at my hotel door, Chance scooped me up off my feet.

"Gotta carry my bride over the threshold."

I wrapped my arms around his neck and sagged into his chest as he unlocked the door with one hand. "Wonder what the history of this is. So the man can show off how strong he is?"

"I think it started because the wife was nervous about losing her virginity."

I snorted. "Well at least we don't have to worry about that one."

Chance's eyes bore into me. He didn't even try to hide the jealousy. It gave me an idea. "Do you want to get married someday?" I asked.

"Someday? I thought I just did." He set me down just inside of my room.

"I mean for real. I wonder who will be carrying me over the threshold when it's my real wedding."

Chance's eyes were serious. "I don't want to think about it."

I kept pushing. "Maybe my new firm will be chock full of eligible bachelors."

"You mean like Harrison?"

I shrugged and sat down to take off my four-inch heels. "I've decided I'm not going to let him keep me down any longer. I've been moping around for two months. When I get settled into California, I'm going to get back on the horse." I looked up and grinned. Chance was still standing near the door. "What, no dirty comment about me getting back on the horse and taking a good ride? You're slipping, Cocky."

His jaw flexed. "Maybe you should take up with that magic wand again, rather than rushing into things."

I stood and walked to him, turning my back and pulling my hair to the side. "Can you unzip me?" The room was silent for a long moment before I felt Chance's hands touch me. One gripped my hip firmly, almost as if he had to hold on tight to keep it in place. The other reached up to my zipper. The sound it made as he slowly unzipped was positively erotic.

Seriously, what was wrong with me?

Neither of us moved. We stood there with thick tension swirling around us.

"Chance?" I breathed. I didn't even recognize my own voice; it was so low and husky.

His fingers dug deeper into my hip. It almost hurt, but turned me on at the same time. I waited for him to say something. Anything. I kept waiting. Neither of us moved.

Still nothing.

"Chance?" I tried to turn around and face him, but his hands kept me in place.

"Don't. I need to go, Aubrey." He paused and blew out a deep breath. "The guy who gets to carry you over that threshold for real, is going to be one lucky bastard."

I didn't turn around until I heard the door to my room click closed behind him. I hadn't wanted to let him see my tears.

It was a good two hours before I heard him return. The door between our adjoining rooms was cracked open enough so I could hear him moving around. My head was spinning, and the thought of never seeing him again after tomorrow seriously had me sick to my stomach. I'd spent more than a year with Harrison, and the day I moved out didn't hurt half as much as this did.

Lying in my own bed, knowing Chance was so physically close, yet I couldn't touch him, made me crazy. I kept on replaying his words over and over in my mind, dissecting each and every conversation I was able to recall. He'd told me I was beautiful. He'd spelled out the things he fantasized about doing to me in vivid detail. He'd said the man who I wound up with was lucky. His words told me he wanted me. His eyes told me he wanted me. His body, his breath, the way he stared at my body like he was clinging to his last thread of control.

I was damn certain he wanted me—that much I'd finally accepted. He just…couldn't. *Couldn't* was the word he'd actually used. Like it was wrong to allow himself. I knew he was trying to protect me from whatever was holding him back. But I didn't *want* to be protected anymore. What I wanted, was to be fucked into oblivion.

And it was time I took control of the situation. I am woman, damn it. Hear me roar.

With adrenaline pumping through my veins, I slipped into my bathroom, washed my face and let my bedtime ponytail loose. I lifted my nightshirt over my head and stared at myself in the mirror. The underwear I was wearing were cute—a pale pink lace demi cup bra with matching boy shorts. But I was done beating around the bush. I shimmied out of my underwear, unhooked my bra and took in my reflection. *Roar.*

My cheeks were flushed, my body was toned, and for the first time in a long time, I liked what I saw. There was no time left. I had to do it now before I chickened out. With each rise and fall of my chest, courage was starting to disappear. I looked at myself one last time, took a deep breath and headed for the door that separated us.

Here comes the lioness.

Chance was walking out of the bathroom as I walked in. He had nothing on but a plush white towel wrapped around his narrow waist. It was dark, but the lights coming from the Vegas strip outside of the bedroom windows illuminated the room enough so I could see. Droplets of water glistened from his chest. He was quite literally breathtaking, because my heart was beating wildly in my chest, and it felt like all of the oxygen was sucked out of my lungs when he caught sight of me.

We stared at each other wordlessly for a moment. The flex of his jaw as he tried to hold my eyes was a testament to how hard he attempted to resist. But he lost the internal battle he had waged when his eyes dropped. I watched each and every second as he took me in. First, my breasts—perky nipples taut and waiting—greeted him. His chest heaved up and down. I felt the caress of his touch on my skin as his eyes continued their descent lower. He took his time to appreciate the narrow of my waist, curve of my hip and flatness of my stomach. Both of our breaths were shallow and fast when his eyes reached still lower, falling on my thin landing strip. Between my legs was soaked, and we hadn't even touched yet. I almost lost it when he licked his lips.

"Aubrey," he groaned in warning. It sounded like he was in actual physical pain. "I—"

He was about to reject me again, and there was no way I could bare it. I wanted him desperately—even knowing I'd only be getting a piece. I pressed my finger to his lips and silenced him. Shock registered on his face when my other hand yanked the towel from around his waist free. I held it up in front of his face and ceremoniously let it drop to the floor.

Chance was gloriously hard, and I wanted him more than I'd ever wanted anything in my life. "We need to consummate our marriage."

He closed his eyes, and for a few agonizing seconds, I waited. When they reopened, everything was different. His pupils were dilated, wild and crazy, filled with desire and raw need. It was like looking in a mirror.

"Get up on the desk." He lifted his chin toward the floor to ceiling windows. A long desk was positioned so you could sit and look out onto the strip while working. There was an edge to his voice, a stern demanding tone that I'd never heard him use before. It made my knees weak as I crossed the room and positioned my ass where he instructed.

"I fantasize about you every night when I go to bed and wake up with a picture of you in my head and a hard-on every morning."

I knew he was attracted to me. But his admission reflected the level of obsessive thoughts I'd been having about him. It made me brave again. "Show me. Show me how you see us when you fantasize. I want to turn your dreams into reality."

His eyes gleamed and lips curled up to a wicked grin. "My dreams don't have rainbows and doves. They have me, pulling your hair as I fuck you up on that desk. You want to be my real live dream, Princess?" He prowled toward me and stood directly in front of where I was perched.

I swallowed hard and nodded.

The dimples appeared. Although the big guns weren't even necessary, I was already a goner. "Spread your legs."

The way he was looking at me made it easy to shed my inhibitions. "You have the most perfect tits I've ever seen in my life. And that pussy…it's even better than I imagined."

I shivered. "You have some dirty mouth on you."

He lowered his mouth to my breasts and looked up at me. Blue number thirteen blazed. "You're going to like my dirty mouth even better after tonight."

I closed my eyes as he drew my right nipple into his mouth. His tongue swirled as he licked and sucked and then caught it between his teeth and tugged hard before moving to the left one.

A soft moan fell from my lips, and I forced my eyes open to watch him. He was devouring me with his sinful mouth. The reality was even better than the fantasy that had played through my head over and over for the last week. After taking time worshiping my breasts, his tongue traced a path from my cleavage down to my belly button. Then he dropped to his knees.

His hands spread my thighs. "Wider."

God I wanted his mouth on me down there. I gripped the edge of the desk so tight, my knuckles turned white.

He took a good long look. I was sitting before him so bare, so exposed, that I had an overwhelming urge to close my legs and hide myself from him. But then he licked his lips again. He was actually salivating to taste me. It was the single most erotic thing I'd ever seen in my life.

He leaned in close and blew a steady stream of air from the bottom to the top of my sex. The cool air connected with my wetness and every nerve in my body zapped to life. My breathing was completely erratic just from the anticipation. I couldn't imagine being able to breathe once his mouth was on me.

He looked up, and our gazes met. "Watch me, Aubrey. I want you to watch me as I eat every last drop of this sweet pussy."

I couldn't respond; anything that came out of my mouth would have been completely incoherent. He didn't wait for an answer anyway. He hauled my ass closer to the edge of the desk and buried his face between my legs. Ravaging me, he sucked and licked, coaxing my body to the brink of orgasm and then pulled back, lessening his suction and slowing his pace. He was not allowing me to fall over the edge. Each time my breathing started to level out, he would start all over again. It was merciless and maddening, and I was beginning to grow desperate.

The third time he started to slow down when I was coming close to orgasm, I gripped his hair. My hands fisted in his thick, damp mane, and I tugged, urging him to continue. "Chance, I…need to…"

"Not yet."

Part of me wanted to kill him, but that part was overruled by the part that needed to desperately find release. "Please. I need to…"

"Not—"

He didn't get the chance to finish. I yanked hard on his hair and pulled his face to me. I heard him chuckle, but it did the trick. After that, he dove in hard—licking and biting, thrusting his tongue in and out of me until he again brought me to the brink. Once I was dangling on the edge, he sucked hard on my clit and sent me spiraling over. I gasped his name as my orgasm rolled through me. He didn't stop until my body felt spineless, and it was difficult to stay in the upright position.

Chance lifted me from the desk and carried me to the bed, gently setting me down. Only a minute ago I had been spent, yet seeing him naked as he stood there, suddenly had me recharged. I heard the crinkle of a condom wrapper and then watched him slip it on. His hand glided down his thick shaft, and my body came alive again. He was beautiful from head to toe, and every firm inch in between.

When he was done, I reached out and threaded my fingers with his. He climbed onto the bed and lifted our entwined hands up over my head, easily restraining my arms. Hovering over me, the head of his cock aligned perfectly with my opening. He searched my face, almost studying it, before our gazes locked. Then he kissed me sweetly as he gently pushed inside of me. He eased in and out a few times slowly before sinking deep. Rooted, he groaned and held himself in place briefly—his face telling me that being buried inside of me felt so good; he didn't want to move a muscle.

I wrapped my legs around his back, the new position allowing him to penetrate even deeper. "Fuck." He closed his eyes and leaned his head back. I loved seeing him struggling for restraint.

We easily found our rhythm together and rocked with a fervent pace. Our bodies slick with sweat, we glided up and down, hips swiveling round and round, until we were both shaking. I moaned as I felt him begin to come undone. His pace quickened, and he drove into me deeper and deeper until we came together while staring into each other's eyes.

It was hours later, drained of many more orgasms, when I finally fell asleep. Filled with new promise and hope, the last thing I remembered thinking as I dozed into dreamland was that I couldn't wait to wake up tomorrow to be with Chance again.

The sun blazed through the tall windows, warming my naked body. I had no idea what time it was, but I knew it was at least early afternoon. I lifted my arms over my head and stretched. My muscles ached, although it was the kind of pain I relished. I'd had boyfriends, a healthy sex life even. Up until last night, I would have gone as far as to say my previous dalliances were somewhat satisfying. But what happened between Chance and me put anything that ever came before it to shame.

Smiling at the thought, I reached back to the bed behind me, anxious to reconnect physically. Finding Chance's spot empty, I turned and listened for signs of where he was. It was quiet, but a minute later a knock at the door answered my question. I wrapped the sheet around my body and padded to the door. A woman dressed in a housekeeping uniform was standing with a cart when I opened it, expecting to find Chance.

"Ummm." I pulled the sheet tighter to my body. "Can you come back in a little while? We have a late checkout today."

The woman looked at her watch and back to me. "Fifteen minutes?"

I had no desire to rush to get ready but nodded anyway. After I closed the door, I looked around both rooms, even though I knew I was alone. There was a nagging feeling in the pit of my stomach—I never wanted this trip to end. Chance had given me no reason to believe things between us would continue once we arrived in California. In fact, he'd been pretty clear that the trip was it for us from the get go. But hadn't last night changed everything? I wanted to allow myself to think it really could have, yet there was that feeling.

In the shower, I closed my eyes and could see Chance hovering over me in the early hours of the morning. It was our third go around, and very different from the first two times. Our desperate, frantic race to be together was behind us, and we slowly poured emotion into every beautiful movement. I'd had sex before, but until that moment in time, I'd never really made love.

The warm water of the shower washed over my skin, and I replayed those last few moments over and over. "You're an amazing woman," Chance said. "Thank you for making my fantasy come alive. I hope all of your dreams come true. You deserve that, Aubrey." In the moment, I'd thought it was a beautiful sentiment. But suddenly, an intense urge to vomit gurgled up from my stomach, and my eyes flashed open. He was saying goodbye.

Chapter Eleven

I checked out of both our rooms and sat in the lobby for six hours. It was ridiculous of me to do. All of his clothes were gone; he obviously had no intention of returning when he'd snuck out while I was sleeping. Yet for some reason, I refused to leave. Sitting on a leather couch in the bustling grand atrium, I stared at the hotel entrance doors. Maybe he'd change his mind? Maybe he'd hopped on a bus and made it half way to California and then regretted leaving? What if he came running back, and I wasn't here? Then, I remembered he had my phone number and hadn't called me. Reality was sinking in even deeper.

A couple walked arm in arm through the front doors. She was wearing a tight white dress and wore a long veil, carrying a round bouquet of red roses. He was wearing a suit with his undone tie hanging loosely around his neck and a rose pinned to his lapel. I watched as he pulled her to him for a long, passionate kiss before heading to the reception desk smiling. Tears rolled down my cheek. It wasn't the first time today.

"Just get married?" An older woman carrying a tub overflowing with quarters sat down across from me. She had white hair styled in a big puffball that looked like it could withstand a typhoon. The blank look on my face was a dead giveaway that my mind was somewhere else.

"I'm sorry?"

Her eyes pointed down to my hands. I was absently twisting the ring on my finger. *My wedding ring.*

"Uh. No. It's not a real wedding band. It was…a joke." *The joke was on me.*

She nodded. "Would have been married fifty years next week."

I assumed she lost her husband. "I'm sorry."

"What for?"

"You said 'would have'. Did your husband pass away?"

"Hell no. I'm not that lucky. Bastard turned out to be a liar, cheat and a gambler."

"So what did you do?"

"Pulled up my big girl panties, kicked him out and divorced his ass almost forty years ago."

I smiled. It was the first one since my shower this morning.

"There you go. Pretty girl like you, that smile should always be on your face."

"Thank you."

"So what did the bastard do?" The name she used for the man who wronged me didn't go unnoticed.

I shook my head. "He left without saying goodbye."

"Sounds like he's a coward."

I was crushed and felt like a fool. But she was right, and I was only making matters worse by sitting around waiting for him—I knew he wasn't coming back for me. I hated to admit it, but Chance *was* a coward. A selfish prick who didn't have the balls to even say goodbye. I let out a frustrated sigh and stood. "Thank you."

"For what?"

"Reminding me to pull up my big girl panties."

The owner of the pet boarding place greeted me with a smile. "Overall, he was very good. Scared the heck out of us when he dropped to the ground at one point. But then we remembered what you said about the occasional fainting. We gave him a bath, so he should smell fresh and clean for your ride back."

Esmerelda Snowflake ran into my arms before circling around me repeatedly. He seemed flustered. Taking him by a leash, we walked out to my packed car in the parking lot. This was the final stop before leaving Vegas.

I was walking around in a daze. None of this seemed real. At any given moment, I still half-expected to hear his voice coming from behind me.

AH-BREE.

"You didn't think I'd really leave you, did you, Princess?"

My chest felt full, like it could burst any moment, but shock was preventing me from letting out the sadness and despair held captive inside of me.

I let Esmerelda into the back and took my place in the driver's seat, unable to garner the energy to start the car. Looking behind me, I said, "This is it. It's just us now. Are you ready?"

The goat startled me by jumping through the center console and into the front. I watched as he sniffed the passenger seat repeatedly and let out a few loud, frantic "baa" sounds. It seemed like he was really trying to communicate something to me.

I wondered if he sensed that Chance wasn't coming back. Animals are funny that way.

"He's gone. No more Chance," I said, rubbing the back of his furry head gently and swallowing the pain of my words. I repeated in a whisper, "He's gone."

The animal started circling around in the seat until he finally stopped and rested his head down.

Nothing could have prepared me for what happened next.

What sounded like a whimper escaped him. *He couldn't be crying.*

As the sounds got louder and louder, I came to the conclusion that he was. This sweet animal wanted Chance and either understood what I just said or had a sixth sense.

When he looked toward me with his sad eyes, it was at that moment that I finally let go. Everything came pouring out as I leaned my forehead against the steering wheel and sobbed. In just a little over a week, I'd found my greatest happiness and suffered my biggest heartbreak. It felt like I was born again only to be destroyed by the very thing that gave me a new lease on life.

Even though we'd slept together less than twenty-four hours ago, Chance seemed so far away now, like it was all a dream. The soreness between my legs from our one night together—our first and last—was the only evidence that it was real.

I wiped my eyes.

Big girl panties. Big girl panties. Big girl panties.

When I finally developed the courage to drive off, it seemed I had a new copilot. Esmerelda stayed curled up into the passenger seat.

As we passed a sign that read, *Leaving Las Vegas,* I wished that the saying were true, that everything that happened in Vegas stayed there. I knew better. What happened to *me* in Vegas would be something that would follow me around for a long time to come.

Two months later and doing my best to settle into my rented bungalow home, I'd come to the conclusion that losing Chance felt a lot like a death. Not only that, I'd pretty much experienced the five stages of grief: Denial, Anger, Bargaining, Depression and Acceptance.

Back in Vegas, at the first realization that he'd left, I was definitely in denial. Throughout the rest of the ride to California, though, anger had started to set in more and more as I focused less on the idea of losing him and more on the simple fact that he'd ditched me.

The bargaining phase hit me shortly after arriving in Temecula and stayed for about a week. *"If only I hadn't thrown myself at him." "If only I'd told him how much he meant to me."* I blamed myself for his leaving.

The fourth phase didn't take long to overshadow all the other stages. Depression was the hardest. It got the best of me for at least a month and a half. Aside from work, I did nothing but come home and wallow in the fact that I would never meet anyone that made me feel like Chance did. Despite how things ended, I truly felt that he'd ruined me for all other men. I'd wake up sweating in the middle of the night, painfully aroused from vivid and recurring dreams of being fucked hard by him as he told me over and over how sorry he was, that he loved me, that he'd made a mistake. I'd then cry myself back to sleep. While the depression never fully went away, as each day passed without any word from him, it gave way to the final stage of grief: acceptance.

As hard as it was, I finally reached a point where I had to accept the fact that he was never coming back for me. I had no choice but to move on with my life. That meant considering getting back into the dating scene even if it killed me. One thing was for certain. There was no way I was going to be able to get over him by continuing to lie in bed at night, reliving how it felt to have him inside of me.

I still longed for him. That might never go away.

If there were such a thing as a sixth stage, it should have been aptly named, *Purge that shit.* I decided that just being in my car was too painful. More than half of our relationship took place inside that BMW. Every time I would look over to my right, I'd hear his laughter or see him sucking on a Pixy stick. Sometimes, I swore I could still smell him. The spirit of Chance would always be alive and well in that car.

When I got to the dealership to trade it in one sunny Saturday afternoon, I was feeling very emotional.

I'd finally settled on an Audi S3. As I was leaving to get into my new car, the woman who'd assisted me with the trade-in called after me.

"Ma'am!"

I turned around to find her holding the Barack Obama bobblehead in her hand. My chest tightened.

"You forgot something. I just pulled it out of your old car. There's a little adhesive left on the dash, but we'll remove it. I thought you might want it."

I almost took it from her. *Almost.* Fighting the tears that were starting to sting my eyes, I held out my palm. "Keep it."

In the months after Chance, letting new things into my life seemed to be a bigger challenge than throwing old things out.

Jeremy Longthorpe was the CEO of a tech company and also a client of mine. We'd spent countless hours together working on a patent application for one of his recent inventions.

Even though he'd made it clear that he was interested in me, I pretended not to notice any of the hints he threw my way. He was really sweet and good-looking enough in a quirky-with-glasses kind of way. Going out with him could have also been a slight conflict of interest, even though the firm had no written rules against dating clients.

The truth was, I just didn't feel ready. My mind was still very much preoccupied with memories of Chance. As much as I tried to rid the physical evidence of him, what remained thereafter couldn't be destroyed as easily no matter how hard I tried. Although he'd hurt me, Chance was still taking up residence inside my head and in my broken heart.

Spending extra time with Jeremy was at the very least, a distraction. He was supposed to be meeting me at the office one Friday evening for a late-night work session. He'd called from the road to let me know he was running a little late and to ask me what kind of takeout I wanted him to bring.

My response was, "Something fast-foodish and really bad for me. It's been that kind of day."

"You got it," he said. *He was so nice.*

The smell of something fried made its way to me before I even noticed him walking through the maze of cubicles and into my corner office. Jeremy was carrying two grease-laden bags. "Since you weren't specific, I got a few different kinds of bad food."

"Thank you. I'm starving."

He slid some papers to the side to make room. "Why don't we just enjoy our dinner before we get to work?"

"Okay," I said, rummaging through the bags.

He'd brought food from Taco Bell, Pizza Hut and Popeyes.

Popeyes.

I just couldn't escape it. Chance was everywhere. Calling dibs on the chicken bites, I started to dig in when Jeremy reached over and grabbed one. "Hey, lay off my bites," I joked. I remembered saying something similar to Chance the first day we met. Little reminders that came in waves unexpectedly like that always seemed to bring the pain back in full force.

I suddenly stopped eating.

Jeremy put his sandwich down. With his mouth full, he asked, "Are you okay?"

"Yeah. I'm fine."

"Were you mad that I took one of your chicken bites?"

I half-smiled. "No, no. It wasn't that at all."

He leaned in. "What is it?"

Looking down, I said, "It's nothing."

"Aubrey, clearly it's not nothing. You were eating like a machine, and you suddenly stopped. What happened?"

The look on my face probably gave me away.

"You can talk to me, you know," he said.

I wanted to tell someone. I hadn't told anyone. Not one single person knew about what happened to me.

"You really want to know?"

"Yeah, I do."

Over the next hour, I told Jeremy everything that went down between Chance and me. He listened intently without passing judgment, and it felt so good to let it all out.

Nodding slowly with his arms crossed, Jeremy's mouth curved into a sympathetic smile. "Well, this explains a lot."

"Meaning?"

"Why you shut down whenever I insinuate that we go out."

"You noticed that, huh?"

"Yes. I notice everything about you." He looked down, almost embarrassed for having admitted his feelings in a roundabout way. When he looked up, he said, "I really like you, Aubrey."

"I like you, too. I don't want you to think my hesitation has anything to do with you."

He placed his hand on my arm. "Look…now that I know the reason why you're closed off, I think it's even more important that we go out. I promise, I'm not going to expect anything. Let me just be your friend. And if things turn into more, fine. If they don't, worst case scenario, we'll have had a good time together."

I smiled. "So, you're asking me out more directly this time."

"Yes. I'm asking you to take a chance. Go out with me."

Take a chance. I hadn't used Chance's name when telling the story. So, I found Jeremy's choice of words ironic.

"Take a chance, huh?"

"Yes."

"Okay, Jeremy. I will."

PART II
Two Years Later
Chance EXIT

CHANCE

My hands were balled into fists as I sat on my bed, bopping my legs up and down. I'd dreaded this day every bit as much as I'd longed for it. The closer it got, the more my apprehension about leaving this place grew. Looking around at the Spartan gray walls, I could hardly believe that this was really it. Today was the day.

Cracking my knuckles, I got up and paced.

"What the hell is wrong with you, man?" my cellmate Eddie said. "This is what you've been waiting for."

"You'll see how it feels when your day comes."

"Yeah. Fucking ecstatic is how I'll feel. You want to trade places? I'd give my right nut to be in your shoes right now."

"I know you would. It's not that I'm ungrateful to be done. It's just that nothing is the same as when I came in here. This place…it's become my normal. Walking out of

131

here is gonna be like walking into a big black hole. At least here I know what to expect."

"It's been two years, not forty."

"A lot can happen in two years, mate. I've learned that all too well." When the words came out of my mouth, my heart immediately felt heavier. Two years ago, I had a mother. Now, I didn't. *My mother was dead.* God, it was so painful to think about her not being around anymore. That was reason enough to want to stay in here and hide from reality.

Mum had suffered an aneurysm while driving about a year ago. The fact that I was locked up and couldn't say goodbye to her when she was clinging to life at the hospital was something that I would never forgive myself for.

There were a lot of things I couldn't forgive myself for.

Eddie's next question threw me for a loop. "Are you gonna try to find her?"

"Who?"

I knew who.

"You know who."

I ran my hands through my hair in frustration. *Why did he have to bring her up?* "No," I said adamantly.

"No?"

My tone was more insistent. "No."

"Why not?"

"Because it's been two fucking years. She's probably married by now, maybe with a baby even. Oh, and there's that minor detail of her hating my guts and wishing I were dead because I broke her fucking heart."

I never intended to tell Eddie about Aubrey. I never intended to tell *anyone* about her, especially the details of how I left her.

132

One night, I had apparently been talking in my sleep in the middle of a dream, saying things like, "Aubrey, I'm sorry. So fucking sorry." I'd woken Eddie up, and he dragged it out of me. The dreams were recurring and continued to happen on and off, to the point where Eddie had dubbed them "Aubreys." *"You had an Aubrey again last night,"* he'd say.

"You don't know for a fact that she wishes you ill will."

"What does it matter, Eddie? Even if she's not married, the whole point of sneaking out that morning was to make her hate me so that she'd move on with her life and not wait two whole years for me while I was stuck in this hell. Why the fuck would I have broken her heart intentionally only to go back and try to be with her again?"

"Aren't you even curious about her?"

Fuck.

Of course I was.

Shrugging my shoulders, I let out a deep breath and sat back down on the bed, staring at the wall. "I hope she's happy and that she's moved on. I really do. But I sure as hell don't want to put myself through witnessing that firsthand."

"Well, it's your decision. I just don't want you to regret it later. From what I can see, that shit traumatized you."

"Oh, you're a shrink now, eh, Ed?"

"I don't have to be a professional to see it. Look, you're a good guy. She'd be proud of you if she saw it the way I do. You've made the best of your time here more than anyone I've seen come and go before."

I'd damn well tried. I'd taken some classes toward finishing my degree and even organized a soccer program for the inmates in the adjoining juvenile hall. I was determined not to let these years be a total waste, to make something good out of them. If being here meant giving up everything, it was damn well not going to be for nothing. There was no doubt I'd be leaving prison a different person—not a happier one—but a stronger one.

Eddie interrupted my thoughts. "Let me ask you this. What if you found out this chick was out there somewhere still single? Don't you think what you had is worth risking disappointment for a shot at a second chance?"

Before I could answer, the long, slow creak of the prison cell door opening echoed through the halls.

I looked at Eddie. "I guess this is it."

He hugged me, patting my back. "When you start to feel down, think about this. If nothing else, Chancey boy, you're still one of the best lookin' dudes ever to leave prison with his ass intact."

I broke out into almost hysterical laughter. I was definitely going to miss him. "You're a good bloke. You've always had a knack for showing me the bright side of things."

"Glad I could do that for you."

"I'll keep in touch, eh?" I said, exiting the cell.

I let out a deep breath as I followed the prison guard through the halls amidst the heckling, swearing and applause of my fellow inmates.

He took me to a room where I signed the release papers. This felt surreal. I definitely expected to be happier about leaving. Instead, the fact that I was about to become a free man left me feeling surprisingly numb.

I waited alone until he returned with a large plastic Ziploc containing my belongings. Opening that bag was like opening a time capsule of an abandoned life. There were my jeans, and navy pullover sweatshirt that I'd been wearing when I turned myself in, along with my wallet, phone and watch.

My iPhone was dead, so I asked the guard if he could find me a charger. Since it was an older phone, no one seemed to have the right kind. Apple had apparently come out with two new versions since my imprisonment began. That figured. The guard was finally able to find someone in the office with a charger that fit my phone.

"You can charge your phone in here, get dressed, and then you're free to go."

I nodded. "Thank you, sir."

I plugged the charger into the wall and proceeded to change into my clothes. After several minutes, a light illuminated the screen of my phone as the device turned on. I waited a bit longer to allow the battery to gain enough juice to last the trip to surprise my sister. I was originally going to have her pick me up, but I decided to keep mum instead.

When it was time to walk out, I felt like a fish out of water. My footsteps past the guard booth were intentionally slow.

The bright sunshine outside the gates was a shock to my system. There I was standing in front of the massive prison building wearing the same clothes from two years ago and having no clue what to do with myself. It felt like the day I turned myself in was just yesterday and a lifetime ago all at once.

How did one become reacquainted with his own life? I felt like asking myself, "Where did we leave things again?"

I looked around me. There should have been a guidebook of what the fuck to do with yourself when you're let out of prison.

When you're locked up, it seems like your life is on pause. You come out expecting and wanting everything to be exactly the same, but knowing damn well that it's not.

All I fucking wanted right then was to go back to exactly where my life left off.

She was where my life left off.

What I wouldn't have given to snap my fingers and have her pull up to the jail in the BMW with that stinking animal in the backseat. One could only dream.

My mind was heading into delusional and dangerous territory. I shook my head and pulled out my phone to look up the number for a car service then remembered I had no data plan. Miraculously, the internet seemed to work. My phone was part of a family plan with my sister, and she must have continued paying the bill. I decided I'd walk to the nearest train station instead of taking a cab. Before I started the trek, I happened to click on my photo library.

Big. Fucking. Mistake.

It opened up to the last picture taken. It was of Aubrey. There she was.

Oh. God.

My heart felt like it came alive again after a two year hiatus.

Princess.

Suddenly, the emotions I was hoping to suppress had appeared in all of their glory, completely overpowering the numbness I'd experienced just minutes earlier.

I'd almost forgotten how beautiful she was. Aubrey never knew I took that picture. I'd snapped it of her sleeping peacefully in the hotel room right before I left. I wanted to always remember that moment.

Our fucking wedding night. It was supposed to be fake, but it felt all too real. Nothing had ever felt more real in my entire life.

Now, I was cursing at myself for ever thinking that taking that photo was a good idea. I should have deleted every single last image of her so that I'd never have to look at what I lost—the heart that I damn well knew I'd shattered into a million pieces.

At the time, I truly felt my leaving her the way I did was for her own good. I knew what kind of person Aubrey was. She would have waited every single day of those two years for me. That wasn't fair. After everything she'd been through, she deserved her fresh start. A new city, a new life…she was on the verge of finally starting to live the life she wanted. I couldn't drag her down, couldn't make her spend two more years lonely and sad. She deserved better.

Fucking her was definitely *not* part of the plan. Several times during the trip, I'd almost lost my control, but that night in Vegas was the last straw. I'd tried with all of my might to avoid giving in. But I wasn't strong enough. I came apart when she stormed into my room. I'd never made love to anyone like that in my life, and to this day, I didn't regret it. That night with her meant everything to me.

My finger lingered over the photo. I couldn't get myself to slide back through to the others. But I also knew I'd never delete them for as long as I lived.

When I stuck my phone back into my pocket, my fingers touched a piece of metal. I took it out. Gleaming in the sunlight was the fake gold wedding band that I'd still been wearing the day I turned myself in. Twirling it between my thumb and index finger, anger started to build up inside of me.

I stood there, staring at the ring, trying to figure out why I was so fucking angry all of a sudden. It was because I was starting to doubt whether I'd made the right decision.

Eddie's question from earlier—the one I never answered—replayed in my head. *"Let me ask you this. What if you found out this chick was out there somewhere, still single. Don't you think what you had is worth risking disappointment for a shot at a second chance?"*

Placing the ring on my finger, I answered the question, "Fuck yes, it would be worth it."

I took the phone out of my pocket. My heart was pounding out of my chest as I typed into Google: *Aubrey Bloom Temecula.*

2 YEARS AND 2 WEEKS AGO

66 "Will the defendant please rise?"

I stood. My lawyer stood with me.

"Mr. Bateman, has your attorney explained the charges that you are pleading guilty to today?"

"Yes, Your Honor."

"Before I can accept your guilty plea, I must be confident that you understand the charges against you, the effect of your guilty plea, and that you are entitled to a trial. The procedure that we do here today is called allocution. I will ask you a series of questions and then you will be given an opportunity to make a statement on your own behalf before sentencing. Do you have any questions about this procedure?"

"No, Your Honor."

"You have been charged with a violation of California penal code 242—Felony Battery With Serious Bodily Injury. Has your attorney explained the elements of this crime to you?"

"Yes, Your Honor. He has."

"And do you understand that you are entitled to a trial by a jury of your peers and that a plea of guilty today will effectively waive that right?"

"I do. Yes, I understand."

"And do you wish to waive that right today and plead guilty to the crime that you have been charged with?"

"I do."

"In your own words, can you please state the elements of the crime that you are charged with?"

"I am charged with physically injuring another person and causing him serious bodily harm."

"Okay, Mr. Bateman. This Court finds that you understand the nature of the crime with which you are charged and the implications for your plea today. The district attorney and your attorney have put forth a plea bargain for the Court to accept. One of the conditions of this plea bargain requires that you provide the explicit details of the crime you have committed and the reason the crime has been committed. This removes any doubt as to the nature of your guilt. Are you prepared to provide the Court with your statement at this time?"

I turned my head and looked back at the mostly empty Court. A bailiff was picking dirt from under his fingernails. A few men in gray suits had their heads down and were texting away on their phones. It was as if nothing earth shattering was happening; this was an every day mundane occurrence. There was only one face that looked shattered in the gallery. I'd done my best to get her not to come—but she insisted. There in the third row of the courtroom, sitting alone on one of the worn, wooden pew style benches, sat my sister Adele. Her nose was red and tears were streaming silently down her face. I hated that she was going to hear the details all over again.

Returning my attention to the waiting Judge, I nodded and spoke quietly. "Yes, Your Honor. I'm ready."

"Alright. What say you, Mr. Bateman? Tell the Court what happened on the night of July 10th?"

I swallowed hard. "On the night of July 10th, I went to the home of a drug dealer and threatened him—"

The Judge interrupted me and spoke to my attorney. "This is an alleged drug dealer, correct? The victim has not been convicted of any crime?"

My attorney responded. "Yes, Your Honor. The victim has not been convicted of any crime."

Ain't that a kick in the ass. I'll be a convicted felon before all of the real criminals.

The Judge directed the next part to me. "Mr. Bateman, you can either refer to the victim as the victim, the alleged drug dealer or by his name. Anything else will not be tolerated. Do you understand?"

My jaw clenched so tight I thought I might crack a pearly white, but I nodded. There was no fucking way I was calling that piece of shit a *victim*. Adele was the only victim in this whole tragedy.

"Go on."

"As I was saying. I went to the home of the *alleged* drug dealer, Darius Marshall, and threatened him. The *alleged* drug dealer was the boyfriend of my sister. It's my understanding that he had a dispute with another *alleged* drug dealer. I threatened Darius to tell me where the other drug dealer was. The police had been looking for the other alleged dealer for two weeks and weren't making any progress. I wanted to help. Darius refused to tell me where the guy was."

"And why were the police looking for this other alleged drug dealer?"

I looked at the bench and then back at my sister. She looked broken. Taking a deep breath, I continued, "He raped my sister. To get even with Darius. And before he left her beaten and scarred, he told her he'd be back again."

It was the first time the Judge's face softened. "And what did you do when Darius Marshall refused to give you the information you wanted?"

It was a small victory, but the Judge finally stopped calling Darius *the victim*, too. "I attacked him."

"Were any weapons involved in the attack?"

I looked to my attorney and back to the judge. "I don't believe so, Your Honor?"

"You don't believe so? Meaning you aren't sure?"

"Well…no weapons were recovered at the scene, and I don't recall having one with me. But, no, I can't be sure."

"And why is that Mr. Bateman?"

"Because I don't remember most of the attack."

"I see. What is the last thing that you are able to recall?"

I knew. But I damn sure didn't want to repeat it out loud. She was so fragile already.

My lawyer whispered to me, "You need to do this, Chance."

I cleared my throat. "Darius said something to me. And that's the last thing I can recall."

"And what is it that he said, Mr. Bateman?"

My attorney had warned me not to show anger. It took every ounce of willpower that I had to unclench my fists and speak. "He said…my sister was a crack whore, and she might as well have gotten the first one under her belt because she would be taking cock down her throat in exchange for a dime bag by next week."

The judge looked sympathetic momentarily. "And do you know the nature of the injuries that Darius Marshall sustained?"

"As far as I've been told, he had a broken nose, a fractured eye socket, a concussion and a few broken ribs."

"And you recall none of the actions that lead to these injuries?"

"No, Your Honor. I don't. I remember what I already told you, and the next thing I can recall is him saying 1925 Harmon Street."

"Alright then, Mr. Bateman. We're almost done here. I have a few additional questions before we will break and then come back this afternoon for sentencing."

I nodded.

"Do you regret your actions, Mr. Bateman?"

The last question was a bone of contention between my lawyer and me. While he didn't outright tell me to lie, I could read between the lines. But I'd come this far. I was going to stand tall. Not three hours after Darius was carted away in an ambulance, the dealer that attacked Adele was arrested. I looked straight into the eyes of the Judge and told the honest to God's truth. "No. I don't regret my actions."

It was nearly four by the time the Judge called us back into the Courtroom. He took off his glasses and rubbed his eyes before speaking. "Mr. Bateman. Do you understand that as a result of your guilty plea, you may lose certain valuable civil rights such as the right to vote, the right to hold public office, the right to serve on a jury and the right to possess a firearm?"

Even after having two months to think about the consequences of my actions, I didn't care about what I lost. Only that Adele could sleep at night again. "I understand, Your Honor."

"Okay, then. Mr. Bateman, your plea deal with the District Attorney to serve two years is found to be an adequate punishment and is therefore accepted by this Court. While the Court sympathizes with what your family has gone through, our legal system must be trusted to serve its intended purposes. We cannot have vigilantes running all over the city avenging crimes as they see fit. Your request for time to get your affairs in order is granted with the condition that you turn in your passport and do not leave the state of California. You are hereby ordered to surrender to the Los Angeles County correctional facility in fourteen days." The judge slammed his gavel and just like that, I was a convicted felon.

Chapter
Fifteen

EXIT

Even though my place was blocks from the beach, the smell of the ocean permeated the air. I took a deep breath and filled my lungs with freedom. *Damn it smelled good.*

The last thing I did before turning myself in for two years of hell, was check my sister into rehab. I knew she did well; I saw it on her face every other Saturday when she came to visit. Yet for some reason, I was suddenly nervous to show up unannounced and surprise her.

When I unlocked the heavy metal door to my place, pop music blasted through the open-air loft I called home. I smiled hearing it, even though her shit taste in music drove me up a wall growing up. "Adele?"

I lived in a renovated warehouse—sound was normally muted from the high ceilings, but it was completely lost to the howlish sound of Taylor Swift blaring through the indoor speakers. "Adele?" I called slightly louder. After everything she'd been through, I didn't want to startle her. I had no idea if she was still skittish. After the attack, she jumped if anyone walked into a room, even when she knew they were there. I dropped my key in the bowl on the table near the door and headed to the kitchen.

A man wearing a dress shirt and boxers was ironing on my granite counter. We spotted each other at the same moment. He held up the iron like a weapon; I held up my hands in surrender. "Is Adele here?"

"Who are you?"

"Relax, Mate." I spoke calmly, keeping my hands in the air where he could see them the entire time. If there was one good thing about spending two years in prison, I'd definitely learned how to defuse a violent situation. "I'm Adele's brother—I live here."

Boxer boy's eyes flared. "Chance?"

Well one of us was filled in. "That's me."

"Shit. Sorry. I thought you were getting out next week."

"Overcrowding." I narrowed my eyes on the iron he was still holding. "You want to put that thing down now, yeah?"

"Yeah. Of course. Sorry." He set the iron on the counter and took two steps toward me, extending his hand. "Harry. Harry Beecham. I've heard so much about you."

You've got to be shitting me? Harry? "Wish I could say the same."

"Do you think we could stop at the—" My sister's voice abruptly halted as she turned the corner into the kitchen. "Oh my God!" She almost knocked me over when she flew into my arms. "You're here! You're home!"

"I am." Adele held me in a death like grip. She was crying, but unlike the last time I hugged her, these were tears of happiness. I pulled back to take a good look at my little sister. I'd seen her every other week, but I'd only gotten glimpses of what she wanted me to see. She was twenty-eight now, dressed in a skirt and girly blouse with her hair fastened on top of her head. She looked a lot like Mum.

"You look…different. Grown up."

She wiped her tears and smoothed her skirt. "This is how I dress for work. I told you. I'm a secretary now."

Harry cleared his throat. The bloke was still standing in his boxers. "I'm late. I should get going. It was great to finally meet you, Chance."

I eyed him. "I hope you put some pants on first."

He gently placed his hand on Adele's shoulder as he passed and spoke softly, "Take the morning off. I'll see you this afternoon."

Adele smiled at Boxer Boy, then looked at me while biting down on her bottom lip. "Sorry. I didn't know…Harold is one of the partners at the accounting firm I work for."

"An accountant?"

"Yeah." My sister smiled. "Not the type I normally go for, huh?"

My sister had a knack for picking one loser after the next. The crowd she hung out with wasn't exactly conducive to meeting CPAs. "As long as he's good to you." I couldn't help myself. "And keeps some damn pants on when I'm around."

Adele and I spent the entire morning catching up. Talking about Mum was the hardest part. Things could have gone either way for my sister after what happened two years ago. Our mother's death could have really set her back. I was relieved to find she truly had turned her life around. It made everything I'd went through worth it in the end. She seemed…happy.

"So." Adele took the mugs we'd been drinking from and placed them in the sink. She leaned her bum against the counter and folded her arms over her chest. "Are you going to go see her?"

"Who?" *Why was I playing this game again? I knew damn well who she was referring to.*

"Your wife." Her eyes pointed to the ring I'd already forgotten was on my finger. I shoved my hand into my pocket.

"She's not my wife."

Adele rolled her eyes. "Your fake wife. Whatever. Are you going to go see her?"

"Don't start, Adele." One lonely visit, I'd turned into a Mary and spilled my guts about Aubrey to my sister. I regretted it instantly. She spent the next twenty-three months trying to talk me into writing to Aubrey and telling her where I was. She even suggested *she* go visit Aubrey to have a chat and keep the hope alive.

"Have you looked her up yet?"

"I've been out for three hours."

My sister squinted. "So that's a yes, then?"

I shook my head, not responding, but she knew the answer. "I'm going to take a long, hot shower. It's been a while."

The look of hope on my sister's face dropped. I walked to her and lifted her chin so our eyes met. "Hey. I'm proud of you. Let's not go backwards anymore. I'm free. You're wearing a damn bun in your hair and dating a guy who thinks a spoon was invented for stirring. Everything turned out pretty good, I'd say, yeah?"

Her eyes welled up again, and she gave me one last hug. My sister was good. I could sleep soundly tonight. It might just be the first time since before I left Aubrey sleeping in Las Vegas. At the thought, I reached up and rubbed at my chest to soothe the ache.

"Will you be here when I get home tonight?"

"I was actually thinking of heading up north. See about a job opportunity," I lied. Suddenly, I was in the mood for another road trip.

My anxiety grew as I merged from State Route 91 to I15 and started to see the first signs for Temecula. I had no idea where I was going, or what the fuck I was going to do when I got there, but I needed to see she was okay.

Stopping at a combo gas station-grocery store, I stocked up on typical stalker snacks. Fun dip, Sour Patch Kids, popcorn and, of course, Pixy Stix. The cashier looked at me like I might be luring kids into the back of my van at the corner of the local elementary school. "Sweet tooth," I offered with a shrug. He didn't really give a shit.

It may be sunny in this part of California three-hundred and thirty days out of three-hundred and sixty five, but it started to rain as I pulled my pickup truck onto Jefferson Avenue in downtown Temecula. It was nearly five o'clock. People dressed in suits were starting to come out of the office buildings that lined the street. I found the tall building marked 4452, parked a half block away, and slumped down in my seat and waited. With low music and a sack full of candy, I could sit here and bask in the simple things for half the night. Who knew I'd be such an expert stalker?

Two hours passed before I saw her. She stepped out from the building and stood under the overhang as the rain pelted down on the sidewalk in front of her. Not wanting to be seen, I slouched even further into my seat, eyeing her just above the steering wheel.

She looked beautiful. Her auburn hair was longer, the waves looser, cascading halfway down her back. An emerald green silky blouse made her contrasting pale skin even more striking. A black skirt hugged her hips and, even though I couldn't see the back, I imagined how the material clung to her shapely ass. Gorgeous. Full of all the class and sass that I knew she was. It had been two years, yet what I felt for her hadn't dimmed one bit. Which is why my knuckles were turning white as I gripped the steering wheel when I saw a man's hand wrap around her tiny waist.

Mother fucker. I hadn't expected her to be single, but I wasn't prepared for what I saw. Some asshat in a navy suit and glasses that looked like Clark Kent's opened an umbrella and snuggled Aubrey close to him. *My Aubrey.* I couldn't breathe as he whisked her into the parking lot across the street, shielding her from the rain, and disappeared out of sight. Minutes later, a car edged out onto the street, waiting for traffic to let it in. I was sure it was them before I even saw the smiling faces in the car. A black goddamn BMW. His name was probably Biffy.

Dejected, I sat in my truck for another two hours, rather than follow them. If just getting a load of her walking with some bloke tore me to shreds, I wasn't ready to see any more. But I also wasn't ready to leave.

Getting piss ant drunk wasn't in my itinerary. Then again, neither was stalking until a few hours ago. I checked into a motel only a few blocks from Aubrey's office on Jefferson and walked to the adjacent bar before even seeing my room. Now, three hours later, I was sufficiently stewed. Carla, the bartender, and I hit it off right away.

"You ready for another one, Aussie?"

I held up my glass and rattled the ice. "Keep 'em coming, Carla babes." She walked over, gave me a sultry smile and filled my glass. This woman was seriously sexy. Like a nineteen forties pinup model, her hair was all done in those vintage old school curls on top of her head. From the neck up she looked like an American throwback. But her arms were full sleeves of colorful ink. A modern day rockin' Jessica Rabbit.

I was normally a light drinker, beer or wine was more my thing than hard liquor, and it had been two years since I last ingested the poison. Finishing my fourth Rum and Coke, I realized I was drunker than I thought as my words were starting to slur. And…I was unloading my problems onto a bartender I never met. I'd already filled Carla Babes in on my whole life story, in less than two hours.

"So what are you afraid of? She asked, leaning her forearms on the bar.

"I don't want to hurt her."

"Sounds like you already did."

She had a point.

"You wanna know what I think?"

"Why else would I be here this evening?"

Carla chuckled. "I think you're afraid *you'll* get hurt."

The next morning, I woke with a wicked hangover. Even though I had a screaming headache and it felt like the desert had taken over my mouth, I hoisted my dragging body out of bed at the ass crack of dawn. Aubrey had left with some suit, looking too comfy for my liking; I needed to see if they arrived together, too.

There was a Starbucks three doors down from her office, and I thought it was a distinct possibility she'd make a pit stop before work. So I parked with a view of the entire block and slumped into position. Three hours passed. I was in desperate need for a second cup of coffee, and there was no sign of Aubrey.

I reached into the glove compartment, pulled out a baseball hat, and slipped on my sunglasses. It wasn't a great disguise, but the chance of running into her by now had to be slim. The moment my feet touched concrete, I saw her turn the corner. *Fuck.* I froze for a moment and then, luckily, instinct took over.

I hopped back into the cab of my pickup and slouched down. She was busy texting on her phone and didn't look up until she hit the door to Starbucks. *That was close.*

A few minutes later, she emerged with her white venti coffee cup and never looked in my direction. *Damn.* She looked just as good going as she did coming. And she was alone.

I did the same thing that afternoon. The five minute glimpses of her were enough to make the whole day worthwhile. So I did it again the next day…and the day after that. Aubrey had a definite routine. I wasn't surprised. She arrived at nine-thirty and left at seven. Two out of three of my evening stalkings, the asshat was with her when she called it a day.

I'd even settled into a routine of sorts. I reported for morning stalking at dawn and ended my day at dusk. In between, I took off for a few hours and went to a gym two towns over. The evenings, I spent drowning my sorrows with Carla Babes.

This particular morning, the hotel hadn't set up the coffee urn by the time I was ready to leave, and I was itching for some caffeine. Seeing as I had Aubrey's routine pretty much down pat, I snuck out of my truck and slipped into her Starbucks. It gave me a thrill to be inside, even though I was certain she wasn't arriving for hours.

I ordered my plain old black coffee, and the young girl behind the counter smiled. "Can I get you anything else?"

"No. I'm good. Thanks." Then a thought escaped my mouth. "Actually. Do you know a woman who comes in every morning about nine twenty? Auburn hair, probably orders a nonfat three-pump vanilla latte, low foam and extra hot?"

"Sure. Aubrey."

I dug a twenty out of my pocket and held it out to the girl. "Her coffee is on me today."

She looked confused.

"Keep the change. And don't give her a description of the guy who wanted to buy her coffee, okay?"

She shrugged and stuck the twenty in the front pocket of her jeans. "Sure thing."

A few hours later, I watched Aubrey go inside, right on schedule. She was texting away as she walked in. But when she came out with a huge smile on her face while carrying her complimentary extra hot, low foam, nonfat three-pump vanilla latte, I knew it wasn't the last time I wanted to be the one to put it there.

Chapter Sixteen

After a few days, I decided to change up my stalking itinerary. I hadn't yet ventured to Aubrey's house. Heading there while she was at work would give me some clues about her life, namely whether she was shacking up with Clark Kent's dorky twin. I'd decided that I needed as much information as possible before confronting her, even if some of it was going to make me ill.

When I pulled up to the small brown bungalow, the exterior looked like typical Aubrey: quirky, a little messy but unconventionally and stunningly beautiful at the same time. The first thing that caught my eye, though, was the grass out front. It looked like it hadn't been cut for months. What the fuck kind of man lets his woman's grass get to nearly a foot high?

Jackass.

With my baseball cap and sunglasses, I looked around me to make sure there were no nosy neighbors. Peeking in the window, I saw that the inside was much tidier than the outside. Her living room had cream-colored furniture, and there were some silk flowers on the coffee table. There was nothing to indicate one way or the other whether a man was living there.

I nearly fell back into the bushes when I saw the shadow of something moving. It couldn't have been Aubrey because I'd waited until she safely disappeared into the office building before coming here.

Who the fuck was in her house?

Adrenaline pumped through me. Deciding to walk to the window at the other side of the house, I trudged through the overgrown grass, swearing under my breath again about it.

I nearly jumped out of my skin when I saw the face plastered against the glass pane. Not just any face.

"No fucking way!" I yelled.

My voice must have scared him, and he went down for the count.

Mutton. *Holy shit. Mutton!*

Through the window, I watched as the goat lay on the ground. He'd fainted. *Of course. Shit.* I kept tapping on the glass to try to wake him.

"Come on, little guy. Wake up."

After a few minutes, he eventually wriggled his body and stood upright. He kept moving around in circles and seemed discombobulated. I needed to get to him and decided to try to break open the window. I'd replace it if I had to. To my surprise, it slid right up on the first nudge.

What was she nuts leaving her window open? She probably slept that way at night, too, making it easy for any crazy lunatics to enter her bedroom whenever they wanted.

I'd have to remember that for the future.

I was halfway through the window. Waving my hands for a blind goat to come toward me, I said, "Bugger! It's me. Come here, Mate."

The animal came right to me and placed his face in my palm. Gently scratching his head like I used to, I said,

"You're a good boy. I can't believe you're still here." I muttered to myself, "You're nuts, Princess. Royally nuts. But I'm glad you kept him."

Call me crazy, but he seemed to remember me. He let out a long, "Baaaaa." The second time, I could've sworn it sounded like "Daaaad."

"What's been going on here, huh? You're my spy. Is she happy? Does she hate me? Tell me."

"Baa."

I scratched his head harder. "Eh, you're no help." He started to lick my face. "Oh, God. I never thought your putrid breath would be a welcome scent."

Mutton wouldn't let me go. It occurred to me that one of the neighbors could suspect I was a burglar. Getting arrested was the last thing I needed at this stage of my life. My eyes wandered around the room and caught a glimpse of a man's suit hanging over the closet door. My heart sank.

I kissed his forehead. "I've got to go. I'll come back and see you again. I promise."

He grunted.

"I know. You don't trust me anymore. You have no reason to right now. I have to earn that back."

For the first time, I noticed that a piece of metal was jingling from around his neck. "What the hell is this? She has a collar on you?" I looked closer at the name.

Pixy.

Hope filled my heart, which suddenly started beating faster. I rubbed my thumb across the engraved lettering. After everything I'd been through over the past two years, don't ask me why this moment was the first that almost caused my eyes to water a little. It was just the right push I needed to keep this going—a little bit of hope that maybe she didn't wish I were dead after all.

It took me a few minutes to get him to let me leave. He was trying to jump out the window to go with me. I was finally able to close it.

When I turned around, the goat's face was still plastered against the window. I suppose I could've broken all the way into the house to get more clues about her life, but that would have been pushing it. Like I told Mutton...*Pixy*...I had to earn my way back into their lives, not steal it.

There was one more piece of business I had to take care of before heading back downtown. I remembered passing a home improvement store on my way to the house.

After a quick trip over there, I returned with a modest Craftsman push mower.

It took me about forty minutes to mow Aubrey's lawn. When I got to the side of the house, Pixy was still waiting at the same spot. A few of the neighbors walked by, and I'd wave with a gigantic smile on my face. I hoped that they'd assume that she dumped Biffy Clark Kent's lazy ass in exchange for a real man who did yard work. Either that, or maybe they just figured I was a landscaper.

Admiring the smooth tracks along the grass, I wiped my forehead with the back of my hand. My work here was done, but the real work was just beginning.

That night, I'd somehow missed her. Either she left in the middle of the afternoon, or she was still inside working late. After waiting until eight-thirty, I finally had to give up and reluctantly left for the bar. A huge feeling of disappointment consumed me. Seeing Aubrey at the end of the day was always my reward, and I felt cheated today.

"Carla Babes, hit me up," I said, assuming position on my usual stool.

She was wiping the counter. "Aussie! You're late tonight. Stalking overtime?"

"Eh. Today wasn't so great."

She stopped wiping to grab my drink. "What happened?"

"I somehow missed her at the end of the day."

"You're losing your touch," she said, slapping my Rum and Coke down on the dark wood counter.

"I'm losing something…my marbles, maybe."

Carla leaned her elbows down on the counter, displaying her massive cleavage. "Anything good at all happen today?"

I started to laugh. "Actually, something great happened. I found my goat."

"Your coat?"

I chuckled again. "My goat. With a *G*."

Her eyes widened. "What?"

I proceeded to tell her the story, everything from how Aubrey and I found him to the shit—quite literally—that happened while on the road.

"Aw…that's so cute. So, he's kind of like your child."

"That was what Aubrey used to say."

She must have noticed a look of melancholy wash over my face. "What's wrong?"

"There was a man's jacket hanging in her room. I think he's living with her. They could be engaged or married for all I know."

"Well, you wouldn't know, would you? Because you haven't *talked* to her." She took her rag and whipped it over my head jokingly.

"This has to be handled carefully. I don't want to fuck it up."

"There's handling it carefully, and there's avoidance. How long are you really gonna camp out like this? You need to just rip the Band Aid off, man."

Taking one last gulp down and slamming the glass on the table, I said, "I hate when you're right, Carla Babes."

"You must hate me all the time then." She winked.

Aubrey looked so incredibly beautiful walking into work the next morning. It was windy, which made her hair especially unruly. As usual, she stopped into Starbucks to grab her coffee before heading into the building.

The ache in my chest was bigger than ever because I knew D-day was nearing. Even though I'd made a vow to "rip the Band Aid off" in the next couple of days, I still hadn't figured out how I was going to approach her.

When she was finally safely inside, I let out a deep breath and exited my truck to head into Starbucks and get my own coffee. Hung over again this morning, I'd slept through my alarm, arriving too late to risk going in earlier and paying for her drink.

I decided to try something new today. I wanted to taste Aubrey. *Well, I wished.* Instead, I decided to order that frou frou drink she always ordered to see what it tasted like.

"I'll have a large nonfat, three-pump vanilla latte, low foam and extra hot."

The young cashier's face always seemed to light up when she saw me. "You're ordering her drink today...for yourself?"

"Changing things up, yeah."

"What's your name?"

"Why do you need my name?"

"It's just procedure with specialty drinks. We write it on the side."

"Oh…Chance."

She wrote my name in black marker on the cup, and I walked over to the other counter where you're supposed to pick up your order.

I watched the barista make a couple of the drinks in line before mine. What a friggin' process between the steaming and the frothing. It better have been complicated for five-bucks a pop.

I heard the cashier's voice. "Aubrey. What are you doing back so soon?"

My eyes quickly darted toward her then I immediately pulled my baseball cap down and turned around toward the back wall. Heart pounding. Chest constricted. Stomach nauseous. A rush of adrenaline.

Oh Fuck.

Fuck.

Fuck.

Fuck.

My heart had never beat so fast. I heard her voice behind me. "My boyfriend came into my office to talk to me and knocked my drink down with his elbow. It spilled all over my desk."

Fucking clutz.

"I'm sorry. Let me get you another one free of charge."

"Thank you so much, Melanie. I appreciate that."

It felt like the walls were closing in on me. The sound of the steaming milk suddenly seemed deafening. I wondered if I could get away with sliding away slowly with my back facing the wall until I was behind her and out the door. Just as I'd started to move, the kid making my drink shouted, "Chance!"

"Did you just say Chance?" Aubrey said.

At this point, I was just behind her.

Melanie, who probably figured Aubrey was just my innocent crush, decided that moment would be a good time to play matchmaker. She outed me. "Chance is the guy who paid for your drink the other day. He's right there."

Aubrey flipped around so fast that she accidentally backed into a display of plastic iced-coffee cups, knocking them down like dominos onto the ground.

Seeming unphased by the disaster she'd just created, she stood staring at me with her hand over her chest as if it were holding her heart in.

I took my baseball cap off and crossed it over my chest. With pleading eyes, I whispered, "Princess."

Looking like she'd just seen a ghost, she slowly shook her head as if to say 'this can't be happening.'

I took one step toward her.

She held her hand out, stopping me in my tracks. "No! Don't you dare come near me."

My heart fell to my stomach, and it felt like my guts were twisting.

This was not how I pictured things going down.

I lifted both of my palms. "I won't. But please, just hear me out."

"You've been stalking me?"

"Not exactly."

We were both silent. Filled with humiliation, I bent down and started picking up the cups she'd knocked over. Aubrey stayed frozen in the same spot.

Nosy Melanie spoke from behind the counter, "Why won't you just listen to what he has to say?"

Aubrey's chest was still rising and falling. She finally spoke, "Let me ask you this, Melanie. If a guy led you to believe that he cared about you, then fucked you and left before the next morning without so much as a sticky note goodbye, would you hear him out?"

"Probably not." She laughed then added, "Well, if he had an ass like Chance, maybe." One of the other female employees giggled.

Aubrey looked at me with daggers in her eyes and continued, "Okay…what if he never contacted you for two whole years after that, then all of a sudden showed up stalking you in your hometown. Would you hear him out?"

"Definitely not," Melanie said. "That's just weird."

"I rest my case."

Aubrey suddenly zipped past me and out the door. She was gone.

Feeling like she'd just ripped my heart out and fed it to me, I stood defeated in the middle of Starbucks.

After a minute of staring blankly outside the store window, I heard a voice inside my head that sounded awfully like Mum. *"Grow some fucking balls and fight for her."*

And that marked the end of my subtlety streak.

I flew out the door and ran down the street, hoping I could track her down before she went inside her building.

There was no sign of Aubrey anywhere. Flying through the revolving doors, I spotted her as she was waiting to get into an elevator. Just as she disappeared into one, I stuck my hand in the doors to open them.

She was alone.

Tears were pouring down her face. *She'd been crying.*

As the elevator rose up, I hit the stop button.

"What the fuck are you doing?" she screamed.

Panting, I said, "If this is the only way I can get you to listen to me, then so be it."

"You can keep me trapped in here for—oh, I don't know—TWO years for all I care. I'm not talking to you. Maybe then, you'll know what it feels like."

Locking her against the wall with one arm on each side of her trembling body, I said, "I'm glad to see you're stubborn as ever, Princess."

Seeming uncomfortable with my close proximity, she swallowed before saying, "I need to get back to the office. Move this elevator, or I'm calling the police."

"I get that you're in shock. You weren't supposed to find out that way."

"Is there a good way to find out that the person who tore your heart to shreds is now stalking you?"

She had a point.

"Probably not. But you have to let me explain."

The words that came out of her mouth next were hard for me to hear. "Do you realize how long it took me to get over you? My life is only just now getting back to normal. You can't come back after two years and expect me to just let you in after I've fought so hard to let go of you. I'd finally let you go. Please. I'm begging you to leave."

My chest was so tight it felt like it might burst.

She'd let me go.

Well, too fucking bad. I'm back.

"I'll go…for now. But I'm not leaving town until you agree to let me explain what happened. If you still want me to go after you've heard it all, then I swear to God, Aubrey, you will never see me again for as long as you live."

Her eyes started to water again as she looked into mine. Without taking my eyes off her, I let go of the stop button and pressed the number for the next floor.

"I'm staying at the Sunrise Motel, room eight. I still have the same cell number as before. You call me when you're ready to listen."

When the doors slid open, I got out, leaving Aubrey in the elevator with the ball in her court. I just hoped she didn't choose to deflate it.

Chapter Seventeen

EXIT

Was it even considered stalking anymore once the victim became clearly aware of the stalker's presence? Now that Aubrey knew I was in town, it was a totally different experience with the risk of getting caught removed from the equation.

Over the next week, I was basically just camping out in Temecula hoping for a miracle. The only real stress was the wait for her to contact me. I'd check my phone constantly, thinking that maybe I'd missed her. But she never called.

Not wanting to piss her off more than I already had, I made a decision to take a break from showing up outside her office for a few days. Instead, I worked out hard at the gym all morning, taking my frustrations out on my body. I hadn't touched a woman in over two years, and the only one I wanted was apparently taken and hated my guts. So, pumping iron was my way of coping with it until I could get her back. I only dreamt of all the ways I could take everything out on Aubrey instead.

After the gym, in the early afternoons, I'd head to her house and continue the landscaping there. Someone had to take care of it, for Christ's sake. I laid down mulch, planted and put in two princess flower bushes. Who knew there was such a thing as a princess flower? They were the perfect choice.

The neighbors were used to seeing me working. With my pickup truck and mower in the back, they just figured landscaping was my job. My skin was now a shade darker after working for days in the sweltering heat. More and more mothers with strollers were walking by lately, too. I'd wave to them with dirt on my hands. These new female spectators seemed to be multiplying by the day.

The best part, though, about spending the afternoons at Aubrey's was my time with the goat. Always waiting at the window, he'd come to expect me.

Pixy.

I still had to get used to calling him that.

I'd bring him lunch. We'd eat together. I was becoming unhealthily attached to the smell of his breath mixed with freshly-cut grass.

Stinking Bugger.

My nighttime schedule was the same as always. I'd head to the bar and unleash all of my troubles onto Carla Babes.

One Friday night, however, there was a surprise change in my routine. I was sitting on my stool at the bar when Carla asked, "What did you say Aubrey looked like?"

"Why?"

"Just describe her to me."

"Petite but curvy, wavy auburn hair, wide eyes, creamy skin…"

"Does she have a leopard print coat by any chance?"

I scratched my chin and remembered she was wearing one into the office one morning. "Yeah…yeah, she does. Why?"

"I think she was just here. Some chick fitting that description was looking over at us through the front window. I just made eye contact with her, and she took off."

I turned around. "What?"

Carla waved her hand towards the door. "Go after her."

Without thinking, I hopped off my stool and ran outside. Sure enough, Aubrey's Audi was exiting the parking lot. My heart was racing as she sped down the road. Since I'd walked to the bar, I couldn't even follow her. My little lead foot Princess jetted away too fast for me to stop her.

I took out my phone and scrolled down to her number to send a text.

Chance: Who's stalking who now?

There was no response. After a few minutes, a return text came in. My heartbeat accelerated.

Aubrey: It was a coincidence.

Chance: Don't text while driving.

Aubrey: Why did you text me then? And don't tell me what to do.

Chance: Pull over, Princess.

Aubrey: I wasn't stalking you.

Chance: Don't text me again until you've pulled over.

Staring down at my screen, I just stood there in the parking lot. After several minutes, the phone vibrated again.

Aubrey: Is that what you do every night? Troll bars around town for women?

Chance: Are you parked?

Aubrey: Yes.

Chance: I've only been trolling around town for one woman. Said woman drives me to drink. Thus, the bar.

Aubrey: I wish you'd just go home. Stop texting me.

Chance: Stop texting? I figured you'd like the vibration.

No response.

That might have taken it too far. It was too soon to joke with her like we used to. I sent another text, giving her the honest response to her request that I go home.

Chance: My home is where you are.

Aubrey: You burned down our home in Vegas after you fucked me and left.

It fucking hurt so badly to see those words. I stared at them for almost a full minute before responding.

Chance: There was a reason I did what I did and I need to explain it to you in person. I won't do it over text.

Aubrey: There is no excuse for what you did.

Chance: Where are you? I'm coming to you.

Aubrey: No. Please don't.

Chance: You have to see me eventually if you ever want to get rid of me.

Aubrey: Why are you doing this?

Because I love you.

Fuck.

Where did that come from?

Chance: Please come back to the bar or I can walk to you where you are. I can't drive because I've been drinking.

Aubrey: I can't see you tonight. I'm not ready.

Chance: Will you ever be?

Aubrey: I don't think so.

Chance: Who is he?

Aubrey: Who?

Chance: Your boyfriend.

Aubrey: You mean, you don't already know? What kind of a stalker are you?

Chance: Tell me his name.

Aubrey: His name is Richard.

Chance: Is he living with you?

Aubrey: That's none of your business.

Chance: I saw his jacket hanging on your closet door.

Aubrey: You've been staring into my bedroom?

Chance: Yes. Only when you're not home. And I never entered your house. I wouldn't.

Aubrey: It's still sick.

Chance: I can't believe you kept him, by the way.

Aubrey: I don't abandon the things I claim to care about.

171

> *Chance: Neither do I. It's why I'm here.*
>
> *Aubrey: After two years?*
>
> *Chance: I came here the first chance I got.*

Even though it was true, I'm sure that confused her. She didn't respond. So, I texted her again.

> *Chance: You named him Pixy. That's proof that you don't hate me.*
>
> *Aubrey: I can't do this anymore.*

I didn't want to upset her any further. So, I stopped the communication.

It surprised me when my phone vibrated again back inside the bar about fifteen minutes later.

> *Aubrey: When have you been doing the gardening?*
>
> *Chance: All day while you're at work.*
>
> *Aubrey: Thank you.*

If it were possible for a heart to smile, I swore mine must have done it in that moment.

> *Chance: You're welcome.*
>
> *Aubrey: Please don't feed him corn anymore. He doesn't digest it and it's not pretty.*

I chuckled.

> *Chance: Whoops.*

That was the end of our conversation that night. It was more than I could have ever hoped for.

Aubrey was still avoiding seeing me at all costs. When another week went by, I knew my approach needed to be more aggressive. With each day that passed, it bothered me more and more that she didn't know the reason behind my leaving. And I still refused to have that conversation any other way but in person.

I understood that she was scared, but it was becoming urgently necessary to find a way to get her alone so that we could talk.

One Thursday afternoon, I got a call from my agent back in Australia about a new potential marketing opportunity. So, I did what anyone in my position would do before entering into a new business deal: I got lawyered up.

Chapter Eighteen EXIT

66 **I** have an appointment at eleven with Ms. Bloom."

The receptionist smiled and looked down at the appointment book. "Mr. Bastardo?"

"The one and only." I was grinning from ear to ear like an idiot. The woman probably thought my excitement was for her. She was a pretty girl; I bet plenty of men lit up around her. But my enthusiasm revolved around only one woman. Even hearing her voice through the intercom made my heart speed up a bit.

"Yes, Kelly?" Aubrey said.

"Your eleven o'clock consult is here."

"Thank you. Would you show him back in five minutes? I need to get organized." I pictured her desk scattered with papers.

Kelly let go of a button and spoke to me. "You can have a seat. I'm actually going to give her ten minutes. She's one of the best attorneys here at the firm, but her desk is usually a disaster."

I sat in the reception area and thumbed through a magazine as I waited, but I couldn't concentrate. I'd been waiting almost a week for this appointment. Yesterday I went and picked up my new suit. It was custom tailored and fit well. When I looked in the mirror, it might have been the first time in two years I didn't hate who stared back at me.

I straightened my tie and hoped the sales lady who helped me pick it out was right. She'd said the blues of the tie brought out the color in my eyes—it would be impossible not to hold a woman captive. Oddly, her choice of words fit what I wanted to do to Aubrey…hold her captive. Quite possibly for the rest of our lives. I may have only spent eight days with this woman, but we learned what takes most people six months of dating. Coming to Temecula confirmed what I spent the last two years thinking about—I was a goner when it came to Aubrey Bloom.

Kelly walked around her desk. "Mr. Bastardo? If you're ready, I'll take you back now."

I took a deep breath. "I'm very ready."

We walked down two long halls and passed a few men in suits. This place was a goddamn smorgasbord of Biffys. Another turn and then Kelly stopped at a door. Corner office.

Nice, Princess. She was appreciated here. I felt a sense of pride.

"Hi, Aubrey. I have Mr. Bastardo for you."

"Thank you."

Kelly stepped aside so I could enter. My attorney was looking down. She spoke before her head came fully up. "It's nice to—"

Aubrey froze. I could have sworn there was a flicker of excitement in her eyes for a second. But it was quickly extinguished…replaced by anger. I'd expected her reaction.

"Mr. Bastardo?" She rolled her eyes. "How did I not figure this one out?"

"Because you don't speak Spanish." I smiled, but she wasn't amused.

"Chance. I'm at work. I can't play your games here. You need to leave."

I buttoned my jacket. "I'm here on business."

"Nice try. I'm a copyright attorney. If you've gone and gotten arrested for public intoxication or lewd and lascivious behavior, you'll need to go three doors down to Celino and Barnes."

"I'm in need of a copyright attorney."

"Is that so?" She wasn't believing a word I was saying.

"It is."

"Well in that case, you'll need to see another attorney." She stepped around her desk and folded her arms over her chest. Fuck if her getting tough with me wasn't the sexiest thing I'd seen in ages.

"I don't want another attorney."

"That's too bad."

We stared at each other for a moment. Then she smiled. It wasn't a happy smile, it was an *I'm about to stick something up your arse and enjoy it* smile. I didn't care. I liked seeing it anyway. I smiled back—twice as broad.

She huffed and left the office.

A few minutes later, she returned. I'd settled in and made myself comfortable in a chair in front of her desk. I stood when she walked in. A man walked in right behind her. The *princess fucker*.

Aubrey looked pretty pleased at herself when she spoke. "Richard. This is Mr. Bateman. Mr. Bateman is in need of a copyright attorney, and I seem to be double booked for this afternoon, so I thought perhaps you could take him on."

The Clark Kent wannabe extended his hand to me. "Richard Kline."

I nodded. "Dick. Good to meet you." The squeeze I gave his hand when I shook it bordered on assault.

I caught the clench in Aubrey's jaw. Then she corrected me. Through gritted teeth, "His name is Richard."

"It's fine." Dick waved her off. "I'm used to it. I don't usually shorten my name, but my dad was a Richard, and everyone called him Dick."

I gave Aubrey a little smile.

She seethed.

"Why don't you come down to my office, and I can see what I can help you with?"

"I'd actually prefer to wait for Ms. Bloom. I was referred to her specifically."

"I'm not available," Aubrey snapped.

Dick seemed taken aback by Aubrey's little attitude. That warmed me for some reason. I *liked* that she didn't give him her sass. Save it all for me, baby. I want all your sass *and* your ass.

"Well." Dick turned to Aubrey. "What else do you have today? Maybe I can handle one of your afternoon appointments?"

"I'd prefer you handle Mr. Bateman."

Dick looked at me apologetically then spoke to her, his tone mildly patronizing. "It seems Mr. Bateman wants his affairs handled by you, personally, Aubrey."

I smiled at Aubrey. "I've been really looking forward to you *handling me.*"

Dick came to my rescue. "Why don't we step into my office and see what I can do to help clear up your schedule so you can get things started with Mr. Bateman?"

178

Dick and Aubrey left the office, and Aubrey returned five minutes later, with the receptionist, Kelly. "Have a seat, Kelly." She'd brought a chaperone.

I was disappointed I wouldn't be getting quality alone time but far from deterred. Aubrey, on the other hand, was *not* happy. With a huff, she pulled a yellow legal pad from her drawer and slammed it down on her desk. "What's the nature of the legal services you need, Mr. Bateman?" Her pen was poised to write and she didn't look up. Kelly looked bewildered at the entire scene playing out before her.

"I have two, actually." I opened the folder I was carrying, took out a large manila envelope and slid it across the desk to her side. "I've received an offer from a company who would like to use some photographs of me in their ad campaign.

She snickered. "Oh. That's right. You're an ass model."

I ignored her. "Anyway. The company that wants to use the photographs in their campaign wants the exclusive rights to the photo, and there's an American company that is using the photo on their website without permission. I need to send them a cease and desist letter to remove it before I sign the contract."

"Fine."

"And I'd like the contract reviewed as well."

"Anything else?"

"Perhaps you'd like to discuss the terms of the contract over dinner?"

"I don't think so."

"Breakfast?"

"Get out, Mr. Bateman."

I stood. I'd pushed pretty hard, and I didn't want to test my limits. "You know how to reach me when you've had an opportunity to look over the documents?"

"Yes." She finally looked up at me. "Apparently, *now* you're available all the time."

She was pissed. But somehow, her being pissed gave me hope. If she didn't care, she would have eased up by now. "Thank you for your time."

"Kelly. Show Mr. *Bastardo* out, please."

Over the next three days, I stuck to my routine. Well, mostly to my routine. I arrived on Jefferson Street at my normal time, only I went inside Starbucks in the morning and read the paper while I had my morning coffee. Each day I paid for Aubrey's coffee and added a little something to the order. Yesterday, it was a banana nut muffin. Today, I decided on chocolate chip coffee cake. I ate the same thing and drank the same coffee. It was as close to having breakfast with Aubrey as I could get right now.

Melanie, my barista, and I were becoming fast friends. She handed me my latte. "She smiles when I tell her you paid, you know."

"She does?"

Melanie nodded. "She tries to cover it up quick. But I see it."

She had no idea she just made my day. "Thanks, Melanie."

She leaned over the counter as if to tell me a secret. "We're all rooting for you."

It was sweet. But they didn't know what I'd done to Aubrey.

At eight o'clock, I went back into my pick up truck. I wanted to be near her but not piss her off by being completely in her face. She didn't acknowledge me, but she knew I was there every morning.

Like clockwork, at nine thirty, Aubrey walked into Starbucks. A few minutes later she walked out. With her coffee and chocolate chip coffee cake in hand, she took two steps toward her office, then stopped, surprising the shit out of me when she headed right for my truck.

I rolled down the window.

"Could you at least make my breakfast lowfat in the future?"

I had to stop myself from saying what I really wanted to say—that I would make her whatever she wanted every morning at her place. Instead, I said, "Sure thing."

She nodded and turned away but halted after only two strides. She didn't turn around when she spoke. "The princess flowers bloomed this morning. They're beautiful." Then she was gone for another ten hours.

I went to the gym and spent a few hours at Home Depot picking up the supplies I'd need for my next project at Aubrey's. When I originally decided to drive down to Temecula, I had taken my pick up truck rather than the motorcycle so I wouldn't be as easily recognizable. Turned out, the truck was coming in handy.

It was a scorching hot afternoon, and I took off my t-shirt to wipe the sweat that was dripping from my forehead. I had unloaded eight trips worth of cedar into Aubrey's backyard in the ninety-degree heat. As I closed up the rear gate to my pickup, a woman who passed by frequently stopped to speak to me.

"Hi. I'm Philomena." She had on one of those short white tennis skirts, knee high rubber rain boots and a skin tight, low cut tank top. The sky was blue, and it hadn't rained for days. My eyes dropped to her cleavage; you couldn't help but notice. She had some major knockers.

"Chance." I nodded.

She lifted her hand, which was in a cast, to gesture down the street. "I live down the block, Chance. I've been watching you out here for a week. I was wondering if you'd like to do me?" She was propositioning me to mow something, but it definitely wasn't her lawn. It had been two years; looking was a given, but I had zero interest.

I caught her eye. "Thank you. But I only do Aubrey."

"Lucky woman. You've really…added some curb appeal to the place."

I looked back at the once drab bungalow. It was looking pretty good now. "Thanks. They're princess flower bushes."

"I wasn't talking about the gardening."

I tried to change the subject. "Hope you didn't injure your hand too badly."

"I tripped over my pig in the middle of the night. It's just me and him. He's the man of the house." She winked, walking away and tossed back over her shoulder, "If you change your mind, my house is number 41. Stop by. *Anytime*."

Later that night, I was recapping my day to Carla Babes when my phone vibrated on the bar. I had texted with Adele earlier and expected the text to be from her again. I was thrilled as shit to find it was from Aubrey.

> **Aubrey: Your photograph was removed from the website today. I also negotiated compensatory damages.**
>
> **Chance: Wow. That's great. You're good.**

Aubrey: I'm good at my job. You'll need to sign a release. I also have some changes to suggest on the contract.

Chance: Where are you? I can come by now.

Aubrey: Come by my office tomorrow at 9:30.

Chance: I'll bring our coffees.

The vibrating stopped, and I thought it was the end of our conversation. A minute later my phone danced on the bar, and my heart danced right along with it. It's pretty amazing what can give you hope when you're desperate to find some.

Aubrey: Are you building a pen for Pixy?

Chance: I am.

Aubrey: He's going to love it.

My phone went quiet after that, but I didn't give a shit. I had a date with Aubrey in the morning.

Green was my new favorite color. It was obvious Aubrey fancied it herself, seeing as it was the second time she'd worn a green blouse since I started my stalking routine. The dark color made her skin look creamy, and the green in her eyes reminded me of Peridot—my mum's birthstone. It was a double hit, thinking of Mum and realizing I'd missed two of Aubrey's birthdays.

I cleared my throat and spoke, "You look beautiful."

"Did you hear a word I said?"

I hadn't actually. I was too busy undressing her with my eyes to concentrate. God, what I wanted to do to her. The desk was making it impossible to focus. She was sitting behind it, but all I envisioned was her ass on top of it with my head buried between her legs. Our eyes locked, and she saw what I was thinking.

"Don't." Her eyes were pleading, and she held up a hand. But I needed to push today.

"We need to talk, Aubrey."

"No. We don't. I'm at work, and this is a business meeting. That's why Kelly is here." She motioned to the receptionist who was again sitting next to me. If Aubrey thought I was above spilling my guts in front of Kelly, she misjudged my level of desperation.

"So see me after work. See me for breakfast. See me at two in the morning. I don't give a shit where or when. Just see me, Aubrey. We need to talk. We both need to set things straight."

"I'm already straight. And I've decided our time together will be limited to this office."

We stared at each other for a minute. The only one to flinch was poor Kelly. She fidgeted in her seat like she needed to go to the bathroom. Finally, I broke our standoff. "Alright, Aubrey. Then you leave me no choice."

"What are you taking about?"

"We're going to have our conversation right here and right now then."

Aubrey stood and folded her hands over her chest. "We are not!"

I rose and joined her, mimicking her posture. "Yes. We are."

Kelly's voice was apprehensive. "Would you like me to leave?"

Aubrey and I answered at the exact same time. Only I said yes and she shouted no.

Kelly stood, then sat back down when Aubrey glared at her.

"Where shall we start then, Aubrey? Since Kelly here doesn't know the whole story, maybe we should start with the last time we were together with a desk in the room?"

Aubrey's eyes flared.

I turned to speak to Kelly. "Have you ever been to Las Vegas? There's a hotel on the—"

"You can go, Kelly." She didn't need to be told twice. Kelly darted out of the room and closed the door behind her. I'd need to remember to thank her for that on my way out.

"Why are you doing this, Chance?" She tried to keep stern, but her voice cracked.

"I just need you to hear me out. I'll leave you alone if you want me to after that. I give you my word."

"Your word?" she scoffed.

"Fifteen minutes. That's all it will take."

"Ten."

That sass. I couldn't help but smile. "Fine. Ten. Can we sit?"

Reluctantly, Aubrey sat down. I'd been waiting for more than two years for this moment, yet suddenly I didn't know where to begin. So I started where the story did.

"Do you remember I told you about my sister, Adele?"

She nodded.

"I told you she went through a rough patch. But I left out just how rough things really got."

Her face softened slightly. I blew out a rush of air and raked my fingers through my hair. There was a burn running from the pit of my stomach up through my throat. Time didn't ease what had happened one bit. I could have been having this conversation with the detective two years ago. The words were just as hard to get out. "Adele was raped."

Aubrey's mouth dropped open, and her hand flew to her chest.

"I wasn't there for her. She got mixed up with a bad crowd."

"I'm so sorry. Is she okay?"

I smiled thinking of my sister the other day. Wearing a damn bun in her hair. "Yeah. She's doing pretty well now."

Aubrey nodded. "So that's why you left?"

"Yes. But there's more."

"More?"

"It's a long story. But the police were having trouble finding the guy, and I did some things."

"What kind of things?"

I held her eyes as I spoke the next part. "I beat a man until he told me where I could find the guy who'd attacked my sister."

One of the biggest fears I had was that my admission would scare her. But Aubrey didn't flinch. *That's my girl. Fearless.* Her reaction gave me the courage to go on. "I injured him badly. I had to pay for what I'd done. The afternoon after I left you, I began a two-year prison sentence."

Aubrey stared at me. I gave her a minute to digest everything I'd just said. Then I finished what I'd come to say. "I got out the day before I showed up here in Temecula. I never planned on meeting you before I went in. I tried everything I could to keep my distance on our trip. But I couldn't."

"Why didn't you tell me?"

"Because you deserved better. I didn't want you waiting around for two years. You had just dumped one loser and were ready to move on. I couldn't saddle you with anymore baggage."

"So instead, you broke my heart?" The question wasn't asked meanly; she was trying to make sense of it all.

I nodded. *And mine, too.*

We were both quiet for a long time. She was staring down at her hands folded on her desk. I had one more thing I needed to say, and she needed to hear me. I shifted in my seat and leaned forward, covering her hands with mine. "Can you look at me?"

She hesitated, but did.

"I'm sorry, Princess. For everything. For hurting you. For leaving you behind. For not being there when you woke up. For not being there every day since then."

Aubrey closed her eyes. There was a look of pain on her face, and I hated that I put it there. I wanted to wrap my arms around her and hold her so badly, but I didn't. I'd pushed enough and anything more was selfish. My heart was pounding in my chest and when she finally opened her eyes again, she was staring at our joined hands—at the ring I was still wearing on my finger. *My wedding band.*

Her eyes watered.

The silence was torture. "I'm sorry you and Adele had to go through that," she finally said, her voice hoarse.

"Me, too. I just want to put it behind me and move on."

Another bout of silence. "I was finally happy. *Richard* makes me happy."

That fucking hurt.

She continued, "I need time to process. I've spent the last two years hating you."

"I understand." *Let me make it up to you, Princess.*

"How long are you staying in town for?"

Until you're mine again.

"I don't really have a plan yet. But I'm sort of in the middle of a project."

That caused the corners of her mouth to twitch up a bit. Although she was quickly serious again. "I need some time," she repeated.

It had been two long years, but I'd finally said my peace. Now I was going to have to wait to see what would bring Aubrey hers.

I'm not sure what I thought I would feel after finally getting to tell Aubrey everything, perhaps a sense of relief. But the reality was, I felt even more anxious than before. Before, we had unfinished business. But now…what if, knowing everything that happened, she forgave me, yet she still had no interest in being with me? We'd either just opened a new door or finally given each other closure.

I sat in my truck for two hours outside of her office, even though I promised I'd give her space. I just needed to see she was okay for myself. My head was pounding, and I shifted my seat back, ready to close my eyes for a few minutes. But a flash of green caught my attention right before my lids shut. Aubrey was standing in front of her building carrying her briefcase. She slipped on sunglasses, looked down and walked across the street. Unlike most days, she wasn't checking her phone or walking with an energetic bounce. Instead, her posture looked defeated, and her walk was more of a trudge. A minute after she disappeared into the lot where she parked her car, I watched her Audi pull out and turn toward home.

Surprising even myself, I didn't follow her.

Instead, I decided to refocus my energy. Being prepared for a fight meant getting to know your opponent. It was about time I got to know a little more about Dick.

At nearly seven, my adversary made an appearance. He rushed to his BMW and took off in the other direction of Aubrey's place. I cut a quick u-turn and followed. The princess fucker took me on a nearly half-hour drive before exiting the highway. I wasn't familiar with this part of California, but it didn't take a geography expert to know we were in a less than idyllic neighborhood.

There were the obvious visible signs—buildings with broken and boarded up windows, graffiti, messy yards, timeworn cars that looked abandoned. The few commercial buildings that held stores, had bars covering the doors and windows. A very visible police car was parked at the corner of a four-way intersection.

Where the fuck did Dick live?

I followed a half-block behind, careful not to call attention to my pickup. He weaved in and out of side streets that made me want to lock my doors. Eventually, he slowed and pulled to the curb. I parked on the opposite side of the street, five or so cars back. If I was going to keep up with this shit, I really needed some fucking binoculars. Dick reached into the back of his car, pulled out a bag, and proceeded to start changing his clothes right there in the front seat of the car.

What the fuck was he doing?

The street we parked on was lined with dilapidated muti-family housing. A half-dozen bandana clad guys hung around on a stoop nearby. I was pretty sure I'd just left a couple of them behind at the state penitentiary. Dick got out, looked around skittishly, and headed to one of the rundown buildings. He disappeared down a set of concrete stairs that looked like it led to a basement entrance.

A few minutes later, another man headed to the same door. This guy had a long, matted beard and wore a wool cap and heavy army jacket, even though it was still close to eighty-five degrees. He was also scratching his face incessantly and looking around frantically as he walked.

Dick was in a crack den? The day was getting a lot more interesting.

After spending two years in a prison full of criminals, I was anxious to get the fuck out of there as night fell. The neighborhood that had seemed desolate was suddenly starting to come alive—with people who didn't go out until they could hide in the shadows of darkness.

But I waited. If Dick could be out here, so could I. More than an hour passed before the Princess Fucker jogged up the stairs and onto the street. With a brown paper bag in his hand, he wasted no time getting in his car. His fancy ride pulled away as soon as his door was shut.

I didn't follow him.

Curiosity had gotten the best of me and before I knew it, I was locking my truck. I hadn't planned what I was going to do once I got to the door—buying a vile of crack as evidence to show Aubrey that Dick was a dick, probably wasn't the smartest thing to do. I would have to settle for understanding what I was up against and worry about what to do with the information later.

The stairwell was narrow, with only a few steps leading to a closed door. When I got to the bottom, I found the door was actually left a crack open. There was also music coming from inside. I edged it open. At first, a little. Then a little bit more. Until the door suddenly swung open, and I nearly fell into the building.

I looked up expecting to find a gun to my head for breaking into a crack house. But what I found couldn't have been more different. A priest was holding open the door and extended his hand into the room behind him, welcoming me.

"Come in. Ladels of Love is happy to feed you this evening."

It took a minute to realize what I'd just walked into. A soup kitchen. The Princess Fucker wasn't buying crack; he was feeding the indigent.

Fuck me.

I was definitely going to need to up my game.

Chapter Twenty

It seemed Aubrey and Dick were quite the pair of philanthropists.

Sitting in my truck on Jefferson a few days later, I opened the local newspaper, and smack dab in the middle of the community section was Aubrey's beautiful smile along with an article about a new animal shelter that had just opened up.

> Local attorneys Aubrey Bloom and Richard Kline of Sherman, Kline and Lefave, LLP attend the grand opening of the Park Street Animal Shelter. Kline and Bloom, a member of the Park Street board of directors, helped raise over five-hundred-thousand dollars to support the shelter's new facility.

At the end of the article, there was a phone number for the shelter. I immediately dialed it.

A girl answered, "Park Street Animal Shelter?"

"Hi, I was wondering if you're looking for any volunteers?"

"Actually, yes, sir. We are in dire need of dog walkers. Is that something you might be interested in?"

"Absolutely. I could come by this afternoon."

"We'll have you fill out some paperwork we need to process, so you may not be able to start until later in the week."

"That's fine. I can't wait to help."

Take that, Princess Fucker.

Stalker, landscaper, goat sitter…add dog walker to the list of new occupations held by Chance Bateman during my stay in Temecula.

The daily routine now consisted of having virtual Starbucks breakfast with Aubrey, hitting the gym, landscaping (aka Pixy time), followed by late afternoon strolls with anywhere from three to five dogs at once. For someone without a real job, I was busier and in better shape than ever before in my life.

One Friday afternoon, I was at a park walking a Great Dane, a German Shepherd mix and a Greyhound when a text from Aubrey came in.

> **Aubrey: Received your new contract today. They need you to sign it this afternoon so they can meet a production deadline.**

Trying to control all three barking dogs with one hand, I used my phone's voice to text feature to respond.

> **Chance: I'm dog walking at Slater Park. I can come there right after.**
>
> **Aubrey: Dog walking?**

I knew that would pique her interest. As a matter of fact, I was banking on it. This was perfect timing to let her know about my newest venture.

> **Chance: I've been volunteering for your shelter. I saw the article. I know that place means a lot to you. Wanted to help.**
>
> **Aubrey: Are you serious?**
>
> **Chance: I'll come by the office around 5:00 after I walk them back?**
>
> **Aubrey: I have plans tonight, so I have to leave the office by then. Why don't I just stop by the park now and have you sign it really quick?**
>
> **Chance: Where should I meet you?**
>
> **Aubrey: By the concession stand at the entrance around 4:15.**
>
> **Chance: See u then.**

Perfect.

If I were being honest, the dogs were really walking me. I let them lead me to wherever they wanted to go. I'd pick up their turds with pink plastic bags provided by the shelter and dump the crap into the public trash.

The things I do for you, Aubrey Bloom.

When it was time to meet Aubrey, reigning the dogs in became a necessity. "Hold your horses, guys. Let's go this way." The two bigger ones really were more like horses than dogs anyway.

I stopped when I spotted her. She didn't see me at first. Aubrey was standing alone with a manila folder tucked under her arm, eating an ice cream cone. My mouth watered as my eyes followed the movement of her tongue sliding along the ice cream. The sunlight caught the natural red highlights in her hair. A light breeze blew her skirt up teasingly. I missed those legs.

Actually, I missed those legs wrapped around my back while I was buried deep inside of her.

My dick twitched at the thought. The dogs weren't happy about having to abruptly stop so that I could gaze at her. They retaliated by suddenly charging toward where she was standing, dragging me behind them.

Aubrey erupted in laughter when she saw me struggling to contain the three barking beasts.

"You've got your hands full." She smiled

All of this was worth it just to earn a genuine smile from her, which was rare lately. She had some ice cream on her bottom lip, and I yearned to suck it off. It seemed the dogs were just as enamored with Aubrey as I was. They started jumping all over her. The Dane snuck some of her ice cream cone. It was covered in slobber, so she let him have the rest. Aubrey seemed to be eating the attention up, though, letting the three of them practically trample her and lick her face. The Shepherd looked like he was about to hump her leg.

Dogs got away with murder.

I'd never wanted to be one so badly in my life.

Tightening my grip on the leashes, I said, "Guys, pipe down. Give poor Aubrey some space."

"Interesting advice coming from you, Mr. Bastardo."

"At least I haven't tried to lick you." I wiggled my brows. "I've thought about it. "

"You have, have you?"

"Yup. Just now, actually. But I can restrain myself when I want to. That's a brownie point in my corner, eh?" I winked.

"Well, congratulations for not acting like an animal."

"It's not easy sometimes, because I know what I'm missing, seeing as though I've already sampled your kibbles n' bits."

Shaking her head, she said, "You're crass."

"You like it."

"No, I don't." She rolled her eyes, but the expression on her face was one of amusement.

There was my dirty girl.

She opened the folder and grabbed a pen from her purse. "We should have you sign your contract. I reviewed it carefully. It includes everything we requested, no surprises, but feel free to look it over before signing."

Scribbling my signature at the bottom as quickly as I could and handing her back the pen, I said, "No need. I trust you completely." Looking straight into her eyes, I added, "I doubt you can say the same about me, but I'm working on that."

She seemed to shut down. "You're right. I can't say the same." She tucked the folder back under her arm. "I better get going. I have to be somewhere."

"You have a date with the Dickster?"

"Stop calling him that. For the last time, his name is Richard."

My tone turned serious. "Come on, Princess. I'm just kidding about all of it...your bits...Dick...everything. You know my sense of humor. You used to like it."

"Really? I did? Funny, because I don't remember much that happened before waking up sore between my legs and finding you gone."

Fuck.

It felt like she punched me in the gut.

When will this ever get easier?

I took a step toward her. "We need to talk more about what happened. I—"

"I really do have to go," Aubrey said, looking down at her watch and backing away.

The dogs were getting antsy and pulling me in the direction of a couple of small Yorkshire Terriers that were running around on the loose. I yelled at them, "Shit! Slow down."

Some wingmen they were.

By the time I turned around again, my girl was gone.

After that fiasco, I went straight to the bar and unloaded the whole story onto Carla Babes.

Pouring me a second drink, she shook her head. "You wanna know what I think? She's just as bad as you."

"Clarify that statement."

"You're both playing games."

I swirled my drink around in the glass. "Well, if it's a game, the fun is starting to wear off."

"She's pretending she doesn't want you here, yet she's been caught stalking you herself. If she really wanted nothing to do with you, she would have never taken your case. She could have told her boyfriend the truth, and he would have kicked you to the curb so fast, client or not. She's hiding you from him because she still has feelings for you and doesn't want him to know. Are you blind, Aussie?"

My heart beat faster, filling with renewed hope. "I never thought of it that way."

"You need to put a stop to this cat and mouse game. Find out what her intentions are. You're a good guy, Chance. I know you hurt her pretty badly, but you're hurt, too. She needs to know that. Stop pretending you're okay with all of this."

"What do you suggest?"

"Cut the patient hero act. How many bushes can you possibly plant, Mr. Green Thumb? It's not helping anything. What you really need is to plant yourself in her bush! Stop wasting time, and tell her what you want."

I cackled. "Forget about green thumb. I think I have a numb green cock at this point."

"The Green Giant," she quipped.

I chimed in, "Shrek."

We were both cracking up. When the laughter subsided, I looked up at her—my sounding board. Her friendship really did mean a lot to me. "What would I do without you, Carla Babes?"

She seemed to blush at my comment. That was unlike her.

Clearing her throat, she leaned her hands against the counter. "Look, in all seriousness, you need to go to her tonight. Tell her how you feel without all of the bullshit. Make sure she knows you're not going to be around forever. Time is precious. There are plenty of other women who would love the opportunity to make you happy if she doesn't care to."

For a split second, the look in her eyes made me wonder if she was referring to herself.

I took the remainder of that weekend off from stalking Aubrey. It was the first time an entire day had gone by where I hadn't at least gotten one glimpse of her. But I really needed time alone to think without the deterrent of her beautiful face and succulent ass.

While the last talk with Carla had boosted my confidence, the more time I spent alone, the more doubt started to creep in.

That Sunday, I spent a good chunk of the day at the laundromat. Watching my clothes spin round and round in the dryer helped me meditate and reflect on everything.

As much as I'd always said that I'd stick around town as long as it took, I wasn't willing to do that if Aubrey had already written me off. If her intention was to stay with Dick come hell or high water, then I really needed to know. It was one thing to get her to forgive me. It was another to get her to forgive me AND give me another chance, leaving a guy that supposedly made her happy and was there for her when I wasn't.

I'd decided that tomorrow night after Aubrey got home from work, I'd try to get my answer once and for all.

Chapter Twenty-One
EXIT

I skipped the Monday morning breakfast routine on Jefferson and went straight to Aubrey's house instead. Today would be a longer day, putting the finishing touches on Pixy's pen and making sure that everything was in order in the event that things didn't turn out in my favor tonight.

I stopped for two of the goat's favorite burritos—sans the corn—and brought lunch over to the window.

Watching him gobble them in just a few bites, I scratched his head. "Listen, I have to tell you something important."

He was too busy licking the burrito wrapper to look up at me.

"I need you to know that if I go away, it's not because of you. Alright?"

"Baa."

"I want nothing more than to see you every day and for the three of us to be together. I just don't know anymore if that's going to be possible. If it's not, I have to go away again. Because it will make me too sad to stay."

He looked at me with his droopy eyes. Even though he was supposedly blind, sometimes I swore he could see me.

"I promise if that happens, I'll never forget you, Bugger, okay?"

Pixy rested his chin in my hand, and I did something I never had before. Reaching down, I kissed his forehead. It wasn't the type of kiss I was hoping for in Temecula, but it was the next best thing. He was the official mascot of my time with Aubrey, always at the center of the good memories that we shared. I'd never forget him. I took a selfie of us. Now I could cross "kiss a goat" off my bucket list.

The rest of the afternoon, I went in search of princess flowers. I didn't want to steal them off the bush I'd planted, so I needed to find a florist who carried them. I was finally able to snag a bouquet and took it back to my motel.

I showered, put on dark jeans and a fitted black shirt and splashed on some cologne. Needing to look and smell my best tonight was going to be important. I decided against calling Aubrey first. I didn't want her to try to talk me out of coming over. So, showing up at her door tonight would be a gamble.

It was a clear evening. The lights from inside her bungalow lit up the otherwise dark street.

She was home.

I was home.

With my heart racing, I parked my truck around the corner and sat there for at least twenty minutes rehearsing what I was going to say. Someone came out of the house I was parked in front of.

The woman was wiggling her ass with her tits hanging out as she approached my truck in a flimsy nightgown and slippers. When I saw the cast on her hand, I remembered it was Aubrey's slutty neighbor, Philomena. Now, it seemed she had a cast on her leg as well. What the fuck? This chick was a hot mess.

"Hey, handsome. I saw your truck out here."

"Sorry, I didn't realize you lived here. I shouldn't have parked right in front of your house."

"Are you kidding? I got all excited, thought maybe you had decided you wanted to mow me after all."

"No, I'm not in the neighborhood on business."

"Maybe you'd like to just come in and fuck me then?"

"Wow, well…um…while that's a tempting offer given your lovely…casts…and all, I'm not really available for that. But thanks."

"Why don't you come in for a drink then? I promise I won't bite."

"No. Actually, I'm heading over to Aubrey's."

She placed her cast on her hip. "You are aware Aubrey has a boyfriend, right?"

"I'm quite aware of that, yes."

"Well, if you change your mind, you know where to find me." She arched her head to see an oncoming car. "Actually, looks like he just turned the corner. This should be interesting."

"Who?"

"That was Aubrey's boyfriend's BMW that just passed by."

My stomach sank. *Fuck*.

After Philomena finally left me alone and went back inside, I just sat for the longest time not knowing what to do. Grabbing the flowers, I eventually got out of the truck, planning to just leave them at her doorstep.

As I approached, what I saw in clear view through the window nearly stopped my heart. Aubrey was sitting on the couch with Richard as she leaned her head on his shoulder. She looked content. *At peace.* It looked like they were watching a movie.

As much as it hurt to see it, I couldn't look away. That vision was the essence of my dream. There was nothing more in the world that I wanted than to come home every night to her and do exactly that—just be with her. With each second that passed as I stood there, the seeds of doubt were growing. Suddenly, for the first time since arriving in Temecula—even with all the stalking—I truly felt like an outsider looking in. It really hit me. While jail had thrown me into a time warp, time had indeed passed. Aubrey had moved on.

She'd moved on.

You fucking fool, Chance.

This was why you did what you did, remember? It was what you supposedly wanted for her.

At least twenty minutes must have gone by after that realization, and I was still standing in the same spot on the very lawn I'd manicured to perfection. I knew why I was feeling sick.

I was mourning her.

Walking away from her the first time left her devastated. My walking away the second time now would devastate *me.* This time, I didn't seem to know how to leave.

I couldn't *not* say goodbye. For now, I'd leave the flowers at the door, maybe send her a message or call her tomorrow to let her know about my plans to return home to Hermosa Beach.

Arriving at her doorstep, I knelt down to place the flowers over the welcome mat. A thump startled me. Pixy must have smelled me or something. He appeared at the dining room window, which was just on the other side of the front door.

He began to "baa" incessantly.

"Shh!" I warned.

Just as I started to walk away, the exterior light flashed on, and the front door opened. I turned around.

Aubrey was standing there. "Chance…"

Lifting my hand slowly, I said, "Hi."

"What are you doing here?" She looked down and spotted the flowers, bending to pick them up. "You were leaving these at my doorstep?"

"That's right. I wasn't planning to come in."

Dick appeared, placing his hand possessively around Aubrey's tiny waist. My eyes landed on it then moved up to meet Aubrey's frightened expression.

"Mr. Bateman," Dick said. "How can we help you?"

We.

Fuck you, Princess Fucker.

"I was just coming by with a little token of my appreciation for Aubrey's assistance with my legal matter."

"That was nice of you, but you should have stopped by the office instead of coming here."

Dick.

"Actually, I'll be leaving early in the morning. So, this was my only opportunity."

Aubrey had been looking down at the flowers. Her head immediately lifted, and her stare was now penetrating my own. "You're leaving town?"

"That's right. My business here is done." I continued looking straight into her eyes, so she understood how serious this was. "I wasn't going to leave without saying goodbye."

She stood there speechless. Pixy was standing right by Aubrey's legs. Knowing what he was angling for, I bent down, closing my eyes to let him lick my face for the last time. When I stood up, Dick, who seemed confused about my instant bond with the goat, looked back and forth between the animal and me.

Tightening his grip on Aubrey, he said, "Well, we wish you the best."

"Thank you." I started to walk away before turning around one last time. My voice was strained. "Take good care of her."

I didn't care how inappropriate that last comment was. It needed to be said.

Swallowing my pain, I walked across the grass without looking back at her. I couldn't. After I turned the corner, I got into my truck and sped off.

I headed straight for my motel room. I'd wanted to go to the bar to say goodbye to Carla but was scared of drinking myself into oblivion. Someday soon, I'd write her a letter or something to let her know how much her friendship meant to me.

Aubrey hadn't called or texted. That only solidified the fact that my leaving was for the best.

Tossing and turning, sleep wasn't happening for me. Unable to rid my body of the excruciating physical ache of knowing I would never touch her again, I conceded to my insomnia. I sat up at the edge of my bed, pulling my hair in frustration as I looked over at my packed suitcase while checking my phone for what seemed like the hundredth time.

Looking down at my hand, I took off the fake gold band from Vegas and threw it angrily in the trash can. While a part of me never expected her to call, a bigger part of me was shattered that she didn't. What bothered me the most was that I still couldn't envision my future without her in it.

A knock at the door startled me.

The motel was in a seedy area, so I made sure to check the peep hole before opening. The view inside was a distorted version of a distraught Aubrey. My confused heart accelerated despite having been emptied earlier of all hope.

I opened the door but said nothing as she walked past me and sat on the bed. I stayed standing across from her. The silence was deafening as we just looked at each other. Then, she started to talk.

"I waited for six hours in the lobby that day…"

When a teardrop fell down her cheek, I grabbed her a tissue and handed it to her before sitting down next to her. My body tensed in anticipation of what she'd say next.

"I was so sure that you were coming back. I kept hearing in my head what you'd told me the night you came home late from getting us dinner in Arizona, when I got scared. You said, 'I would never do that to you.' So, I held out hope for a while. I felt like a fool because even though all of your belongings were gone, I still believed you were coming back. I know it was only eight days with you, but I felt closer to you than anyone. I saw a future with you."

My chest constricted. "Tell me what happened when you got to Temecula. I need to know everything even if it hurts to hear it."

"I was very depressed for a long while. I threw myself into the new job. A couple of months after the move, I met a guy. He became a really good friend. His name was Jeremy. He was so sweet and good to me. We were friends for six months before he became my boyfriend. He knew everything about what happened between you and me." She laughed a little, looking over at me for the first time. "He hated you."

I smiled even though that made me hurt on the inside.

She continued, "I put up a wall, wouldn't let him in. I was still so wrapped up in you even though you were gone, and you'd hurt me. You were still all I wanted, all I yearned for. Everywhere I went, everything reminded me of you. Jeremy knew it. He wanted more from me than I could give him. He wanted my heart, and even though you'd broken it, it still belonged to you."

"How did you end up meeting Richard?"

"After things ended with Jeremy, I decided I really needed help. Between my career, my relationships, even my family dealings…I felt…stuck. I started seeing a therapist. She helped me to make some changes and stop blaming myself for your leaving. She helped me move on somewhat from the trust and abandonment issues. I'm still working on them. She also made me see that I had to accept that you weren't coming back. By the time Richard entered my life seven months ago, I was ready to let someone in again. He was hired as a partner at the firm. That's how we met."

"As much as I rank on his name, he seems like a nice guy."

"I've never told him about you. Yes, he is a wonderful person. He and I have a lot of common interests. He encourages me to follow my passion. He's the reason I started getting involved in the animal shelter."

"That's a good thing."

"He wasn't the first person to inspire me that way. That was the one thing you did for me, Chance. You taught me so much in a short amount of time about how to live life. Even though you broke my heart, I never regretted meeting you. I still wouldn't go back and change it. That was the thing that always seemed so fucked up to me. A lot of who I am now is because of you."

"Do you love him?"

Without hesitation, she said, "Yes." Her answer felt like a gunshot to the chest at point blank range.

Swallowing, I said, "Okay…"

"I've been very confused. As much as I care about Richard, I'm not going to lie. Your showing up has turned my world upside down. I could have never guessed the real reason that you were gone. Everything I believed to be true…isn't. I assumed you abandoned me for other reasons."

"I thought I was doing you a favor."

"Why didn't you want me to wait for you?" Sounding pained, she added, "I would have waited every single one of those days."

I caressed her hair. I couldn't help it. "I never doubted that. But I thought you'd grow to resent me. I didn't know what being in jail would do to me and didn't want you waiting for a man who I wasn't sure would be worth it. In reality, the experience made me a stronger person, but I had no way of knowing that back then. More than anything, you didn't deserve to have to put your life on hold just when you were trying for a fresh start."

"Even though I now understand things more clearly, the way you left was still traumatizing. Even if things were different with Richard, I don't know that I could ever fully trust you not to leave again."

Hearing that made me uneasy. I stopped beating around the bush.

"Just answer me this. Am I really too late?"

My heart was pounding. She hesitated, and something in her eyes gave me a glimmer of hope. This moment felt like my last opportunity, and I wasn't too proud to beg.

She was still sitting on the bed when I fell to my knees below her, resting my head on her stomach. "Just tell me what to do, Aubrey." I repeated, "Just tell me what I need to do to get you to give me another chance."

I hadn't been touched by a woman in over two years, so when she raked her fingers through my hair, it seemed to feel better than anything I'd ever experienced in my life. My breath hitched. Her breathing was ragged. Each sound that escaped her went straight to my cock. Being so close like this made me desperate for a taste of her. I wasn't beyond taking advantage of her sexual attraction to me.

If I had to play dirty, I would. Speaking slowly over her stomach, I said, "Let me make it up to you. I swear you'll forget all the pain. You won't even remember your own name."

"No," she breathed.

I lowered my mouth and spoke over the skin just below her belly button. "Does he pleasure you? Does he give you what you really need?"

Her legs were quivering. "Chance, stop."

Her body's reaction was enough of an answer for me.

I was back in the game.

"Princess, look over there. My suitcase is packed. I'm ready to leave in the morning. Do I have any reason to stay? You tell me."

A look of torment washed over her pretty face. "I can't promise anything."

"I didn't ask for a promise. I asked for a chance. I'd like to start by just being your friend again…the way we began."

She got up and started to pace. "I'm still with Richard. I won't cheat on him."

"I didn't ask you to." I walked toward her slowly, trying not to seem like a lion on the prowl despite my predatory feelings. "So, let me ask you again. Do you want me to stay?"

She looked up into my eyes and whispered, "Yes."

"Then, I'm here."

She backed away. "I have to go. I told him I was going out to get ice cream and put gas in my car."

"You'd better actually go get some then. Be careful. It's late. When will I see you again?"

"Richard has an early meeting. Meet me tomorrow for breakfast at Starbucks at nine."

"Us? Together? At Starbucks?"

"Yes. Just don't order the same thing as me. It's creepy."

I grinned.

When the door closed behind her, my previously subtle smile transformed into a huge beaming one.

I walked over to the trash can, dug up my ring and placed it back on my finger.

Slow and steady wins the race.

Chapter Twenty-Two

EXIT

I stayed up half the night trying to come up with some grand scheme of making Aubrey trust me again. It had been two long years, and I wanted back in so badly—both figuratively and literally—I felt like I could explode. But in the end, I knew there was no grand scheme. It needed to happen the way *we* happened. Just us being us, a little at a time.

Now, that didn't mean I wasn't going to try to use every available advantage I could come up with. It just meant that I'd have to sprinkle those advantages around lightly over time.

In the shower, I thought back to the things that made Aubrey's eyes sparkle. The first time I saw her eyes glaze over, we were in a diner, and I'd fed her from my plate. The greasy eggs and sausage were dripping with Sriracha, and all I could think about was how I could never enjoy a meal again alone after watching her eat from my hands. I was also quite certain she had an affinity for my accent. With these two small things in my mind, my shower might have taken a bit longer than I anticipated. But I was ready for my breakfast date. And damn was I hungry for Aubrey.

I stopped by a local deli and picked up some things, prepping for my Australian breakfast. Before I left my place, I'd swiped some of my favorites from my sister's food stash. I headed over to Starbucks early with a large brown bag, wanting to clear my bringing breakfast in with Melanie before Aubrey arrived.

"You're late this morning." Melanie pulled out a cup and began to write on it with a marker for the barista behind her.

"Could you make it two of those? I'm meeting someone for breakfast." My cocky smile was enough to tell Melanie who that someone was.

Melanie's eyes widened. She truly looked excited for me. "You mean you'll be sharing coffee with her this morning, instead of just picking up the tab?"

"I will."

She clapped her hands together. "I knew it! Richard's a nice guy and all. But it's not the same. You've brought out a side of Aubrey we've never seen."

I hoped that side was the real Aubrey, and she'd still kept it hidden for me. I wondered if good 'ole Dick knew my girl liked to fight and had a dirty streak in her. I was banking on the fact that he was fucking clueless. "Listen, Melanie. Do you mind if I bring in some breakfast this morning? I picked up some things to share with Aubrey."

"Of course not. By all means. Do whatever is necessary."

"Thanks, Melanie."

I picked the coziest seats I could find. They were in the corner, two brown distressed leather chairs with a small table between them. I pulled the chairs closer together before I set out our breakfast. Aubrey showed right at nine.

I stood when she arrived at our table. There was an awkward moment at first. I wanted to lean in and kiss her, even if it was only on her cheek. But her body language was rigid—almost nervous. "Morning." I nodded.

She forced a timid smile. "Hi."

I gestured to the table behind me. "I already got us coffee and picked us up some breakfast."

She sat. "What is all this?"

"It's an Australian breakfast."

"An Australian breakfast? Here at Starbucks?"

"I sort of brought it in. Melanie was good with it."

Aubrey looked back over her shoulder at the register. Melanie and two others were blatantly watching us with huge smiles on their faces. She rolled her eyes when she looked back at me. "Tell me what you're feeding me?"

I smirked. She frowned. "We need to set some ground rules."

"You're setting me up to fail then."

"What are you talking about?"

"You know if you set up rules, I won't be able to help myself. I'll need to break them."

"Rule number one. No breaking the rules."

"That's a little extreme isn't it? If I break rule number four then I've gone and broken two rules. You're being difficult already."

"I could leave."

"Why would you do that? I like you best when you're difficult."

"You would."

"Why don't we get something in you? I think you're extra cranky because you haven't eaten yet."

"Fine." She looked at the food on the table and licked her lips.

Fuck me. This was going to be harder than I thought.

I lifted the toast to show it to her. "This is Vegemite. It's an Aussie favorite." My sister and I might have left Australia behind, but there were certain things we couldn't part with.

"It sounds sort of…gross."

"If you eat it alone, it could be. But when you slather it with butter, it's fan-fucking-tastic."

I offered her a bite of the toast. She attempted to take it from my hand. I pulled the offering back from her reach. "Australian tradition, you feed each other the Vegemite. It's sort of a peace offering between new friends." Okay, so that part, I totally made up. But I'd skipped the hello kiss, so I needed something.

She shook her head, but looked amused. "Fine." Aubrey opened her mouth and closed her eyes.

Jesus Christ. This woman was going to be the death of me. *Two years.* Now I had to look at the woman I'd been dreaming about for all that time with her painted lips opened and eyes shut waiting for me. And I thought prison was a test of restraint.

Unlike most Americans, Aubrey liked the Vegemite. For some odd reason, I knew she would. Together we devoured everything I brought as we danced around real conversation with small talk. I knew in order to start to win back her trust, she needed to see what Adele meant to me. I also wanted to open myself up to her—transparency invites trust. Dr. Phil was one of the approved shows in prison.

"When Adele and I were kids, I used to like to play practical jokes on her. Saran wrap her body to the bed while she slept. Saran wrap the toilet bowl so she would pee on the floor. Hide under her bed until she got into it and turned the light off. Then I'd jump out and scare the crap out of her."

"And I used to feel deprived for not having a sibling."

"Yeah, well. She got even with me once." I offered her the last bite of the toast, and she didn't hesitate to open. Why did I love that she ordered salads with Dick and let me fill her with carbohydrates and empty calories?

"What did she do?"

"She was maybe eight or nine, so I was probably ten or soon to be eleven. I'd just found both soccer and girls. There was a girl I'd taken notice of, and she seemed to have noticed me, too. Izzy. She was on the sidelines of my practice one day, and I was showing off…bouncing the ball all over my knee and my head. Izzy was impressed. I had her just where I wanted her. Until I turned around."

"What did Adele do?"

"She'd painted the back of my white soccer uniform with Vegemite. You ate it between two pieces of toast. But it's not a pretty sight."

She laughed. "I'm glad you told me that *after* we finished eating."

"Izzy lost interest, and I became Chance dirty pants."

We both cracked up. "And to think, years later, that dirty pants ass would become famous."

"You know, that poster has my face on it, too. It's only a little of my arse showing."

"Trust me. It's the ass that sold it."

"Are you saying you like my ass better than my face?"

She shook her head and didn't answer, but her cheeks pinked up a bit. "So how did you get even with Adele?"

"I didn't." I shrugged. "I was proud of her, actually."

We talked for two more hours. About nothing. About everything. I could have sat there for days. When Aubrey's phone buzzed on the table, both our eyes caught the name flashing before our gazes locked. Richard. *Dick*.

"I should go. I can't believe we've been sitting here for close to two and a half hours. I didn't even tell my office I was going to be late." She stood, and I joined her. "What are your plans for today?"

"Go walk some mutts, weed a flower bed for my lawyer. The usual."

She dug into her pocketbook and pulled out a set of keys. Slipping one off her key ring, she offered it to me. "Here. In case you need to use the bathroom or anything while you're working."

It meant so much more than just a place to relieve myself. I took the key from her hand, then linked my fingers with hers. "Thank you."

I took a step closer. *Fuck, she smelled good.* "Private Collection Tuberose Gardenia," I mumbled. Pavlov himself would have drooled at how the smell had conditioned me. It brought me back to the first night in our hotel rooms. The smell permeated her bathroom, and those black lacy underwear were on the counter. *Shit*. Taking care of myself did nothing to quench the thirst I had around her. My pants were growing snug.

"You remembered the name of my perfume."

I couldn't help myself this time. I wrapped my arm around her neck and pulled her against me tightly for a hug. "I remember everything about you," I whispered in her ear.

She was flush when we separated, but her face grew crimson when she looked down to escape my stare and caught sight of the obvious bulge in my jeans.

"It's been more than two years," I offered quietly as an explanation.

"You haven't—"

"Been inside a woman in two years." Then I thought better of my phrasing. "I haven't touched another women since I met you. And I don't plan on it."

I watched her throat swallow before she spoke. "Thank you for breakfast."

"When will I see you again, Princess?"

"I have to go out of town tomorrow morning. I'll probably be getting on the road early and back late. I'll text you the day after tomorrow, maybe."

I hated that answer. But I took it. "Have a safe trip."

I walked some dogs, went to the gym and decided to skip Aubrey's for today. After my time with her this morning, I didn't want to screw things up by being inside stalking when she arrived back home. And there was no doubt once I walked inside her house, I'd be doing a full investigation. So instead, I showered and headed for some quality time with my favorite bartender. The place was always empty at this time.

"You look particularly gorgeous today, Carla Babes." She had on a red shirt with large white polka dots that was tied just under her ample tits, revealing a shitload of smooth skin. Her pinup girl style hair was done up with a red scarf.

She poured me a drink. "You're in a good mood today. Finally grow some balls and go after that woman?"

"I'm working on it."

"You've been working on it for two weeks now."

"It's a marathon, not a sprint." I sucked back a mouthful of my drink.

"What are you, the Dalai Lama?"

"I'm starting to feel like a Buddhist Monk. They don't get laid either, do they?"

"Let me ask you something. Why don't you go to a bar and pick up a willing woman and get the dirty deed over with? It's been a long time. Just have sex. Sweaty, body slapping, meaningless, dirty sex. It might make you feel better."

Honestly, I'd noticed a few women lately. I'd have to be dead not to. Yet my body didn't have the desire to be with anyone else. "I would feel like I was cheating."

"Even though she's screwing someone else?"

That fucking hurt. "Thanks, Carla."

"Sorry." She grinned. "But let me know if you change your mind."

I looked down at the ring on my finger. They may have been vows spoken in front of Elvis with a buzz on, but I was committed all the same. It made me wonder if she remembered our vows, now that I was back in her life again.

Chapter Twenty-Three

EXIT

They say that the rate of recidivism for criminals is upwards of fifty percent. I was becoming a damn statistic. Even though I had a key and wasn't technically a criminal, my little snooping gauntlet had me feeling like the felon that I was.

It started innocently enough. I let myself in to go to the bathroom; then Pixy was looking thirsty. So I went through half of the kitchen cabinets to find a bowl. Nothing too incriminating there. Some fancy wine glasses, coffee mugs with law firms etched into them, canned goods with the labels all facing the front. I smiled when I saw two bottles of the red sauce with a pompous rooster proudly displayed on the front. *My girl liked the cock sauce.*

From there, I moved onto more conspicuous investigating. The bathroom had only one pink toothbrush. The tub was filled with only girly crap. I might have opened the canister of cream on the countertop and taken a giant whiff. It smelled like Aubrey. I was smiling like an idiot again. Until I opened the mirrored bathroom closet. Tylenol, deodorant, razors, extra this and that and...*birth control pills*. I opened the little oval container and saw Monday, Tuesday and Wednesday had already been popped out of the silver foil this week. The urge to flush the remnants of the month down the toilet was powerful. But the ramifications from doing that was something I couldn't even allow myself to think about. I ventured down the hall further.

Inside her bedroom, I opened the sliding closet doors. One of the doors was off the track and almost came crashing down onto my head. *Princess fucker fixes nothing, I see.* There was no sign of men's clothes in the closet, which made me feel somewhat vindicated after the bathroom medicine cabinet find.

On top of her dresser, there were a few framed photographs, one of which I presumed to be Aubrey and her dad at her law school graduation. She was looking at him as he looked at the camera proudly. I remembered he was a lawyer, too. There were a few others. One of her and a friend as teenagers. Another of an older woman and Aubrey. They looked alike; it must have been her grandmother. The last picture caused a crushing sensation in my chest. It was of her and Dick...with Pixy sitting between them. *Mutton, you damn traitor.* As much as it hurt to look at it, I couldn't stop staring at it for a full five minutes. Aubrey was smiling widely. She looked...happy. *That should have been me.*

I'd seen just about all I could take and was about to walk out of her bedroom, when I stopped in front of the last dresser drawers. My eyes fixated on the top drawer, which was square—the type you keep your underwear in. Seeing as I was already an asshole today, I slid it open. Inside was filled with lace. And a note.

Cocky – since you have nothing better to do, how about fixing the closet doors?

I laughed for a full five minutes. We knew each other so well. Then I fixed the closet doors.

I hadn't heard from her since yesterday morning. I was hopeful maybe tomorrow she would text, excited as hell when my phone flashed her name at almost nine in the evening.

> *Aubrey: Thank you for fixing the doors, pervert.*
>
> *Chance: Anything for you.*

A few minutes passed. I wasn't sure if I should apologize for my obvious snooping or not.

> *Aubrey: You didn't try any on, did you?*
>
> *Chance: I'm more of a sniffer than a cross dresser. Plus, I like your ass in lace, not mine.*
>
> *Aubrey: Very funny.*
>
> *Chance: I wasn't kidding about liking your ass in lace.*

My phone went quiet. Clearly, I'd moved this conversation from friend territory. I figured why not push my luck a bit more.

> *Chance: I miss you. When can I see you again?*
>
> *Aubrey: How about a dog walk tomorrow afternoon? My last appointment at the office should be done by 4.*
>
> *Chance: I'll meet you at the shelter at 4:30*
>
> *Aubrey: OK.*
>
> *Chance: Good night, Princess.*

Aubrey: Night, Chance.

The next afternoon, we met at the shelter. Aubrey arrived after me, looking as beautiful as always in her fancy suit. But when she disappeared into the bathroom and came out wearing jeans, a white t-shirt, flip flops and a pony tail, she looked fucking phenomenal. I couldn't help but stare at her as we each leashed up two dogs and headed for the park.

"What? You're looking at me like something is wrong?"

"Just looking at you. I'm not sure if it's possible, but I think you get more beautiful every time I see you."

She was quiet as we entered the park. We walked for a while and then sat on a bench. "Can I ask you something?"

"Anything."

"What was it like? In prison, I mean?"

I suppose it made sense for her to wonder what I'd spent the last two years actually doing. Seeing as all I had done for two years was wonder what she was up to. She was catching up.

"It was…degrading. Overcrowded, yet solidary at the same time."

"Did you have any visitors?"

"Adele came to see me, every other Saturday."

"What about your Mom? Is she still taking care of your ill grandmother?"

"No, she passed."

Aubrey looked over at me. Her face fell. "I'm sorry. That was thoughtless. Your grandmother was ill. I should have realized."

"You couldn't have known." I cleared my throat. "They're both gone now, actually. Mum died of an aneurysm the first year."

"Oh my God, Chance. I'm sorry."

"Thank you."

I opened the water bottle I was carrying and fed some to the panting pooches. Aubrey was still looking at me when the bottle was empty. So I gave her my full attention and waited to hear what she was thinking about.

A tear rolled down her face before she spoke. "You've lost so much."

I wiped it away and cupped her cheek. She leaned into my touch. I could barely breathe remembering all that I lost. "Yes. I did." I closed my eyes briefly to pull myself together. When I reopened them, Aubrey was still watching me. So I continued. "Sometimes, it takes losing everything to make you realize what you really need."

She laced my fingers with hers and squeezed. We sat on the bench like that for another hour before the four dogs we were exercising decided it was time to get back up. I told her about the soccer clinic I started in prison. She told me about everything she did to get the animal shelter up and running. Her firm allowed her to do a sizeable amount of pro bono work, which made her happy. It sounded as if she had found the type of balance she was still figuring out she wanted two years ago.

After we returned the dogs to the shelter, I wasn't ready to let her go. We were standing out front, and it felt like an awkward end to a first date. "Could we go get a bite to eat?" I asked.

She bit her bottom lip. "I sort of have plans tonight."

Dick. I nodded and looked down.

"But—"

I glanced back up hopeful. I wasn't beyond puppy dog eyes.

"They were sort of loose plans. Maybe I could change them."

I answered honestly, "I would really love that. I'm not ready to give you back tonight."

She nodded and excused herself for a minute, walking away to make a phone call out of earshot. When she returned, she dropped her phone into her purse. "What are you in the mood for? I need to stop home and change for wherever we go. The dogs got me all dirty, and I don't want to put back on my suit from work."

"How about we order in?"

She thought about it for a few seconds. "I don't think that's a good idea, Chance."

I held up three fingers. "I'll be on my best behavior. Boy Scout's promise."

She squinted at me as she considered the idea. "Fine."

My other hand was behind my back with two fingers crossed.

We ordered spaghetti carbonara and chicken cutlet parmigiana from the Italian restaurant a few blocks from her house. Sharing, we both dug in as soon as it arrived. She dipped a piece of bread into the sauce after we polished off both dishes. "I see you've lifted your ban on carbohydrates. I seem to remember you only allowing yourself one cheat meal a month."

"I decided I liked food too much. So I traded bread and pasta for a strict regimen at the gym. Richard got me into running, and I realized I could burn off a slice of cheesecake in less than thirty minutes. Totally worth the half hour."

I looked away. Hearing her talk about him, and all the good he'd done for her, left me conflicted. I was happy she was enjoying things more but sad I wasn't the person who helped her learn to enjoy what life had to offer. If I was truthful, hearing his name from her lips also made me feel cross.

"Sorry." She caught my long face and offered sincerely.

"I'm being an arse. I'm glad that you're eating and exercising." I needed a minute, so I got up and took our plates to the sink. Aubrey cleaned up the table while I loaded and started the dishwasher. It felt so…domestic. So right. I wondered if she felt like this with him, too.

It was only eight o'clock when dinner was done. I didn't want to outstay my welcome, yet I never wanted to leave. I stared down at the kitchen floor. There were some cracks in the grout—a project for another day. "Do you want me to go?" My head was still bowed, but my eyes looked up at her filled with hope.

She shook her head and spoke softly. "How about we watch a movie?"

Pixy joined us in the living room. The minute we sat on the couch, the bugger hopped up on the adjoining loveseat. He propped his head up on the armrest and stared at us. "It's sort of his seat," she offered.

We argued about what to watch before we finally settled on a series on Netflix that Aubrey babbled on about. It was a show about a motorcycle gang with the mum from that old TV show, Married with Children. We had a TV in the day room in prison, but there was no way a show about bikers was on the approved list of programs. I was a few years behind on even the meaningless things like television shows.

"You know, when I first saw your motorcycle that day in the rest stop parking lot, I imagined myself riding on the back of it, my arms wrapped around that guy." She pointed to some blonde bloke on the television, riding a Harley with bright white sneakers. "I wondered what it would feel like to ride."

"Oh yeah?" She lifted her legs onto the couch and stretched them out. Her knees were bent, but her feet reached my thigh. Without thinking, I took one of her feet into my hands and started to rub. She looked pensive at first, but her shoulders quickly relaxed. "Feel good?"

"Mmmm...hmmm."

"Guess I'll be taking a trip back down to Hermosa Beach."

"Why is that?"

"To get my bike. I owe you a ride."

She closed her eyes as I kneaded her feet. "I'd like that."

Me too, Princess. Me, too.

"You wanna know what I thought the first time I saw you?"

She chuckled. "Probably not."

"I couldn't keep my eyes off of you. You were gorgeous, but something about the way you smiled as you played with that bobblehead just did something to me."

"I thought you hated me."

"I wondered what it would feel like to ride, too. Only I wasn't thinking about the bike one bit."

Our eyes caught, and I watched as her pupils actually dilated. *Fuck.* She was getting turned on. I pressed my thumbs into the arch of one of her feet, and she closed her eyes and let out a small moan. "God, I love that sound." I heard the thickness in my own voice. My cock was growing to match it.

As I rubbed, I felt the tightness from her muscles flee. But it was replaced by a different type of tension. A raw sexual energy filled the air around us. She was relishing my touch, slowly giving into how it made her feel. My hands at her feet moved up to her calf. Her breathing became jagged with each knead. God, I missed the feel of her skin beneath my fingers. I wanted her body under mine so badly, it was almost painful to keep myself from pushing too fast. My hand slid up to the back of her knee, and I inched closer to her. Her body was so responsive to my touch.

"Chance," she moaned with her eyes shut.

I leaned into her slowly. "Aub—"

The sound of the doorbell was the equivalent to throwing a bucket of ice water over Aubrey. Her eyes flew open and bulged from her head, and her body became rigid. It didn't take a rocket scientist to figure out who she thought was at the door.

"What if it's…Richard?"

"So what? We didn't do anything wrong."

"But…I didn't tell him about us. You showed up the other night on my doorstep and said you were leaving town. I'm pretty sure that raised his suspicion enough. If he finds you here, he'll think something is going on between us."

I was suddenly defensive. I stood. "There is something going on between us."

"You know what I mean."

The doorbell rang again. I wanted nothing more than to stomp to the front door, swing it open and tell Dick to take a hike. But Aubrey was looking panicked. I raked my fingers through my hair. "What do you want me to do? Slip out the back door?" I was being sarcastic. Although, the way she looked at me told me it was exactly what she wanted. "You've got to be kidding me."

"I'm sorry. I really am. I...I...just can't let him find you here."

We stared at each other for a long moment. Leaving like this felt monumental to me. Like *I* was the other guy. Not Dick. It hurt like hell, but I did what she wanted. Without another word, I left out the back door.

I waited by the back window until I saw him inside, then walked around to the front. I couldn't watch from the outside in again. It would kill me. And there was no way in hell I could stick around to possibly watch his car spend the night. So, I left. There might have been tire marks on the street outside of her house—but I left.

Steamed, I got on the highway and headed back toward Hermosa Beach. It was either that or wallow in my own self-pity with Carla, and I didn't trust myself to stick around at the moment. I made it about an hour before my gas light was flashing. Pulling into the combo rest stop-gas station, I parked and leaned my head on the steering wheel for a few minutes.

What was I doing? Aubrey was happy. At least she was before I selfishly showed up back in her life. I wanted her to want me back so badly, I questioned if I was seeing something that was no longer there. The hour drive had me flip flopping back and forth between being certain she only needed time to learn to trust me again and being certain I was doing the wrong thing for sticking around.

Just as I was about to get out of the car, the sky opened up. Rain started to teem, bouncing off the hot California blacktop making it steam like dry ice. It was eerie looking, really. Lonely, almost. Maybe it was a sign.

I jogged into the rest stop. Unable to beat the raindrops, my clothes were drenched as I headed to the bathroom. I splashed some water on my face, looked in the mirror and tried to give myself a pep talk. I couldn't even convince my own sorry ass that everything was going to turn out fine, yet I was trying to convince Aubrey. My phone buzzed in my pocket and, for a second, I let my hopes rise. It was a text from my carrier telling me I'd nearly reached the end of my data plan usage allotment. *Now, there's a damn sign. I was running out of time.*

Grumbling to myself, I walked out of the restroom and decided to grab a bite before filling the tank and getting back on the road. I laughed when I saw my choices: Starbucks or Popeyes Chicken. It was ironic, really. Perhaps, I'd stop in the small gift shop and look for an Obama bobblehead on my way out. I was internally berating myself for being such a pathetic fuckwad.

Anxious to get the hell out of there, I ordered some chicken and reached into my pocket for my billfold to pay. Something tumbled from my pocket and clanked loudly on the floor. It was the key Aubrey had given me. I picked it up and closed it into the palm of my hand as I paid for my meal.

It hit me then. Here I was looking for a stupid sign, when all along I'd had the key. *Dick* rang the bell. They'd been together seven months, and she hadn't given the princess fucker a key. I'm *not* the other guy. She just hadn't admitted it to herself yet. Now that was something I could give her a hand in doing.

Adele was sitting on the couch with her legs crossed. "So, you're going back tonight?"

I nodded. "I don't have time to waste. Every second that I'm here, he's getting more of an upper hand. I just came back to throw my bike into the back of my truck." I wriggled my forehead. "She wants me to take her for a ride."

"That's great and all. I just hope she's not taking *you* for a ride."

"That's kind of what I've been angling for, Sis."

"You know what I mean! Stringing you along. The fact that she has a boyfriend who seems like a good guy makes this complicated. She's not going to want to hurt him."

"I'm aware this isn't ideal. But here is the key to what I needed to know." I stuck my hand in my back pocket, pulling out Aubrey's house key. "Right here."

"That's a literal key."

"Exactly." I winked. "He doesn't have one. She gave one to me. Granted, it was to be able to use the toilet at my leisure while I'm doing her lawn. But what does the fact that he doesn't have one say?"

"That he's not cutting her grass." She laughed. "Believe me, I want to think that you're going to get the girl in the end, but the alternative makes me nervous. That's all. What happens then?"

"Then, your dear old brokenhearted brother camps out on his couch eating a shitload of Tim Tams all day in his pajamas."

She threw a pillow at me. "That's what scares me."

"You're worried about me." I threw the pillow back. "That's cute but unnecessary."

"I really hope you're right."

Back in Temecula, with my bike gassed up, I was anxious to see her. It was Friday afternoon, so she was still in work. Unable to contain my excitement, I sent her a text.

> **Chance: In the mood to straddle me?**
>
> **Aubrey: Excuse me?**
>
> **Chance: Get your mind out of the gutter, dirty girl. I brought the Harley back from Hermosa Beach. Care to live out your little biker fantasy with me?**
>
> **Aubrey: You want to take me out?**
>
> **Chance: Among other things, yes.**
>
> **Aubrey: When?**
>
> **Chance: This weekend sometime if you're free. I was thinking we could take a little road trip.**
>
> **Aubrey: The last time I did that with you, it got me into trouble.**

Chance: Come on, Princess. I'll let you call me Charlie Hummer.

Aubrey: Hunnam. LOL. Charlie Hunnam!

Chance: I like Hummer better.

Aubrey: I'm sure you do, pervert.

Chance: Who's the pervert? I was talking about the vehicle. What were you talking about? Better yet...can you demonstrate?

Aubrey: You're unbelievable.

Chance: Are you smiling?

Aubrey: Maybe.

Chance: Good. So, what do you say?

Aubrey: I can't do it tomorrow. What about Sunday?

Not wanting to wait an entire day to spend time with her, disappointment set in.

Chance: I happen to be available Sunday.

Aubrey: Do I need to bring anything?

Chance: I've got it taken care of.

Aubrey: That scares me.

Chance: LOL. It should.

Aubrey: See you Sunday then.

Chance: What time shall I pick you up?

Aubrey: Noon?

Chance: Sounds good.

She didn't respond. I couldn't help sending one last text.

Chance: I can't wait.

I spent the rest of Friday afternoon and evening preparing for our Sunday trip. First order of business: buying Aubrey a helmet. At the store, I nearly died in laughter when I spotted one that was supposed to look like the green skin of a watermelon. It had a triangle sliced into it that made it appear like a chunk was cut off. I figured she'd kill me if I made her wear that. I settled on a different one that was perfect for her.

Not used to riding with anyone, I also adjusted the rear suspension on the bike in preparation for my passenger.

Back at the motel, I went online in search of a route that we could take and a good place where we could stop. I found a town called Julian that was about seventy-six miles away. That would mean about a two-hour ride. It was a mountainous area about an hour east of San Diego and apparently known for its apple pies. Apple pie for my apple-bottom girl. *Julian it was.*

I kept fantasizing about finding a bed and breakfast there where we could stay the night but knew that she would never go for that. So, our destination had to be easily doable in a round trip, getting us back to Temecula at a decent hour.

Sunday finally rolled around. I made sure I pulled out all the stops in looking every bit like Aubrey's biker boy fantasy. Wearing a distressed brown leather jacket, blue jeans and my shiny black helmet, I was ready to claim the only woman I ever wanted on the back of my ride. Charlie Hummer better watch out.

Rather than go to her door, I revved the engine of the bike right in front of her house, prompting her to come outside. The entire neighborhood was now aware of my arrival.

Aubrey came out, and it warmed my heart to see her smiling. She was wearing a short, tight black leather jacket that hugged her tits. *Fuck me*. Her hair was down, and she wore high black leather boots over her jeans.

As I held out her helmet, my mouth spread into a huge smile. "God, you look fucking hot."

She covered her mouth in laughter when she looked down at the pink helmet I'd picked out that had the words *Biker Princess* etched onto the side. "Biker Princess? Did you have this made?"

"No. They had it at the bike shop. How perfect is that? It was fate."

"What would really be perfect is if yours said *Cocky Bastard.*" She winked. I was thrilled to see that the version of her that showed up today was *feisty Aubrey*. My dick was even more thrilled.

"Ready to roll, Princess?"

"Honestly, I'm a little scared. I've never been on one of these in my life."

"You know the feeling you have when you're riding in a convertible?"

"Yeah?"

"Well, times that by ten. That's what it's gonna be like. Fucking awesome, Aubrey."

She still looked nervous.

"Are you nervous, baby?"

"I can't help it."

"Don't be scared. Just don't let go of me. That's the main thing you have to remember."

Please don't ever let go of me.

"Believe me. I won't," she said.

"Is that a promise?"

She blushed knowing what I was really getting at and ignored the question.

"This is my first time too, you know," I said.

"What do you mean? You've been on a motorcycle plenty of times."

"Yes, but you're the first woman that's ever ridden behind me."

"Really?"

"Really." I put the helmet over her head. "Here, let me help you." Adjusting the strap, I looked into her beautiful eyes, and said, "Now, I'm gonna teach you some things before we leave. I read up on some safety stuff."

"Alright." She looked adorable with that huge pink helmet on her head.

I sat on the bike. "Hop on behind me."

She did as I said.

"Wrap your arms around my waist."

I stilled for a moment at the feel of them wrapped around me tightly. "See what you're doing now? Just keep doing it. Hold onto me as tightly you can."

"Okay."

I looked behind her. "Now this is very important. When I turn a corner, just relax your body. Don't lean against the turn. That's going to be your impulse, but don't do it. Alright?"

"Alright."

"The other thing is, it's going to be hard for us to hear each other unless we really yell. So, if you don't want to scream and for any reason, you need me to stop, just tap me on the shoulder. But that's the only time you're allowed to let go."

My rules regarding holding on for dear life were a bit of an exaggeration. But I was going to milk the experience of being close to her for all it was worth.

"Let's get going. Ready?"

She shrugged. "As ready as I'll ever be."

I cranked the engine, and we took off down some side roads before entering the highway. Aubrey never did let go. Not once. I never imagined how good it would feel to have someone behind me. Well, I suppose it was because it was *her* behind me. I'd forgotten how much I missed riding too, that feeling of shifting through the gears, the wind hitting my face and the sensory overload. It was the next best thing to sex—a feeling of absolute power. Having to focus intently on the road and everything around me brought about a strange sense of calm.

As much fun as it was, I was all too aware of how careful I needed to be with Aubrey's life in my hands. Being on a bike makes you overly conscious of your own mortality, particularly when you're on the freeway. Our route alternated between the highway and open country roads that were surrounded by mountains. Even though the scenery was breathtaking, I missed her beautiful face. I couldn't wait to see her all wind-burned with her hair messed up.

One of the most fun parts of the ride for me was trying to communicate with Aubrey. She couldn't really hear what I was saying. So, I'd shout things for the fuck of it that I wished I could say to her.

We were riding along, almost at our destination when I shouted, "I can't wait till you sit on my face."

"What's that?"

"I said, I can't wait to show you this place."

Another time it was, "I think we should get married for real."

"What?"

"Whatever happened to Captain and Tennille?"

When we arrived in Julian, Aubrey looked exactly as I expected she would. Her face was red from the wind, her hair wild. It took everything in me not to smash my lips into hers.

Shaking out her hair, she asked, "What are we doing first?"

I was so fixated on her, the question hadn't immediately registered. "Huh?"

She repeated, "Where are we going?"

"I heard this place is known for their apple pie. Why don't we go find some?"

Aubrey chuckled. "We travelled nearly two hours by motorcycle for apple pie?"

"Pretty much, yes."

"Only you would do that. That's one of the things I like most about you. Everything can somehow seem like an adventure. Even just getting apple pie."

"Is that a compliment?"

"It is." She flashed the sweetest smile. "And I would love nothing more than to have apple pie with you."

Something had definitely softened her. Maybe it was the ride. That whole experience is very intimate, especially for the passenger, given that you're putting your life in someone else's hands. I guess I impressed her.

Score one, Bateman.

Dick…Zero.

We walked to the Julian Café where they boasted the best apple pie in the entire town. The two of us sat in a cozy corner table up against a brick wall. They served us generous slices of warm apples baked with cinnamon into a buttery crust with dollops of vanilla ice cream on top. They weren't kidding; it was the best I'd ever tasted. At least this day would include *something* orgasmic.

Our conversation started out easy enough. We talked more about the shelter, her plans to convert her guest bedroom into an office, a new type of yoga she was trying. *I hoped to God I'd get to reap the benefits of that someday.* I told her about my brief visit back to Hermosa Beach and my plans to put a small shed on her property to store my garden equipment. Then, I sort of went and ruined the mood.

"So, where does Dick…uh…Richard think you are today?"

"Meeting a friend."

I let out a sarcastic laugh. "Okay. Stretching the truth just a bit."

"Why is that so funny? Aren't we supposedly trying to be friends? That was your idea."

"I use the term friend very loosely. Sort of like—oh, I don't know—*girlfriend*."

"I'm not your girlfriend."

"No, you're my fucking wife."

"Chance…"

"Relax. I'm kidding." *Not really.* "Look, my point is, you can convince yourself that this is innocent for now, but I doubt Dick would want you spending time with a supposed friend whose ultimate goal is to steal you from him. Said friend also happens to have a key to your place when he doesn't. Don't think I didn't catch that. Make no mistake about it, Aubrey. Stealing you away from him is my ulterior motive in case I hadn't made that crystal clear. I'm your friend for now, but that's not enough for me. Never will be. I want you beneath me every night and across from me every morning at the breakfast table. Fuck that, I want *you* for breakfast. I won't be satisfied until I own all of you." Pissed at myself for losing my composure on what was supposed to be a peaceful trip for pie, I pulled at my hair and looked down at my empty plate. My voice lowered. "I'm sorry. I just can't fucking pretend."

Taken aback, she was quiet but nodded in understanding. "It's okay."

After my awkward outburst, we needed a change of scenery. I got up out of my seat. "You want to take a walk around, see the sights, before we head back on the road?"

"I'd love to."

We went for a stroll and ended up stopping inside a small bookstore that also sold trinkets. Aubrey was eying this bracelet that had some Buddhist peace symbol on it. When she became immersed in a Deepak Chopra book, I took one of the bracelets to the register and bought it.

Once we stepped outside, I handed it to her. "Here. I wanted to get you something so that you remember your first trip by motorcycle. I hope it's not the last."

"As if I could ever forget this day," she said. "But that was really sweet of you. Thank you. I love it so much."

"I know. I saw you looking at it. I was looking at *you*, because I can't keep my eyes off you. So…" I put my hands in my pockets and looked around as my words trailed off.

She placed it on her tiny wrist. "Maybe this will help channel some much needed peace in my life."

As we stood there on the sidewalk, it really hit me that this situation was equally hard on her. I spent so much time immersed in my own fears that I had a tendency to forget what all of this might have been like for Aubrey. To have me come back practically from the dead just when she was getting her life in order. It turned her world upside down.

So tempted to hold her hand, I grinded my teeth and refrained. Instead, I said, "Hiking is big around here. If we had more time, we could have stayed at one of the cabins, made a weekend out of it. I know you have to get back."

"Maybe another time." She smiled.

"Yeah."

About an hour later, we were back on the open road. Something about the tone of the ride home was much different than the first trip. As the reddish sun was setting on the horizon, her grip on me had definitely relaxed a bit. We were both quiet, and about halfway through, Aubrey rested her chin on my back. It was a small gesture but sent what felt like electricity through me. It meant everything. It was easy to envision us taking trips like this every weekend. There was nothing like the feeling of having your woman on the back of your bike.

She *was* my woman. Whether or not I was her man was the question that remained.

When we pulled up to her bungalow, the sound of crickets replaced the roaring engine of the bike as I shut it off. We both sat there in silence. She wasn't getting off and hadn't let go of my waist, so I didn't move.

Finally, she spoke. Her voice was quiet. "I won't string you along forever, Chance. I promise. It's not fair. I have to figure this out."

I lifted her hands that were still wrapped around my waist and clutched them tightly around my chest. "I'm not going anywhere anytime soon, Princess."

She let out a deep breath and jumped off the bike while I stayed on. I could see Pixy in the window watching us. *Blind goat, my ass.*

I tugged at the front of her leather jacket flirtatiously. "When will I see you again?"

"I'm not sure."

"Think about it."

"Thank you for today. I'll never forget it."

Her last comment didn't sit well in my stomach.

I'll never forget it.

"You did great, Princess. I can't wait to do this again."

On the ride home that night, I made a tough decision. I was going to lie low for a bit, give her some space. They say if you let something go and it doesn't come back to you, it was never really yours to begin with. But considering I was the one who initially left in this situation, all bets were off.

Chapter Twenty-Five

Two days later, I started to put up the new shed on Aubrey's property. It was going to be nice to be able to keep all of my lawn equipment in one place without having to transport it back and forth. I had to admit, Aubrey must have had the most beautiful garden in all of Temecula by now.

It was a particularly hot day, and it became necessary to cool off. Starting to feel dehydrated, I was thinking of calling it a day here.

Using my key, I entered the house for a drink and to use the toilet before leaving. Pixy was so used to hearing me come in now, he no longer even flinched when I walked inside.

I hadn't texted Aubrey at all since our road trip and had no idea where her head was at. It felt like forever since we'd spoken. My only clues would have been inside of this house, but snooping always made me feel like shit. Thankfully, there was no obvious evidence of Dick having been here in the past couple of days, so that was good. The house was Dickless, just the way I liked it.

Sweat was dripping off my body as the goat followed me around. I wondered if Aubrey would care if I took a quick shower in her bathroom. Seeing as though I made a vow not to contact her, texting her to check wasn't an option. I couldn't see why it would be a problem, though.

"You won't tell, will you, Mutton?"

"Baa."

"Good boy."

I stripped down and left my dirty clothes in a pile just outside the bathroom. Under the lukewarm water, my thoughts, of course, turned to her. Lathering her fruity soaps and shampoo over me was like bathing in a sea of Aubrey. Sweet, sweet torture. I gripped my cock and started to jerk myself off but stopped after thinking better of it. Even though the urge was intense, there was no way I was going to be able to finish myself off in her shower. With my luck, I'd accidentally leave a trace of spluge behind. *Wel-cum Home, Aubrey!* She'd know it was me. That wasn't going to help my cause. Horny as hell, though, I'd definitely need to rub one off back at the motel.

As I exited the shower, the bathroom filled with steam. Wiping myself down, I looked in the mirror at my sculpted body and flexed my muscles.

Shit, I looked good.

With all of the time in the sun and my workouts, my body was truly in the best shape of my life. Sadly, I couldn't even use it on anyone at the moment.

Rubbing the towel vigorously over my wet hair, I walked back out into Aubrey's bedroom. A painting on the wall showing a woman with her breasts exposed caught my eye. It wasn't there the last time I was in here. Must have been new. *Holy shit.* It was classy but still not something I expected her to have.

As I stared up at it, I thought about all the things I never had an opportunity to learn about her. Aubrey was definitely a sexual being, and it made me sad that I never really had a chance to tap more into that side, to push boundaries with her and take her places sexually that she'd never been. All that we could have done in those two years.

Fuck. I was getting hard again. A bead of precum formed at the tip of my dick. I was really hard up.

My body shook at the sound of her voice.

She screamed, "Oh my God!"

I turned around exposing my fully hard cock in all of its glory. "Shit!" I quickly wrapped the towel around my waist to cover my privates. Not only had she seen my ass as she walked in but also got the full frontal experience when I'd turned around.

She sounded breathless. "What are you doing?"

"I..uh…okay…so, I was really hot. I needed to cool down. I took a shower." I laughed nervously. "I didn't think you'd mind."

"I guess I don't mind, but Jesus, do you normally just stand there in the middle of the room stark naked staring at the wall?"

"I was staring at your lovely painting, actually." My eyes trailed down the length of her body. She was wearing her workout clothes, a purple sports bra that squished her beautiful tits together and tight spandex. Dressed like that, she clearly wasn't expecting me to be here this late in the afternoon. I normally didn't stay here so long, but since I'd been building the shed, I lost track of time. She never came home this early.

"Why are you here?" I asked.

"Shouldn't I be asking you that? This is my house."

"I know, but you're normally not home until after five sometime."

"I had a doctor's appointment, so I didn't go back to the office. I went to the gym instead and came home early to shower."

"I just missed you then. We could have done that together."

She rolled her eyes but cracked a tiny smile.

There was nothing hotter than the sight of Aubrey sweaty. My erection was impossible to control. So were my feelings. As I stood there still wrapped in the towel with my dick protruding through it, I slowly approached where she was standing. Her body stiffened and went into some sort of protective mode.

"I've missed you, Aubrey. You could probably tell I've been trying to give you space."

Her chest was heaving. "I know you have. Just not right now, apparently."

"That's right. Not right now."

Her eyes lowered to my abs and back up again. She wasn't just sneaking a look at me. She was blatantly checking me out. Her pupils even seemed to dilate.

Inching even closer to her, I couldn't help telling her how I felt. "You wanted to know why I was staring at the wall. You know what I was thinking about when you walked in?"

"What?"

"I was thinking about how you present yourself as this prim and proper girl but that secretly you're a little minx. That picture on the wall there proves it. You're sexual by nature, someone who will never be fully satisfied by vanilla things. You're someone who—whether you admit it or not—wants to try everything, push boundaries. I know if we were together, you'd let me do all the things I want to your body. And you'd fucking love it."

"What kind of things?" she whispered. Her question surprised me.

Good girl. Play along, baby.

"Let's talk about what I'd want to do right now if I could. I want to slowly lick every ounce of salty sweat off your body, starting with those beautiful tits. I'd clean you off with my tongue and fuck you hard until you come even harder with every drop of my cum inside of you where it belongs."

She looked like she was squirming. "What else?" she asked as she backed away from me, which only made me walk toward her until my face was only inches from hers.

"Then, I'd fuck you all over again with my mouth. I'd love to try eating you out while you take my cock down your throat. I think you'd like that. I want to have you in every way; on top of me, under me and over my knee with my hand marks in pink on your beautiful pale ass. I can't wait to fuck you again. When I say fuck, I really mean make love hard, because that's all it could ever be with us, loving hard and fucking hard."

"Oh God," she muttered, closing her eyes.

Capitalizing on her weakness, I pressed my hungry mouth into hers and shamelessly took what I'd been starving to taste for two years. She opened for me as my tongue invaded her mouth, searching for hers. The moan she let out seemed to travel down my throat in a straight shot to my dick. She ran her fingers through my wet hair as I backed her into the wall, nearly knocking her lamp off of the bedside table. Still in nothing but a towel, I knew I needed to pull back but didn't know how.

Finally, Aubrey pried herself away from me. "Please. Stop."

In between panting breaths, I shouted, "Can't you see how you react to me? Isn't it obvious that we belong together?"

She walked to the opposite side of the room and started to pace. "Relationships aren't all about sexual chemistry, Chance."

"Bullshit. It's extremely important. I don't care how nice of a Dick he is, if he doesn't know how to *use* his dick to please you, he won't keep you happy forever. That's beside the point anyway. You know damn well we have chemistry in *every* way. It's far more than physical. In fact, the emotional connection between us is what scares you the most. So, what's missing here? Trust? Because I'd give my left arm at this point to prove that you can trust me."

She held her hands up and shook her head. "This is too much right now. I wasn't expecting you to be here."

"When won't it be too much? Will it ever be the right time?" I yelled and immediately regretted having raised my voice.

Pixy let out a noise. Bugger was sitting in the corner watching this go down like a movie.

"You're scaring him," she said.

"If he hasn't fainted, he's fine."

She headed for the bathroom, and I trailed behind her.

"Stop running from me as soon as you start to feel something." I put my hands on her shoulders to stop her. "Look at me, Princess."

She turned around, appearing as if she was about to cry. "What?"

Here it was. I knew it was now or never. I shut my eyes then opened them before taking a deep breath. "I love you, Aubrey. Can't you see that? I am head over heels in fucking love with you. I love you more than anything in this entire world. When I look into your eyes, I don't just see you, I see my children. Hell, I see an entire farm of children and deaf, dumb and blind goats. I see my entire future. Without you, I see nothing. *Nothing.* Even those two years locked up, memories of you were what gave me the strength to go on every day. I know you have to resolve things with him, and I don't expect a confirmation right now with me standing here in this towel. I'll wait. In the meantime, I'm here. You have me. The question is, do you want to keep me, or will you throw me away?"

When she opened her mouth, what came out was the last thing I ever expected. "Richard told me some time ago that the firm is dissolving and closing up shop by the end of the year. He was offered a position at a Boston patent law firm as a partner there. I just found this out yesterday. He wants to try to hire me. Either way, he asked me to go with him."

Adrenaline rushed through me as my body was gearing up for a fight. I swallowed the massive lump in my throat. "When does he leave?"

A teardrop fell down her cheek. "Two weeks."

Chapter Twenty-Six

I barely slept after the bomb Aubrey dropped last night. I knew I was starting to get to her, although she was still fighting it. Two weeks was not a lot of time to gain back her trust. But what choice did I have at this point?

Thirteen days. I picked up my cell phone and stared at the time. The damn minutes seemed to tick away faster than they ever had. In prison, waiting for a day to pass seemed like an eternity. Yet now, it felt like the hands on the clock were spinning at warp speed.

I buzzed by Starbucks, picked up a coffee and paid for Aubrey's. I also ordered an apple fritter and gave Melanie instructions to warm it for my girl before she gave it to her. I hoped it would subliminally remind her of our bike excursion for apple pie.

My brain was still frazzled, and I needed to work off the growing feeling of frustration, so I headed to the gym. It was noon by the time I finally made my muscles burn enough to think about something other than *thirteen days*.

Not knowing what else to do with myself, I headed to Aubrey's with a dozen more flats of flowers. It was busy work, and in only two weeks time, someone else could be appreciating the garden. But I couldn't let myself think about that now.

I was coming from the backyard with a wheelbarrow full of mulch when I saw Dick pull up outside of Aubrey's. He looked right at me, and I had no desire to hide anymore anyway.

Maybe the Princess Fucker wouldn't recognize me shirtless and sweaty. I continued down the driveway as he approached.

"Mr. Bateman?" He squinted, clearly confused by my appearance.

"That's me. What can I do you for?"

"What are you doing here?"

I looked down at the wheelbarrow and back up at Dick with a face that said 'can't you figure that shit out yourself?' "Planting flowers." I shrugged.

"I can see that. But why are you *here* planting flowers?"

"I guess that would be because Aubrey likes flowers." Something you obviously didn't know or give a shit about seeing as what the place looked like when I first arrived.

Dick folded his arms over his chest. "I thought you were going back to Australia?"

My jaw clenched. I was torn between telling off the asshole for not taking care of Aubrey's property and punching him in the face for trying to take the woman I loved away. Just then, Aubrey's car turned the corner. No matter how bad I wanted to ruin things, I couldn't do it to her.

"Ohhh." I nodded my head as if something just dawned on me. "You must think I'm my brother, Chance."

"Excuse me?"

"Chance. He's the better looking brother for sure. But we're identical twins. I'm Harry." I extended my hand.

He was skeptical for a moment, but the dumb bloke fell for my line of shit easy enough. My hand was hot, sweaty and dirty. The suit wearing snob looked like he wanted to find somewhere to wipe off his hand after we shook. *Not used to man hands, are you, Dick?*

"Well that explains it then. Your brother was a client of Aubrey's. I met him in the office."

"Yes. I referred him to Aubrey. There's no one else that the Bateman brothers would allow to touch their tockley. Except Aubrey."

"Pardon?"

"Tockley—it's an Australian term for important paperwork."

He nodded and looked over at the curb as Aubrey parked.

Dumb fuck. Suck my tockley.

Now that I wasn't supposed to know who he was, I could screw with the guy a bit. "So what do you think of the place? Coming along really well, don't you think? Place was a real mess when I got here. I'm surprised Aubrey doesn't have a man around the house to take care of things properly."

Dick cleared his throat. "She does. Just not one who has the time or inclination to do this sort of work."

"That's a shame. Aubrey could use a man that takes care of all her needs."

Dick narrowed his eyes at me, as Aubrey rushed from her car. She looked pale and frazzled.

"You didn't tell me, Mr. Bateman's brother was your landscaper?" Dick said to Aubrey.

"Brother?" Aubrey looked to me and I grinned.

"I thought Harry here was Chance when I pulled up." Then the idiot added, "Now I can see the difference, of course. Twins always look different around the eyes."

"Harry?" Aubrey's panicked face cracked a tiny smile.

I spoke to Dick. "Aubrey calls me Harrison. She's a stickler for proper names, isn't she?"

He ignored my comment. I got the feeling this tool ignored anyone who wasn't wearing a suit. Instead he spoke to her. "I was just about to tell Harry that his services are no longer going to be needed. Seeing as we'll be heading to Boston soon enough."

Aubrey spoke quietly. "That's not decided yet."

"I told you. It's just a formality. I've already spoken to the partners. They want you." Dick put his hand on the small of Aubrey's back. I was barely able to stop myself from physically removing it.

"Nice to meet you, Mr. Bateman." He didn't bother to look at me. "We better grab that file, sweetheart. Or we'll be late for the deposition."

Aubrey nodded. She looked back over her shoulder twice before disappearing into the house. A few minutes later, they came out together again. Dick nodded at me, and Aubrey looked down as they passed. I had started to dig a hole to put flowers in when they went inside, but I'd forgotten to stop. I now had a waist deep crater. I couldn't look over at the curb as they got into their cars. My restraint was hanging on by a thread.

One car pulled away. Not hearing the second start, eventually I looked out to the street. Dick was gone, but Aubrey was still sitting in her car. Her head was leaning against the steering wheel. I walked over and got into the passenger seat.

Neither of us said a word for a minute. "What am I supposed to do?" She eventually whispered.

I blew out a heavy stream of air. "Do what's in your heart, Aubrey. If that's not being with me—it will suck—I'm not going to lie. But I want you to be happy. That's how I'm sure I'm in love with you. If the choice is you being happy or me…there is no choice. You come first."

She shook her head. "I believe you, you know."

I took her hand from the steering wheel and lifted it to my lips, kissing the top. "You should. Because I mean it. There's nothing I won't do for you, Princess."

She smiled. It was a step in the right direction. *She believed me.*

"I better go. We have a deposition in fifteen minutes across town, and I've been so preoccupied, I didn't even realize that the file was at home."

I opened the car door. If we had more time, I would have preferred to leave things for today. But, *thirteen days.* I had to ask. "Come home with me this weekend?"

"Chance…"

"I know. But I don't have the luxury of time anymore. You have a decision to make. And Dick gets you all the time. I want to take you home with me. Show you what our life can be like. No crazy road trips. No interruptions. Just me and you. Give me a fair shot if you're making this choice."

"I told you. I can't be with you like that. Richard is a good man. It wouldn't be fair to cheat on him. Our kiss the other night was bad enough."

"Bad? I thought it was pretty fucking phenomenal."

"That's not what I meant, and you know it."

"Fine. I won't touch you. Sexually, I mean. I won't."

She looked at me like she didn't believe my intentions were genuine.

"Trust me. You have my word. I will not lay a finger on you in a sexual way." It looked like she was considering it. I probably should have just kept my mouth shut. But, I wouldn't be me if I did. "And when you make a move on me, I'll refute it."

Her eyebrows jumped. "When?"

"That's right. When."

"Pretty sure of yourself, aren't you, Cocky?"

She had no idea how much hearing her call me Cocky, did for me. "I am. Sounds like the only one that can't control themselves is you."

"I can absolutely control myself around you."

I leaned in. "Then come with me. Give me a weekend before you decide. Please."

She looked torn. "Let me think about it."

That was better than a no. "Alright."

"I really better go now."

I exited the car and stood next to it as she started the engine. Right before pulling away, she rolled down the window. "Nice name, by the way." Then, she disappeared.

It was the end of the second day since I'd spoken to Aubrey on her front lawn, and I still hadn't heard from her. *Eleven days.* Time was ticking, and there wasn't shit I could do about it.

Except get drunk.

It was a distinct possibility that I might have drank more sitting at that little bar across the street from the motel, than I had in the last five years of my life.

"Carla Babes. Hit me up again."

"Don't you think you've had enough, hot stuff?"

My brain was still working. "Nope. Not even close." I held up the glass and clanked the ice around.

She took it, filled it with what I suspected from the color was pure club soda, and then proceeded to come around the other side of the bar and sit next to me. It was nearly closing time, and I had been sitting on that stool for close to six hours. We were the only two left in the bar.

Carla waited until I looked her straight in the eyes before she spoke. "She's an idiot. You're a great guy. I don't even have to know Dick in order to be certain she's making a big mistake. And it's not just because you're hot as fuck and have a body I'm pretty sure matches that perfect face. It's because you're committed."

I scoffed. "I should be committed, alright."

"I mean it, Chance. If a guy put in half the effort you do, I'd be impressed. You're willing to lay it all out there day after day, even knowing that she could very well stomp on your heart."

"Thanks, Carla Babes."

"No problem. But it's the truth. Plus…I've watched a dozen women try to pick you up in this place, and you never once even gave it any real thought. Considering you haven't been laid in over two years, that's a feat unto itself."

"Eleven days. I suppose I might have to figure out how to get back in the saddle after all if things don't pan out."

"I tell you what. Closing time in eleven days. Things don't work out. You meet me right here. I'd be honored to help you out with that. No talking. No strings. We'll just walk across to your room, and I'll let you ride all your frustrations away, cowboy."

"You'd do that for me, Carla Babes?"

"*For you?* I've thought about doing that *to you*, since the day you walked in the door." She gave me a quick kiss on the lips and sent me packing.

Chapter Twenty-Seven

The next morning, I overslept and had to rush to Starbucks. It was almost nine when I got there, and the line was longer than usual. I hadn't yet checked my phone, so I powered it on as I waited for my turn to order. The damn thing started to buzz in my hand.

I got excited when I saw a new text arrived.

Aubrey: OK. Friday 6pm. I'm yours for the weekend.

I let out a deep breath. It felt like I'd been holding it for days. Melanie called my name as I continued to stare down at my phone.

"Two coffees?"

I couldn't stop smiling. "You bet."

"And what will Aubrey be having for breakfast this morning?"

I leaned back and looked in the case. "I'll take two of those chocolate chip muffins, an iced lemon pound cake, three of those salted caramel pecan squares, an oatmeal cookie and one of those fancy yogurt parfaits you have there."

Melanie looked at me like I was nuts. At that point, I pretty much had lost my mind, so she wasn't too far off. "You want those all in a box? They're all for Aubrey?"

"Yep." I paid and glanced at the time on my phone. She usually didn't come by until half past nine. "Mel, hold my coffee. I'll be right back. Okay?"

I hauled ass to the florist I'd been eyeing a few doors down and came back with a gigantic bouquet; it was bordering on ridiculous. But I didn't care. Aubrey was going to be *mine* for a weekend. This was cause for celebration.

Melanie smiled at me so big, I could see her full mouth of teeth—top and bottom. "Can you give her these with breakfast today?"

"Of course."

I parked my truck around the corner and stood in the doorway a few stores down from Starbucks. If I wasn't on such a high, this new stalking technique might have felt a little creepy. Right at nine-thirty, Aubrey walked out of Starbucks with a box and the giant flowers. She was sporting the hugest smile.

I stood there for another ten minutes. Eventually, another text came.

> **Aubrey: Was I especially hungry this morning?**
>
> **Chance: Sorry. I got carried away. We're celebrating.**
>
> **Aubrey: What are we celebrating?**
>
> **Chance: You. Coming home with me this weekend.**

My phone went quiet. A few minutes later, it buzzed again.

Aubrey: I'm nervous. I'm not sure it's a good idea.

So am I, but I wasn't about to admit that. The consequences of blowing this were too much to even consider.

Chance: Trust me. Please.

A few minutes later, a final text came in.

Aubrey: OK

I arrived at her place Friday at six, ready for our weekend. I knocked, and she came to the door looking almost exactly like a recurring fantasy I'd had of her over the last two years. She was wearing a tight white tank top, tiny white shorts and had on a pair of silver sandals. It was a particularly humid day, and her hair was down and wilder than usual. *Trust me?* That was the promise I'd made to her. *Fuuuck.*

"What's wrong?" She noticed the worry on my face. "Are we taking the motorcycle after all? Do I need to change?"

"No. Yes. No."

Her brows drew down, so I explained. "No. We're not taking the motorcycle. Yes, you need to change."

She looked down at her outfit. "What's wrong with what I'm wearing?"

"Absolutely nothing. It's perfect."

"But—"

I raked my fingers through my hair. "Except that I had this recurring fantasy of you wearing all white."

She smiled. "That's sweet. Like I was an angel?"

My mouth spread into a wicked grin. "Not exactly."

Her cheeks blushed. "Oh."

I chuckled. "You don't have to change. But you should know, if I'm quiet on the ride to my place, it's because I'm replaying that fantasy over and over in my mind." I winked.

There was a red suitcase next to the door, so I grabbed it.

"I just need to get my purse."

Mutton was rubbing at my leg, wanting attention. "And Mutton's leash. I don't have a big yard like you. We'll have to walk him."

Aubrey turned around. "You want to bring Pixy?"

"Of course. We're a family."

It was like the damn goat understood what we were talking about. He nuzzled into my hands and let out a soft "Baaaa."

"That's right, buddy. It's just going to be me and you and Mommy." I scratched the top of his head. "You like that, don't you."

"All set." Aubrey returned with her purse and the leash. "I just need to stop at Philomena's and tell her she doesn't need to take care of Pixy."

"Philomena's?"

"My neighbor. She takes care of Pixy when I work late sometimes. When I went over to ask her to take care of him yesterday, she raved about my gardens. She said she would love to steal you from me. Then she went on a tirade about the mailman delivering her four Magic Bullets that she didn't order and insisted I take one home with me." Aubrey pointed to an unopened box on the counter. "She's a bit on the odd side but very nice."

"Magic Bullet? Is that like your magic wand? You still playing with that?"

"No! It's a blender…for smoothies."

It was normally a two-hour drive from Temecula to Hermosa Beach, but the rush hour traffic made it almost double that. I didn't give a shit, though. The sun was shining, I was free, and my girl was coming to my place for the weekend. Since I couldn't do what I really wanted to do with her, I decided to show Aubrey what a normal weekend with us together would be like. We both knew we had chemistry, but something told me one of the things holding her back, aside from trust, was she wasn't convinced we had *more* than chemistry.

Adele was still at my place when we arrived. She pretended to have been running late, but I knew she really wanted to meet Aubrey.

"Sorry. I was hoping to be at Harry's by the time you got home. I was just cleaning up a bit."

Aubrey looked at me in disbelief. "Harry?"

"I shit you not. First day out, I come home and find some bloke in his boxers ironing at my kitchen counter. He tells me his name is Harry."

Aubrey and I both laughed. Adele didn't get the joke, but was smiling from ear to ear anyway. My sister extended her hand. "I'm so glad to meet you, Aubrey. I've heard so much about you."

Aubrey and Adele stared at each other for a long moment. I had no idea what was going on, but something strange seemed to be taking place. Then the two practically collided, wrapping each other in their arms for a hug. It was like they were long lost best friends. They didn't let go for the longest time.

Watching it, I became a bit choked up. Both women had tears in their eyes when they separated. I heard my sister whisper, "We both lost a lot. I'm finding my way back. I hope you do, too."

I cleared my throat and hugged my sister goodbye a few minutes later. She was carrying an overnight bag to spend the weekend at Harry's. "I stocked the cabinets with your essentials."

"Snags, Tim Tams and Pixy sticks?"

"Of course. And I got this guy here some treats, too." She gave Pixy a good rub before leaving.

When it was just the two of us, I gave Aubrey a tour. My place was an old converted warehouse. It had high ceilings and a wide open floor plan. There were three bedrooms, but I'd converted one into an art studio. My sister was using the other one since she came to stay with me. When I told her Aubrey would be staying in the guest room, she sounded like she didn't believe me but prepped it for a guest nonetheless.

I stopped at my bedroom first. "This is our bedroom."

"Chance—"

"I know. Not tonight. But if we decide to live down here near the beach, this will be our room." The fucked up thing was, I already thought of it as *our* bedroom.

"It's very nice. Is that a Klimt painting?"

I smiled. *Love my dirty girl.* "It is. It's the Three Ages of Women. See, we have a lot in common. We both like women's breasts in paintings. Although when we're in here, I won't notice anything but those babies." My eyes pointed to her great rack.

"You're a perv."

"And you love it."

I gave her the rest of the tour, regretfully dropping her bag in the guest room. The last room on the tour was my art studio. I hadn't made anything in a long, long time. There were canvas drop cloths covering most projects I was working on before my life became a clusterfuck. I flicked on the light and meant to pass the room right by, but Aubrey wandered inside.

"Did you make that?" She pointed to a large motorcycle made of recycled parts. It had been in a few art shows, but now there was an inch of dust covering it.

"I did."

"Wow. It's…incredible." She walked around, inspecting it carefully. "Everything on here is junk?"

"I don't use any purchased materials. Only recycled objects that I find."

"You're really good. I'm not sure what I expected. But this seems to tell a story." I smiled. Of course, she totally got it. I always felt every individual piece that I collected could tell a different tale. The way they all blended together was sort of like reading a book to me. I walked around to the other side of the bike and pointed to a few different things, telling her where each piece had come from.

If it were possible, I fell just a little more for her right then.

That night, we ordered in Chinese food and ate straight from the cartons. Aubrey fell asleep with her head on my lap as we watched a movie. Keeping to my word, I covered her with a blanket and went to my own bed to sleep.

The next morning, she was still sleeping when I slipped out to take Pixy for a walk. But she was awake when I walked in carrying two coffees and an assortment of overpriced crap from Starbucks.

"Morning."

She sat up on the couch and stretched her arms over her head. Her shirt pulled up, exposing her beautiful soft skin. I wanted to fucking bite it. I had to turn the other way.

"You get some strange ass looks when you walk a goat."

Aubrey chuckled. "Yeah. I know." She came into the kitchen and sat on a stool on the other side of the island.

"Let me ask you something. This promise I stupidly made. It only includes touching. I can say whatever I want, right?"

She sipped her coffee. "I'm afraid to say yes. But…yes. I suppose words aren't off limits."

"Good. Because I gotta tell you. Your tits saluting me are better than seeing the sunrise in the morning."

She shook her head. "You have a wicked tongue, Mr. Bateman."

"Oh, if only I could show you, Mrs. Bloom Bateman."

"Mrs. Bloom Bateman, huh?"

"Well, you are my wife. I figured you'd want to keep your name, too. Seeing as how you're a working woman and all."

"You make me sound like a hooker."

"Prostitute…lawyer." I grinned. "Same thing."

"Very nice. And to think…I was going to give up the Bloom name and take my husband's. Now I'm not so sure."

"Oh yeah? I would have taken you for a hyphenator."

She slid the bag on the counter over to her and dug inside. "Nah. Not me. I'm old school. I plan to give everything to my husband."

"I'm glad to hear that Mrs. Bateman. Because I plan to take everything. On a daily basis."

I wanted to show her the area. Now that her firm was closing up, maybe we would live in Hermosa Beach. Being near the water was important to me. Although, I'd live in the desert if it meant getting to be with Aubrey. After lunch, we walked down to the boardwalk. It was a gorgeous day, and she didn't pull away when I took her hand in mine.

"How about a swim?" I was glad I told her to put on a suit when we left this morning. It was hot as hell.

"Okay."

We walked down to the water's edge, and I pulled my shirt off. Following my lead, she slipped out of hers, and my eyes almost bulged from my head. *Fuck. Maybe this wasn't such a good idea after all.* She had on a little red string bikini top, and her fantastic tits looked like they longed to spill out. When she shimmied out of her shorts, I was blatantly leering at her and didn't give a damn. If I couldn't touch, I most certainly was going to get my visual fill. "I almost feel bad for you."

"Me? Why?"

"Because when you finally let me have you." I raked my eyes up and down her luscious body. "I'm going to be like a savage making up for lost time."

I needed to cool off, and Aubrey was coming with me. Surprising her, I bent and lifted, tossing her over my shoulder fireman style before running for the water. She screamed and kicked the entire time, but I could tell from her tone that she was smiling. I smacked her ass hard before launching us both into the water.

Together we swam and walked along the beach until the sun set. I never wanted the day to end.

"We should get back," she said. "Pixy probably needs to go out."

"Kids. They're always ruining a good time," I joked.

On the walk back, our conversation took a serious turn. "Do you want kids?"

I answered honestly, "I never really thought about it. Until I met you. But now. I want nothing more than for you to bear my spawn."

She laughed. "How many do you want?"

"Six," I answered quickly.

"Six?" She stopped in her tracks.

"I have no idea why. But the thought of you pregnant does something to me. I'm getting turned on now just thinking about it."

"You really need help. I think you might be a sex addict."

"I'd be the first sex addict that hasn't gotten laid in a few years."

She looked at me with sincerity. "Sorry. That must be hard."

"When I look at you in that bathing suit. It sure is."

"Do you...you know."

"What?"

"You know."

"I don't." I certainly did.

"You know. Take care of yourself."

"You mean like shower and get haircuts. Yes. I take care of myself. I even exercise."

She laughed. "You want me to say it, don't you?"

"You'd totally make my day, Princess."

We arrived on my block. I was holding her left hand, but she turned and walked backwards, taking both of mine into hers. She cocked her head to the side when she spoke. "Do you masturbate, Chance?"

Fuck yeah. I loved hearing her even say the word. "I do. Frequently, in fact, lately. All I have to do is smell you, and my cock strains. I'd be walking around with a nasty case of blue balls if I didn't."

"I'm sorry."

I pulled her closer to me. "You wanna know something else?"

She bit her lip, but nodded.

"It will all be worth it when I'm back inside of you, Princess."

We went into the house, and I offered Aubrey the shower first. After our day on the beach, I had sand in places there shouldn't be. While she was in the shower, I cranked up the music, put two Coronas in the freezer to chill, and might have danced with a goat.

I heard the faint sound of Aubrey's voice in between verses. "Chance?"

The full bath was in the master bedroom. I answered through the cracked door, "Everything okay?"

"I forgot to grab a towel. Are there any in here?"

The shower water was still running. "No. They're in the closet out here. I'll grab you one."

I picked the fluffiest, girliest looking towel I could find. Without thinking, I opened the door. The shower had glass sliders. They were foggy with steam, but I could still see her sexy silhouette. Her back was facing me, giving me a fan-fucking-tastic view of her succulent ass. I couldn't move. My restraint was rapidly slipping through my fingers.

When she turned around and caught me staring, she didn't make an effort to cover up. Instead, she reached up and began to wash her breasts.

273

Fucking incredible.

I took a step toward the shower but stopped myself from going further. With the door behind me open and the cool air blowing in, the fog was getting heavier on the shower doors.

"Princess—" The word came out a cross between a groan and a plea. "I vowed not to touch you."

I could barely hear her whispered words over the rain of the shower. "I know. I thought maybe…you'd like it if…I…" She paused. My girl's walls were crumbling. *She* was pushing the boundaries. And it was the sexiest thing I'd ever seen in my life. She said the last sentence louder and with more conviction. "I thought maybe you'd like to watch me touch myself."

There she is. My beautiful, sweet dirty girl.

"Oh baby. I could go blind after watching you and never feel like I'd missed seeing anything. Will you let me help? I'll tell you what I want you to do to yourself, and you can do it for me. That way we'll be doing it together. Is that okay?"

She nodded.

"That's good, baby. So fucking good. Would you like it if I stroked myself while I watched you?"

"Yes."

I dropped my shorts and stood before her. Even if I wasn't already fully erect, I would have been after seeing the way she was looking at me. Her eyes were glued to my cock. I watched them follow my hand as I leisurely stroked up and down.

"This is what you do to me. Every day. I dream about being deep inside of you. In your heart and in your body. I want to suck on those beautiful nipples you're touching. Tug them between my teeth until sweet pain shoots through every nerve in your gorgeous body." Aubrey's head lulled back a bit as she started to relax into my voice and her own touch. Her hands that were gently swirling around her nipples slowed, and I watched her pinch. "Harder. Pinch harder." She did, and her lips parted as she felt it travel south.

"Spread your legs a bit." Without hesitation, she did as I asked. "I want to spread you out on my bed and lick every inch of you until you can barely breathe. Then I want to hear you beg for my cock. Will you do that, Aubrey. Will you beg for me?"

"I will. I'll beg for it."

"Do it. Do it now. Tell me that you want my cock, and I'll let you put your fingers inside yourself."

Her hand started to travel painstakingly slowly down her body. I had to strain to hear her voice. "I dream about you being inside of me again. The way you bury yourself like you can't get deep enough. Please. I miss you being inside of me." Her voice was uneven, and her hand trembled as it hovered over her sweet pussy.

"Rub your fingers along your clit. But don't put them inside yet. I'll tell you when."

Her body was sun kissed from the beach today, and her cheeks were pink from arousal. The image before me was better than anything I could possibly have imagined. I fisted my cock harder and faster. It was getting difficult to speak.

I took two steps closer to the shower door. It took every ounce of willpower not to open it. But I needed to at least be closer to hear the jagged edge to her breath. "Please, Chance."

It made me wild to know she was willing to beg for me. That she wanted me inside of her as much as I longed to sink into her. "Slip two fingers inside. Keep your eyes closed and pretend it's me. Feel my cock inside of you."

When her fingers disappeared, I couldn't hold back any longer. It took less than two minutes—she was pumping in and out as fast as I was tugging at my cock. Her mouth parted, and I knew she was beginning. "Chance…"

"Come baby. Together." It was the most spectacular sight in the world as she became undone right before my eyes. The sound of her moaning my name as she brought herself to her own climax was purely erotic.

It took a while after we both finished to regain control of our panting breaths. Eventually, Aubrey's body went slack, and she leaned against the tiled wall of the shower. She didn't open her eyes as I reached in and turned off the water. I scooped her into my arms and carried her to my bed. Climbing in behind her, I slipped under the sheet, careful not to press myself against her. That would be breaking the rules. And oddly, I was sated for now.

Not fifteen minutes later, she mumbled the words 'I'm sorry' right before I heard the light sound of her sleep.

I fell asleep not long after that, feeling relief and content with the woman I loved sleeping next to me in our bed.

Unfortunately, the feeling was gone the next morning when I woke up, and it wouldn't take me long to figure out why.

Chapter Twenty-Eight

Talk about going from your highest high to your lowest low. For the first time, I realized exactly how Aubrey might have felt the moment she woke up and found that I'd abandoned her at the hotel in Vegas.

She was gone.

So was Pixy.

The morning sun streamed into the loft. My heart raced as a piece of white paper on the kitchen counter caught my eye. Unfolding it, I rubbed my groggy eyes in order to read each and every word clearly.

> *Chance,*
>
> *Yesterday was beyond amazing. But I got carried away last night. It proved once again that I don't have any willpower against my attraction to you. As long as I'm with Richard, my giving in like that is not fair to him. I didn't want to risk things going any further if I stayed another day. I'm pretty sure I can't resist you physically anymore. I'm sorry. I know I promised you the whole weekend. I'm just trying to do the right thing.*

Crumbling the letter and throwing it across the room, I yelled, "Fuck." My voice echoed into the empty kitchen. So, that was it? Yesterday was my final chance to make any kind of a lasting impression on her before she made a decision, and the last thing I did was jerk myself off before we passed out. After everything, that was how it was going to end? *Well played, Bateman.* How the hell did she even get transportation that fast back to Temecula with a goat? She must have researched an exit plan prior to agreeing to the trip. Aubrey probably had a car company on standby. *"Chance took out his dick, so you can come pick me up now!"*

Feeling hopeless, I leaned my elbows against the counter and rubbed my temples. I debated whether to call her and decided against it for the time being. It was the first time since reentering her life that I had no strategy. I honestly didn't know what to do from here.

A couple of hours later, Adele came by after I'd called to let her know that Aubrey left.

Pacing across the loft, I ran my hands through my hair. "I'm thinking of going back to Temecula tonight."

"Don't."

"Don't?"

"Don't." She put her hands on my arms to stop me from pacing. "Look, I really like her. I hope that it works out, but you've done everything you possibly can to show her how you feel. It's time to step back and give her the space she needs to hopefully come to the right conclusion— that you're the one. I could see in her eyes how much she still cares about you. She was crying, for Christ's sake. The only thing holding her back is fear of getting hurt."

"What if she lets fear win and ends up with dickwad?"

"Then, you have to move on."

Could I move on? I couldn't fathom wanting anyone in the same way or as badly ever again in my lifetime. But if she chose him, I knew I would have to get on with my life eventually, date other women and finally end my two year celibacy.

She opened a package of Tim Tams and poured two tall servings of milk. Since you can't get that brand of cookies in America, Adele had a friend from Melbourne who shipped them to her in bulk.

I dunked one of the chocolate-covered wafers into my glass and took a bite as I spoke with my mouth full. "How the fuck am I gonna stay here wasting away in Hermosa Beach, knowing that I may never see her again if she decides to move away with him? He's leaving in just a matter of days."

Adele looked confused. "How fast could she possibly move to Boston? Wouldn't she have to sell her house, get rid of all her shit?"

"She rents the house and mentioned that most of the furniture was there when she moved in. The biggest problem is going to be transporting our goat."

"You realize you said *our* goat, right? As in your goat, too?"

"Fuck. I meant her goat."

Adele smiled sympathetically. "No, you didn't."

"You're right. I didn't."

Later that evening after Adele returned to Harry's, anger started to override all other emotions. I sent a text to Aubrey.

Chance: The chase is over. I'm giving you the space you want. If you need me, you know where to find me.

She sent a simple response.

Aubrey: Thank you.

I was pretty damn proud of myself the first few days of that following week. I didn't call or text Aubrey and kept occupied at home in Hermosa Beach, working on a new junk art project and taking care of some long neglected repairs around the house. Even though I was keeping busy, deep down, I was miserable.

It was hard not to contact her, but I'd been taking my sister's advice, keeping my distance in the hopes that Aubrey would make the right decision on her own.

As the end of the week neared, I was starting to grow impatient. One night, while trying unsuccessfully to distract myself with an episode of Top Gear, I impulsively broke my vow and texted her.

Chance: You there?

Aubrey: I'm here.

Chance: Hi

Aubrey: Sorry I haven't been in touch.

Chance: It's fine. I've been intentionally staying away so you can sort your head out.

Aubrey: Are you back in Temecula?

Chance: No. There's nothing for me there besides you, and I'm giving you space. My home is here. Although, now that you've been here, it doesn't seem whole anymore without you.

Aubrey: I'm sorry that you regret taking me home.

Chance: The only thing I regret is not bursting through that shower door, Princess.

She didn't immediately respond. A few minutes later, my phone vibrated.

Aubrey: Thank you for not doing that.

Chance: You would still be here if I had.

Aubrey: Is that right?

Chance: You might have trouble walking, but you'd still be here.

Aubrey: I see.

She never texted back, so I typed again.

Chance: Are you okay?

Aubrey: Yes. I can't text much more. I promise to call you this weekend.

Chance: Is he there with you?

Aubrey: Yes

Jealousy hit me like a ton of bricks. There was that voice again that sounded awfully like Mum. *"Get off your hiney and get your woman!"* Suddenly, it just clicked. What was keeping me here? Pride? Fuck pride. She was all that mattered. Getting her back was more important.

I was not okay. *This* was not okay. I knew in my heart that she loved me. I could see it in her eyes. She was just scared of getting hurt again. Sitting back like this was only giving him the upper hand. If I was going to let her go, it sure as hell wasn't going to be without a fight. I needed to be near her.

Change of plans.

Grabbing my keys, I got into my truck and hit the highway toward Temecula. The road was barren, so I was going about eighty-five miles per hour.

The plan was to spend the night at the motel and be ready bright and early for whatever the day held. I wasn't sure what tomorrow would bring. I just knew that I was going to be there with her till the end, regardless of how it turned out.

I'm in for the fucking long haul, Princess.

I turned the radio onto an instrumental channel for the entire ride. My nerves couldn't seem to handle anything else.

It was late by the time I finally got to the motel. By some miracle, I fell asleep. I wanted to be parked at Jefferson bright and early in the morning to get her breakfast. Tomorrow couldn't come fast enough.

The next day started out normally. The hustle and bustle outside of Aubrey's office building was just like usual. When I walked into Starbucks to place her breakfast order, it became abundantly clear that this was no ordinary morning.

"G'day, Melanie."

"Chance. I thought you left town."

"I'm back."

"I'm surprised."

"Why do you say that?"

"You don't know?"

"Know what?"

"Aubrey's last day was yesterday. She came in to say goodbye to us."

What?

"She's not here anymore?"

"No. I'm sorry. I thought you guys were friends now. So, I figured you knew she quit her job."

"Friends. Yeah. We are. She must have neglected to mention that little piece of information, though. Did she say where she was going?"

"She just said she quit and wouldn't be seeing us every morning anymore."

Scratching my chin, I stared into space trying to absorb that news.

Melanie interrupted my thought process. "Can I get you anything?"

Without even paying attention, I said, "Sure. A nonfat three-pump vanilla latte, low foam and extra hot."

"You're getting Aubrey's drink?"

"Uh…yeah." I hadn't even realized that I'd ordered it. "Why not?" I shrugged. "For old time's sake."

As I sat at the corner table, swirling the foamy milk around in my cup, I tried to convince myself that her leaving the job and not telling me didn't necessarily mean that she'd chosen to move to Boston with Dick. I could have texted her, but a part of me wasn't ready for the answer. Maybe she only decided to quit, seeing as though the firm was shutting down anyway. Either way, this would likely be my last hurrah at the Starbucks that served as the backdrop for my time here with Aubrey. I wouldn't be spending any more mornings stalking her on Jefferson if she didn't work here anymore. I emptied my wallet of the cash inside and stuffed over a hundred dollars in the tip jar.

"Thank you, Mates. Appreciate your help all these weeks."

Melanie's eyes widened. "Wow, thank you. You won't be back?"

"Afraid not."

When I pulled up to Aubrey's house, a white and blue sign on the front lawn was the first thing that caught my eye. My heart started to pound furiously.

What in the hell?

As I got out close enough to read it, I saw that it said, *For Rent.* My heart seemed to fall to my stomach. Taking my key out, I rushed to the front door and opened it. Mutton's water bowl was still in the kitchen, but it was empty. No sign of the goat anywhere. All of the furniture was still in place, but it seemed all of Aubrey's personal belongings were gone.

I was practically flying through the house. A sweep of her bedroom also confirmed the worst. Every last item of clothing in her closet was also gone. Sitting on her bed and looking around the room, reality was starting to sink in. Adrenaline pumped through me.

Calm down, Chance.

In a daze, I returned outside into the blinding sun. I opened the shed and started packing my lawn equipment into the back of the truck. That was when I heard a whistle.

Turning around, I realized it was Aubrey's nutty neighbor, Philomena. She'd run outside to meet the UPS guy and was carrying a brown box.

She sauntered over to me, dragging her slippers on the pavement. She had rollers in her hair, and her lips were sloppily outlined with bright pink pencil but no lipstick. "Hey, hot stuff."

Trying to act friendly despite my rotten mood, I said, "Nice to see you again, Philomena. What do you have there in the box?"

"Who knows? I order stuff in my sleep and don't even remember." She snorted.

"Ah, that's right. The four Magic Bullets. You gave Aubrey one."

"You want one? I'll trade you for a ride on your mower."

"That's alright. I'm retired from the lawn care business as of today."

"You mean now that she's gone?"

My eyes darted toward hers. "You know where she went?"

"I didn't have a chance to talk to her, saw her leaving with the boyfriend yesterday. She was inside packing. I asked him what was going on, and he said she was moving to Boston with him. Next thing I knew, there was a sign up out front this morning."

My ears felt like they were burning. "Really..."

"Yeah."

I couldn't remember what I said to Philomena after that. I didn't even have a recollection of the ride back to the motel. I would have expected to feel angry or confused, but everything was just numb.

Holding my phone in my hands as I sat on the bed, I wanted to text her, but the more I thought about it, the less it seemed like a good idea. If she really were moving to Boston, she didn't even bother to tell me that she'd made her decision. Was she there already? Was she even going to call me this weekend like she'd promised? Suddenly, the numbness was wearing off, replaced by pure rage.

Grabbing my wallet, I walked across the way to the bar. I didn't want to feel the emotions of losing her. I didn't want to feel anything tonight.

The words rolled off my tongue bitterly. "Hit me up, Carla Babes."

Carla looked absolutely shocked to see me sitting in my usual spot. "I didn't think I'd ever see you again, Aussie."

"Well, I came to say goodbye. I'm leaving to head home tomorrow, and I'm not coming back."

She poured my drink faster than ever, sensing I needed it badly. "What happened?"

I took a swig and slammed the glass down on the bar. "It's over."

"That's it? Over? Aubrey stayed with Dick?"

It pleased me that she'd also adopted my nickname for him.

"Yes. I went to her house today, and everything was cleaned out. There was a sign out front advertising the place for rent. The dickhead told the neighbor Aubrey was going to Boston with him."

"Are you fucking kidding me?"

"End of story."

"So, she didn't even have the decency to tell you herself?"

"The decency or the guts, not sure which."

"How did you leave things with her?"

"I'd gone back to Hermosa Beach for a while. She thinks I'm still there. She was supposed to call me this weekend. I decided to come back anyway and check on things. Now, I know what she was planning to tell me when she called."

"I'm so sorry."

"Not your fault."

"I was really hoping things would work out for you. You deserved to have a happy ending."

"Can we not talk about this anymore? About her?" I swallowed as if it were painful.

"Okay. Whatever you want."

Carla quietly placed drink after drink in front of me. She knew that I was in no mood to talk, so she let me be. At one point, she cut me off, refusing to serve me anymore. I lay my head on the counter as she wiped down the tables. The bar was getting ready to close. I had no concept of what time it even was. The sound of the television and a few patrons talking was muffled.

She tapped me on the shoulder. "Come on, big guy. I'll drive you across the street."

I got into Carla's red Prius and rested my head back on the seat with my eyes closed. I was still a little drunk but starting to sober up. I would have probably had to drink myself to death to get to the level of inebriation necessary to forget this day. So, in a sense, I was pissed at Carla for refusing to serve me more alcohol but grateful to her for looking out for me.

She walked me to my room and quietly followed me inside. Lying back on my bed, I crossed my arms and closed my eyes. When I opened them, Carla had disappeared. The water was running, and I realized she was in the bathroom.

I closed my eyes again. This time, when I opened them, Carla was standing by my bed. She'd taken down her hair, which was usually up in a retro style. She'd washed off the heavy red lipstick she wore. Most notable was the fact that she'd taken off all of her clothes except for her red lace bra and matching underwear. Her breasts were spilling out of the material, and the panties barely covered her curvy bottom.

My voice sounded sleepy. "What are you doing?"

"Remember what we talked about? The offer still stands. Let me make you forget everything. No strings, Chance. Just you and me and a really good fuck."

My dick twitched, my body unable to control the natural reaction to that proposition.

"Carla Babes, you don't have to."

"I want to. God, Chance, I want to so badly. You have no idea what you do to me."

Shit.

Before I could form words, she began to straddle me over my jeans, grinding against my half-stiff cock. "I think you're ready for me," she muttered over my lips.

She kissed me, and I reluctantly returned it, unsure of whether to accept her offer or push her off of me.

"Do you have a condom?" she whispered.

"No."

"It's okay. You don't have to worry. I'm on the pill, and I'm clean."

Carla lifted my shirt over my head as I closed my eyes again. She was kissing down my chest as my intoxicated mind imagined it was Aubrey.

Aubrey.

Aubrey.

Aubrey.

Carla gently pushed me back further onto the bed. She started to open my belt buckle as I continued to lay down. When my cock sprung free into the cold air and she started to stroke me, I knew she was about to take me into her mouth. Something deep within me screamed, *"Don't do it."*

I slid my body back suddenly before pulling up my underwear. Standing up, I zipped my pants.

Moving my fingers through my hair, I looked down at the ground and shook my head. "I can't do this." Grabbing my shirt and slipping it back over my head, I said, "I'm so sorry."

With her hands on her hips, Carla bit her lower lip and nodded in understanding. "It's okay, Aussie."

"It's not you…it's just—"

"Her. I know. It's her."

"I'm just not ready to—"

She spoke louder. "You don't have to explain, Chance."

Carla looked sad. I hated hurting her feelings, but being with her like that didn't feel right at all.

"I'll get dressed and go, okay?"

"You don't have to leave."

"I really should."

After she put her clothes on, Carla came over to where I was standing and kissed me gently on the cheek. "One day she's going to wake up and regret it. I hope by that time, you've found the one you're really meant to be with. Because it's not her."

"Thank you, Carla Babes. Thank you for everything."

"Please come back someday when your head's on straight again, will you, Aussie? I want to know that you're happy."

"I will. I promise."

Just like that, Carla drove away into the night.

Left with a minor case of blue balls, I retreated to the shower. Letting the warm water run down on me, I squirted some shampoo into my palm and fisted my cock into my hands, jerking it roughly. Despite best efforts to block her from my mind, all I could think about was Aubrey as I stroked myself. Visions of her rubbing her clit while we masturbated together in my bathroom infiltrated my brain. I jerked myself harder and imagined coming inside of her instead of my hand. As I finished, my thoughts were spiraling out of control. I leaned against the tile wall, overcome with emotion as the orgasm shook me.

Fuck you, Aubrey.

Fuck you.

I hate you.,

I love you.

I hate you.

I love you.

Shit.

I still love you so much.

Chapter
Twenty-Nine

EXIT

ack in Hermosa Beach the following Sunday, I still hadn't heard from her. I refused to reach out first, especially knowing what I knew. If she didn't care enough to at least call me to let me know what was going on, then I wasn't going to give her the satisfaction of contacting her.

A flock of seagulls followed me as I walked along the beach near my loft. Kicking the sand, I wondered where my life would go from here, how I would spend my days without the focus on getting Aubrey back. More than anything, I wondered how I could possibly make myself forget her long enough to move on.

Picking a spot, I sat down and gazed out into the ocean. The water was rough. A brisk wind blew some sand into my eyes. A few surfers rode the choppy waves in the distance. A group of people were playing volleyball a few feet away. One of the girls ran over to me.

"Hey, we need another player. Want to join?"

Why the hell not? A distraction certainly couldn't hurt. "Yeah. Alright." Lifting my sluggish body off the ground, I joined a guy and a girl on one side of the net. Repeatedly serving the ball under arm, I kept my team in the lead for several games.

At one point, we took a break, and the only other guy player went to fetch some waters for us from the beach concession stand. When he returned, he was cracking up.

"Dude, you're never gonna believe what I just saw."

"What's that, Mate?"

"There was a chick in line with a goat on a leash."

I dropped the ball. "Say what?"

"A goddamn goat on a leash! This smoking hot chick, too. She wa—"

"Where?"

He pointed in the direction from which he came.

When I immediately took off, one of the girls yelled from behind me. "Hey, don't leave! We're starting another game."

"Play without me," I shouted without looking back.

My heart felt like it was beating unnaturally fast.

When I got to the concession stand, no one was in line. Looking around frantically, I wondered if it were possible that this were just a coincidence. A goat on a leash? No way. She was here.

Then, I saw her.

Aubrey.

My God.

She and Mutton were sitting alone on the sand. She was feeding him an ice cream cone as she looked out towards the water. The wind was blowing her hair around. She looked heart-stoppingly beautiful. Staring at her in disbelief, I stood there for the longest time without saying anything.

Somehow, he noticed me first. The "blind" goat suddenly bolted toward me, nearly knocking me down in the process.

Not knowing why the animal took off, Aubrey jumped up in a panic before she realized he was in my arms.

She stood up and brushed sand off of her pale yellow sundress. "Chance."

"Princess. What are you doing here?"

"I'm parked at your house. You didn't get my text?"

I took my phone out of my pocket and realized I had missed a text from her. It must have come in during the volleyball game. "No, but I see it now."

Trying not to get overly excited, I reminded myself that she could very well have come here just to deliver the bad news in person. Despite my wanting to reach out and touch her, my body stiffened instead as a self-protective mechanism.

"Can we walk to your house? I don't want to have this talk here." She wasn't smiling. Her expression was only confirming my worst fears.

A feeling of dread developed at the pit of my stomach. "Sure."

The short walk to my place was quiet. When we arrived, Aubrey's car was parked out front. We sat outside on the front steps to the loft. Mutton chewed on the grass next to us. She rubbed her palms together nervously.

"Go on, Aubrey. Just get it over with."

She looked like she was about to cry, and her question caught me off guard. "Are you seeing someone?"

My tone was abrupt. "Am *I* seeing someone?"

"Just answer me."

"No, Aubrey. I've done nothing but eat, sleep and breathe you for weeks." My tone bordered on angry. "Why would you ask me that?"

"The other night, I returned to my house to get some things I forgot during the move. Philomena saw my car and came out to tell me that you had been there earlier in the day. So, I went to your motel that night. There was a car parked outside. When I peeked in the window, a girl was with you, and she was putting a shirt over her head. I think it was that bartender."

Fuck.

Fuck.

Fuck.

Are you kidding me?

Fuck.

"Princess, listen to me." I placed my hand under her chin, directing her to look at me. "I promise you, I will never lie to you. Do you believe me?"

"Just tell me the truth."

"That was Carla. She's a friend. You're right. She's the bartender at the bar I frequented. She followed me back to my room because I drank too much that night. She took off her clothes and came on to me, but I stopped it. Nothing happened."

"Really?"

"I swear on my Mum's grave. Carla kissed me and started to undress me, but I told her I couldn't do anything, nor did I want to."

She let out a huge breath. "Oh my God. I've been losing sleep. I know I don't even have a right to be upset after the way I've treated you."

"My judgment was off that night. I was devastated after I found out you decided to go to Boston. It felt like my life was over."

"Boston? I never decided to go to Boston."

"What? But all of your stuff was gone."

"Yes. I moved out…but not to go to Boston."

"Philomena talked to Dick while you were packing. He told her you'd made up your mind to go with him."

"No. That's not true."

"Fuck, Princess. That's why I got so sloshed that night. I thought I'd lost you."

"Richard was hopeful. Maybe that's why he told Philomena I was moving with him. He kept thinking he could convince me, dangling the promise of a job and all. I hadn't told him about you until the next day. I wanted to pack my stuff before things got ugly."

"Wait. Are you telling me…"

"I never intended to go to Boston, Chance. My mind was basically made up a long time before that, but I was still scared to give in to you completely. The fear is always going to be there. I will always be afraid to lose you because of how much I love you. Spending that one day with you here, though, it felt so right. I'd never been more certain of anything in my life. I knew I had to go back and tie up my loose ends. I knew I had to end it with him."

"You broke up with Dick?"

"Yes. It was a mess. I told him everything. He accused me of fucking you and your twin brother, Harry the landscaper."

We both burst out into laughter, startling the goat who miraculously stayed conscious for once.

"If *only* I were two people and could double team you. Did you tell him I don't really have a twin?"

"No. Once he accused me of being a slut, I didn't care to clarify."

"Dumbass."

"He really was a good guy, but from the moment you came back, Chance, you need to know there was never really any contest."

I let out a huge sigh of relief as my mind started to piece together what was happening. "You quit your job...not to go to Boston but to..."

"I wasn't happy there anyway. Plus, if I were going to move to Hermosa Beach, I—"

"Move here?" A huge smile spread across my face. At that moment, I squinted my eyes to take a closer look at Aubrey's Audi and noticed for the first time that it was packed to the rim with all of her crap just like the first week we met. Holy shit. We'd come full circle.

"All of your shit is in there?"

"Yes." She placed her hand on my heart. "But I don't need anything but this."

Leaning in, I kissed her with everything in me and lifted her up into the air. People were driving by and honking.

When I put her down, she had tears in her eyes as she wrapped her arms around my neck. "I hope this complex allows goats."

"If anyone gives us shit, we'll just move. I'm thinking we need a house anyway where I can grow you another garden."

My breathing quickened as the magnitude of everything started to hit me. I became overwhelmed with an animalistic urge to claim what I finally knew with absolute certainty was mine. I couldn't wait a second longer to be inside of her. "Princess, hope you don't have any plans for a while."

She lifted her brow. "Why is that?"

"Because we have two years' worth of fucking to do."

I took Aubrey by the hand, and she followed me into the apartment as we practically stumbled through the door. Anticipating what was about to happen, my dick was excruciatingly hard.

I grabbed the biggest bowl I could find and filled it with water so that Pixy wouldn't dehydrate in case we didn't come out of our room for hours.

"Go to town, Bugger," I said, placing the bowl in front of him. "That's exactly what I intend to do on your mother."

As she stood in front of me, it felt like a huge weight had lifted. It was the first time that I could truly be with Aubrey without apprehension and uncertainty.

I pulled at my hair as I stared down at her and shook my head. "I don't even know where to start. There's so much I want to do to you."

"I'm ready for anything."

"You sure?"

"Yes."

"I think I need to fuck you hard then. Are you okay with that?"

She answered by pulling her sundress over her head. As she kicked her panties to the ground, I stripped out of my own clothes. The way she was staring at my body excited me even more. All of the restraint I exhibited over the past several weeks was completely non-existent now.

"Good God," I breathed out as I got a look at her stark naked body in pure daylight. She'd shaved a thin line of hair down the middle of her beautiful mound. I so wanted to savor her, but not this time. That would be later. Right now, I needed her desperately.

I gripped the side of her waist and pulled her toward me. Within seconds, her legs were wrapped around me as I lifted her onto my starving cock.

"Aaagh," I yelled out at how incredible it felt as I sunk deep inside of her. It felt better than anything I could remember before it.

We hadn't even bothered to move from the same spot. Her back was against my bedroom door as I pounded into her relentlessly, breaking her in while she begged for it harder. I wasn't sure if it was because I was with the woman I loved or because it had been so long, but never had a pussy wrapped around my cock ever felt tighter, hotter, wetter…more perfect or made for me in my entire life.

Gripping her ass tightly, within minutes, I felt her muscles spasm around me.

"Come, Aubrey. Come all over my dick, Princess. Let go."

"Say my name when you come. I love when you say my name," she whispered over my mouth.

As I came inside of her, I muttered her name repeatedly with each thrust of my hips. "Aubrey…Fuck…Aubrey…God…Aubrey…Aubrey…Aubrey."

We stayed connected, leaning our foreheads together.

"I love you, Aubrey."

"It was a long road to get here, but it was worth it," she said.

"Worth every second."

We stayed holding each other for a long time before I finally put her down. "You hungry?"

"A little."

"Let's get something in you…besides me. You're gonna need the energy for round two."

I threw my underwear on and placed my t-shirt over her head. I loved looking at her nipples peeking through my clothing. As she followed me into the kitchen, she placed her hand over her mouth in disbelief as reality set in. "Holy shit. I don't have a job. I've never been unemployed before."

"You're in luck, Mrs. Bateman. I have an opening for a sex slave."

"After what you just did to me in there, I would gladly volunteer for that position, Mr. Bateman."

"We'll find you a job here doing something you're passionate about," I said seriously.

"I'm passionate about you, and I'd like to do *you* over and over again."

"Then, it's settled. Sex slave it is."

"But seriously, though, I don't want to be dependent. I would literally be mooching off of your ass money."

"Seeing as though I'll be claiming your ass later, sounds like that's only fair. An ass for an ass."

AUBREY
VEGAS – ONE YEAR
LATER

Chance and I stood at the door of the little white chapel, home to our fake wedding over three years ago. Goosebumps peppered my skin because it all seemed just like yesterday. Being here was nostalgic and at the same time, made me a little sad for the years that we lost in between.

With her red frizzy hair and over the top multi-colored smock, Zelda looked almost exactly the same as I remembered her.

She squinted her eyes and looked right at Chance. "Haven't you been in here before?"

He beamed. Returning here had been his idea. "Very perceptive. This time we have an appointment. It's under Bateman. Six o'clock," Chance said, lifting up the piece of paper. "And an actual marriage license. We're doing the real deal this time."

She snapped her finger. "That's right. You're the Aussie guy...those vows...how could I forget? I should have known that you two were for real. One of the few couples I actually wondered about after they left. What took you so long?"

"Eh, hit a few bumps during the rest of our road trip. But we landed on our feet, didn't we, Princess?"

Hearing him say that was bittersweet. Anytime I thought about the two years we were apart, it made me incredibly sad. He looked down at me with adoring eyes. God, how did I get so lucky to find a man who loved me so hard?

"Are you ready to get started?" she asked.

"Yes." I smiled, still looking up into Chance's number thirteen blues.

Adele and her boyfriend Harry were with us to serve as witnesses. Since we drove, we brought Pixy along. He was the honorary best man.

Already decked out in a dress of my choice, I'd come prepared this time. Chance looked incredibly sexy in a white linen shirt rolled up at the sleeves and dress pants that hugged his gorgeous ass—the ass that still helped support us to this day. I'd given up my law career for a much more fulfilling job running the local animal shelter in Hermosa Beach. The pay was crap, but I looked forward to getting up and being with the animals every day and never dreaded going into work. Chance still made a good living off royalties from his soccer-model career but also opened up his own landscaping business with a full staff of employees. He still dabbled in junk art on the side.

As I made my way down the aisle, the song that Chance had chosen caught me off guard: *The Long and Winding Road* by the Beatles. It was unconventional, but the meaning was completely perfect for us.

You'd think after all this time, I wouldn't have been nervous, but my hands were shaking as the ceremony started. It was no different than our first go round here.

Elvis spoke, "If anyone can show just cause why they may not be lawfully joined together, let them speak now or forever hold their peace."

As if on cue, Pixy let out a long "Baaaaaa."

Chance turned around and joked, "You *would* stir up trouble right now, wouldn't you, Bugger?"

"Who gives this woman to be married to this man?"

Adele spoke from behind me, "I do." She and I had become like sisters to each other. I was grateful for my new family.

It touched me when Chance took my hands in his and said, "I wish Mum could have met you."

Elvis interrupted our private moment. "Will you be using standard vows, or do you have your own?"

We answered at the same exact time.

"Standard," Chance said while I spoke over him, "I have my own."

He looked stunned as he leaned in and whispered, "Princess, you wrote vows? I just wanted to be officially married to you as fast as possible. I was gonna forego them this time."

Nodding, I said, "It's my turn. I have something to say."

When Chance got through repeating after Elvis, I cleared my throat.

How could I possibly put into words what he meant to me?

Taking a deep breath, I composed my thoughts before speaking. "Chance, when we met, I didn't know what hit me. All I knew was that for the first time in my life, I was living in the moment. You taught me so much in a little over a week about what's important in life. You taught me how to enjoy life and not take myself so seriously. You made me fall so crazy in love with you that even later when I believed you'd hurt me, I still couldn't shake you. I could only *pretend* not to care anymore. I thought I loved you then. But little did I know that our real love story hadn't even begun to play out. I never loved you more than when you came back and fought for me with everything that you had. Day in and day out, you threw away your pride and never gave up on me even when I made it really hard to believe that things would ever work out for us. You earned back my trust and then some. You said you wished your mother could have met me. Well, I wish she were here too, so I could thank her for the way she brought you up. To think that if I took even one wrong turn, I might never have met you when I did at the rest stop in Nebraska. A single minute can change an entire life. Yet, I still feel like somehow we would have met anyway. That's because I know now that you're my soulmate. The road that led us here wasn't always easy, but it made us stronger and more ready than ever for where it takes us next. I can't wait for the next adventure. I love you, Chance."

I don't think I'd ever seen Chance cry, but his eyes were starting to glisten as he silently mouthed, "I love you, Princess."

Elvis prompted us to exchange rings. Chance had always refused to take the old fake one off even though it had turned his finger green. I slid a new platinum band on his finger instead this time. Chance had surprised me with—what else—a princess cut diamond ring a few months ago. He placed a diamond eternity band on my hand in front of it.

"By the power vested in me by the state of Nevada, you may now kiss the bride."

Chance lifted me up into his arms and kissed me like there was no tomorrow. His warm lips enveloping mine along with knowing that he was officially my husband felt like heaven. Pixy was growing impatient and started to "baa" again while Adele and Harry clapped.

Chance put me down, and Zelda spoke from behind us. "That kiss! Now, I know exactly why I remember you two."

Zelda took pictures of Chance and me alone and then some with Adele and Pixy.

We booked a room at the same hotel where we stayed three years ago and planned to stay in Vegas for a mini honeymoon. Adele and Harry took Pixy back into their SUV. We hugged them goodbye, since they'd be driving right back to Hermosa Beach.

As we stepped out into the dry heat with the Vegas sun setting, I had a special surprise waiting for Chance in front of the chapel.

He broke out in laughter when he saw the black BMW, the same make and model as the one from our road trip.

"You rented a Beemer?"

BEE-MA. My love for his accent never waned.

"I know we were going to fly home, but I thought it would be a nice touch."

I had Adele decorate the car with sparkly writing on the back that read: *Just Married…Again.* I was most excited to show him something that was inside.

"It's perfect. Shall I drive, Mrs. Bateman?"

"Yes. I think I'd like to just stare at my handsome husband without any distractions."

When we got in, a wide smile spread across his face the moment he spotted it on the dash, "Mr. Obama! You kept him all these years?"

"I have to tell you a story. Back when I first got to Temecula and traded in the BMW, I left the bobblehead inside. The clerk at the dealership ran after me and asked me if I wanted it. I told her to keep it. I was trying to get rid of all physical signs of you, because losing you hurt so badly. You were still in my heart, and that wasn't going away, so I did what I could to remove all other reminders. A few weeks later, I was parked at a gas station. A boy around twelve was waiting in the car next to me for his father to come out of the mini-mart. I noticed the bobblehead on his dash. I just couldn't believe it. I knew it had to be ours. I asked him where he got it. He said his father gave it to him. Turns out, the dad worked at the dealership. I didn't know what it meant, but it somehow felt like it was a sign that I wasn't supposed to let you go. I asked him how much money I could give him to buy it back. He charged me ten bucks, but I would have paid just about anything. I was a blubbering mess that day. Even though I still forced myself to move on, when you showed up again, I thought back to the bobblehead and knew that the universe had been trying to tell me to wait for you, not to give up." Tears began falling from my eyes as I thought about how lucky I was to have gotten him back and so much more.

"That story is amazing, Princess." Chance swiped his fingers along the tears falling from my eyes and said, "Thank you for giving me that second chance." He leaned down and kissed my five-months pregnant belly that stretched through the lace of my empire waist gown. The baby boy we were expecting would be named after its daddy.

My second Chance.

Chance kept his head on my stomach. I ran my fingers through his hair and said, "Only fair. I gave you your second chance, and now you're giving me mine."

Dear Readers,

Thank you so much for all of your amazing support! Please sign up for our newsletters so that we can stay in touch. Members receive access to exclusive sneak peeks and contests!

Easy one-click signup

http://eepurl.com/brAPo9

Thank you to all the amazing bloggers who have helped spread the word about our first collaboration. We are forever grateful for your hard work in helping bring new readers to us every day.

To Julie – You are our sounding board. Thank you for putting up with our silliness at times over this project!

To Dallison and Kim – Thank you for your attention to detail in making sure Chance was nice and clean for public consumption.

To Luna – Your eyes ensured that Chance was the best Australian he could be. Can't wait to see what goat teasers you come up with!

To Lisa – For organizing the release tour and all of your support.

To Letitia – All of your covers rock, but this one just may be a favorite! Thanks for tweaking it to perfection.

To our agents, Kimberly Brower and Mark Gottlieb – For your hard work and thank you in advance for your roles in getting Cocky Bastard onto the big screen. (We can dream, right?)

To our readers – Thank you for allowing us to take you on a ride with Chance and Aubrey and for your continued support and enthusiasm for our books! We would be nothing without you!

Much love

Penelope & Vi

Stepbrother Dearest

A New York Times, USA Today and Wall Street Journal Bestseller.

You're not supposed to want the one who torments you.

When my stepbrother, Elec, came to live with us my senior year, I wasn't prepared for how much of a jerk he'd be.

I hated that he took it out on me because he didn't want to be here.

I hated that he brought girls from our high school back to his room.

But what I hated the most was the unwanted way my body reacted to him.

At first, I thought all he had going for him were his rock-hard tattooed abs and chiseled face. But things started changing between us, and it all came to a head one night.

Then, just as quickly as he'd come into my life, he was gone back to California.

It had been years since I'd seen Elec.

When tragedy struck our family, I'd have to face him again.

And holy hell, the teenager who made me crazy was now a man that drove me insane.

I had a feeling my heart was about to get broken again.

Stepbrother Dearest is a standalone novel.

**Contains graphic sexual content and harsh language. It is only appropriate for adult readers age 18+

<u>BEAT</u>
—Life On Stage Series

From *New York Times* and *USA Today* Bestseller, Vi Keeland, comes a steamy new standalone novel about a rockstar. *Or two.*

Dimpled smile of a boy

Hard body of a man

Sings like an angel

Fucks like the devil

I was stuck between a rock(star) and a hard place.

At fifteen, his poster hung on my bedroom wall. At twenty-five his body hovered over mine. Every girl's fantasy became my reality. *I was dating a rockstar.* Yet I was slowly falling for another man. The problem was—the two men—they shared a tour bus.

Flynn Beckham was the opening act.

Dylan Ryder was the headliner.

What happens when the opening act begins to shine so bright, it seems to dim everything else in its wake?

I'll tell you what happens. Things get ugly.

Author's note - Beat is a full-length standalone novel. Due to strong language and sexual content, this book is not intended for readers under the age of 18.

JAKE UNDONE

From the New York Times Bestelling author of Stepbrother Dearest...

Nina Kennedy was alive...but not living...until she met him.

Planes, trains, heights...you name it, Nina was afraid of it and led a sheltered life ruled by irrational fears and phobias.

When she moves to Brooklyn for nursing school, that life is turned upside down, as she develops an intense but unwanted attraction to her gorgeous roommate, who's pierced, tattooed and just happens to be the smartest person she's ever met.

Behind Jake Green's rough exterior and devilish smile, lies a heart of gold. He makes it his mission to change Nina's outlook on life. When he agrees to tutor her, they forge a bet and the stakes are high as Jake forces Nina to face her demons. He just wasn't expecting to fall hard for her in the process.

What Nina doesn't realize, is that Jake has been living his own private hell. Once he drops a bombshell, will their love survive it?

Told in two parts from both Nina and Jake's points of view, Jake Undone is a STANDALONE story and a companion to the novel, Gemini.

***Author's note: Due to strong language and sexual content, this book is not intended for readers under the age of 18.

THROB
—Life On Stage Series

The rules:

> No dating.
>
> No sex outside of the game.
>
> No disclosing the terms of the contract.

Rules were made to be broken, right?

Eight weeks ago I signed a contract. One that seemed like a good idea at the time. A handsome bachelor, luxury accommodations, and a chance to win a prize my family desperately needed. There were some rules though. Lots of them actually. Follow the script, no dating, sex, or disclosing the terms of the deal. After my self-imposed moratorium on men the last year, it wouldn't be hard to live up to my end of the bargain...so I thought. Until I realized the deal I'd made was with the devil...and I was in love with his dirty-talking brother.

My Skylar
(Mitch and Skylar's Story)

A USA Today Bestseller.

From the author of the #1 bestselling romance, *Jake Undone*, comes a friends-to-lovers story of longing, passion, betrayal and redemption...with a twist that will rip your heart out.

Skylar was my best friend, but I secretly pined for her. One thing after another kept us apart, and I've spent the last decade in fear of losing her forever.

First, it was the cancer, but she survived only to face the unthinkable at my hands. Because of me, she left town. For years, I thought I'd never see her again.

But now she's back...and living with *him*.

I don't deserve her after everything I've put her through, but I can't live without her. This is my last chance, because she's about to make the biggest mistake of her life. I can see it her eyes: she doesn't love him. She still loves me...which is why I have to stop her before it's too late.

My Skylar is a standalone story and a companion to the novel, *Jake Undone*.

Worth The Fight
—MMA Fighter Series

It didn't matter that the ref called it a clean hit. Nico Hunter would never be the same.

Elle has a good life. A job she loves, a great apartment, and the guy she's been dating for more than two years is a catch and a half. But it's boring...and she strives to keep it that way. Too many emotions are dangerous. Her own past is living proof of what can happen when you lose control.

Then Nico walks into Elle's office and everything changes...for both of them. But what can the tattooed, hard-bodied MMA fighter and the beautiful and always steady attorney have in common? A lot more than they bargained for.

Author's note THIS IS A STAND-ALONE NOVEL. Due to strong language and sexual content, this book is not intended for readers under the age of 18.

JAKE UNDERSTOOD

From the New York Times Bestselling author of *Jake Undone*, **comes a full-length companion novel and sequel.**

A different side to the story: Jake's side.

"We're getting a new roommate," they said.

I thought nothing of it…until she walked in the door. Her hand trembled in mine as she looked at me with fearful eyes. My entire world spun on its axis.

Nina…

It was a mismatch made in heaven: innocent girl from the boonies moves in with tattooed, pierced, badboy engineer.

I came up with a bet, a plan to tutor her in math and coach her through her phobias. What I wasn't betting on was becoming addicted to her.

But I was living a double life on weekends, and once she found out about it, she'd be gone.

I had to protect myself and that meant one thing: I couldn't fall in love.

*In *Jake Understood*, pivotal scenes from *Jake Undone* are retold from Jake's point of view, combined with all-new material from both the past and present time where Jake Undone left off. It can stand alone, but if both books are read, should follow *Jake Undone*.

Contains graphic sexual content and harsh language. It is only appropriate for adult readers age 18+.

<u>Worth The Chance</u>
—MMA Fighter Series

Meet Liv Michaels

It may have been seven years, but I'd know him anywhere. Sure, he's grown, filled out in all the right places, but his captivating blue eyes and cocky grin are exactly the way I remember. Even though I'd much rather forget.

Liv Michaels is almost there. She's smart, determined and weeks away from landing the job she's dreamed about for years. Time healed old wounds, even her broken heart from the devastation of being crushed by her first love.

Meet Vince Stone

Women love a fighter, especially a good one. Lucky for me, I'm damn good. But there's one woman that isn't interested. Not again, anyway.

Vince 'The Invincible' Stone is every woman's fantasy...strong, sexy, confident and completely in control. Growing up surrounded by chaos, he's learned never to get too attached. Love will drag you down. He adores women, treats them well, puts their own needs before his own...for the night anyway. With the biggest fight of his life coming up, his focus should be on training.

When fate brings Vince & Liv back together again, there's no denying the chemistry is still there. But can Vince erase the old scars their past left behind? Or will Liv hurt him instead?

Author's note THIS IS A STAND-ALONE NOVEL. Due to strong language and sexual content, this book is not intended for readers under the 18.

GEMINI
(Allison and Cedric's story)

An Amazon Bestseller.

Diner waitress Allison Abraham had no idea her mundane life was about to dramatically change the day she serves a devastatingly handsome customer.

Allison is immediately captivated by the mysterious man who stared through her soul with his electric blue eyes. After he abruptly leaves the restaurant, she can't get him out of her head.

She has no idea that he had actually come on a mission to find her.

Cedric Callahan wasn't expecting to fall in love at first sight with the pretty waitress he'd set out to find. In fact, she was the last woman on Earth he should be having feelings for. But his selfish heart had other plans. Feeling compelled to know her before revealing himself, he makes her believe their meetings are coincidental.

After a passionate romance ignites, Cedric's lies and secrets are finally revealed, changing both of their lives forever.

Worth Forgiving
—MMA Fighter Series

They say men like a lady in the living room and a whore in the bedroom. I never knew the sentiment was reciprocal. Until I met Jax Knight. A gentleman in public, a commanding, dirty talking rogue in the bedroom.

Daughter of legendary fighter "The Saint," Lily St. Claire knows firsthand how fighters can be. As the owner of a chain of MMA gyms, she's no stranger to aggressive, dominating, and possessive men. That's why she's always kept her distance. But the day Jax Knight walks through her door she's captivated by his charm. Stunningly handsome, well mannered, Ivy League educated, and confident, he shatters all the preconceived notions she'd come to think were true about men who trained to fight.

But falling for someone so soon after her breakup wasn't something she'd planned on. And definitely not something her ex plans to allow.

Belong To You
—Cole Series

My honeymoon was almost everything I dreamed it would be, a tropical paradise, turquoise water, romantic walks on the beach, and loads and loads of mind shattering sex. The only thing missing was the groom.

After seven years of coasting through a relationship with Michael, my senses were numb. A week of passion with a stranger was just what I needed to clear my head and take back control of my life. But how do you move on when the man that was only supposed to be a fling somehow seeps into your soul and steals your heart?

Made For You
—Cole Series

Jack and Syd spent a week in paradise. It was only supposed to be a fling. But life can be funny sometimes, and circumstances brought them back together again. Together they seemed to have found their happy ever after. But when

Sydney is offered a chance at the career she has always wanted, she must leave Jack behind to follow her dreams. Can their love survive long distance? Sydney's touring with a man every woman wants, but he only has eyes for Syd. And an unexpected tragedy leaves Jack feeling remorseful. Can the two find a way through to forever?

First Thing I See

Life changed for me in three days — the day my mother died, the day my dad married Candice and the day I met Kennedy Jenner.

From the moment I saw him, I was drawn to him. Like a moth to a flame, I couldn't keep away from the irresistible heat of the fire. That knowing, confident smile...those beautiful pale blue eyes...and those dimples...simply delicious. Who could resist such a beautiful strong man?

Hope York transformed herself from boring small town girl into a flawless beauty on the outside. But inside, she never changed. Kennedy Jenner was a successful, wealthy and jaw dropping handsome man that could have whatever he wanted, on his own terms. And he wanted Hope. But would he still want her after he saw her for who she really was, instead of what she carefully planned for everyone to see? And will his own secret past stand in his way for getting what he really wants?

Left Behind

Two stories so deeply intertwined, you'll think you know how they intersect...but you'll be wrong....

Zack Martin

The day I met Emily Bennett my whole world changed. Sure, we were just kids, but I was old enough to know my life would never be the same. She was my best friend. My destiny. My fate. I wasn't wrong...I just didn't know how twisted fate could be.

Nikki Fallon

After the death of my mother, moving from my dark and dreary trailer park to sunny California, I was focused on one thing — finding a sister I'd only just learned existed. Falling in love with him wasn't part of the plan. But he filled a void I never knew was possible to fill. He had to be my fate. My destiny. Until the day I finally found out who my sister was...and how twisted fate could be.

Penelope Ward

enelope Ward is a **New York Times, USA Today** and **Wall Street Journal** Bestselling author.

She grew up in Boston with five older brothers and spent most of her twenties as a television news anchor, before switching to a more family-friendly career.

Penelope lives for reading books in the new adult genre, coffee and hanging out with her friends and family on weekends.

She is the proud mother of a beautiful 10-year-old girl with autism (the inspiration for the character Callie in Gemini) and an 8-year-old boy, both of whom are the lights of her life.

Penelope, her husband and kids reside in Rhode Island.

Contact Penelope

Facebook

www.facebook.com/penelopewardauthor

Website

www.penelopewardauthor.com

Twitter

twitter.com/PenelopeAuthor

Instagram

@penelopewardauthor

Pinterest

www.pinterest.com/penelopewardaut/

Goodreads

www.goodreads.com/author/show/7105545.Penelope_Ward

Vi Keeland

Vi Keeland is a native New Yorker with three children that occupy most of her free time, which she complains about often, but wouldn't change for the world. She is a bookworm and has been known to read her kindle at stop lights, while styling her hair, cleaning, walking, during sporting events, and frequently while pretending to work. She is a boring attorney by day, and an exciting *New York Times* & *USA Today* Best Selling smut author by night!

Contact Vi

Facebook
www.facebook.com/vi.keeland or www.facebook.com/pages/Author-Vi-Keeland/435952616513958

Website
www.vikeeland.com

Twitter
@ViKeeland

Instagram
@Vi_Keeland

Pinterest
www.pinterest.com/vikeeland/pins/

Goodreads
www.goodreads.com/author/show/6887119.Vi_Keeland

9 781682 304280